AN UNCONVENTIONAL WOMAN

Jean Tahija was born in East Brunswick, in Victoria, Australia, on 3 February 1916. After graduating as a dentist, she worked at Melbourne's Dental Hospital until her marriage to Julius Tahija in 1946. Since that time, Jean Tahija has lived with her husband and two sons in Indonesia, where she is now a citizen.

An Unconventional Woman

Jean Tahija

The author and publisher would like to thank *The Herald* and *Weekly Times* for permission to include 'Black Hero Returns for White Wife', from *The Herald*, 21 October 1948; and the Australian Picture Library for permission to include UPI photographs in the photograph section.

Viking
Penguin Books Australia Ltd
487 Maroondah Highway, PO Box 257
Ringwood, Victoria 3134, Australia
Penguin Books Ltd
Harmondsworth, Middlesex, England
Penguin Putnam Inc.
375 Hudson street, New York, New York 10014, USA
Penguin Books Canada Limited
10 Alcorn Avenue, Toronto, Ontario, Canada M4V 3B2
Penguin Books (N.Z.) Ltd
Cnr Rosedale and Airborne Roads, Albany, Auckland, New Zealand
Penguin Books (South Africa) (Pty) Ltd
4 Pallinghurst Road, Parktown 2193, South Africa

First published by Penguin Books Australia Ltd 1998

1 3 5 7 9 10 8 6 4 2

Cover design by Sandy Cull, Penguin Design Studio
Typeset in 14/18½ pt Centaur by Post Pre-press Group, Brisbane
Printed and bound in Australia by Australian Print Group, Maryborough, Victoria

National Library of Australia
Cataloguing-in-Publication data

Tahija, Jean.
An unconventional woman.

Includes index.

ISBN 0 670 88193 7.

1. Tahija, Jean. 2. Businesspeople – Indonesia – Biography.
3. Millionaires – Indonesia – Biography. 4 Australians –
Indonesia – Biography. I. Title.

338.092

TO JULIUS

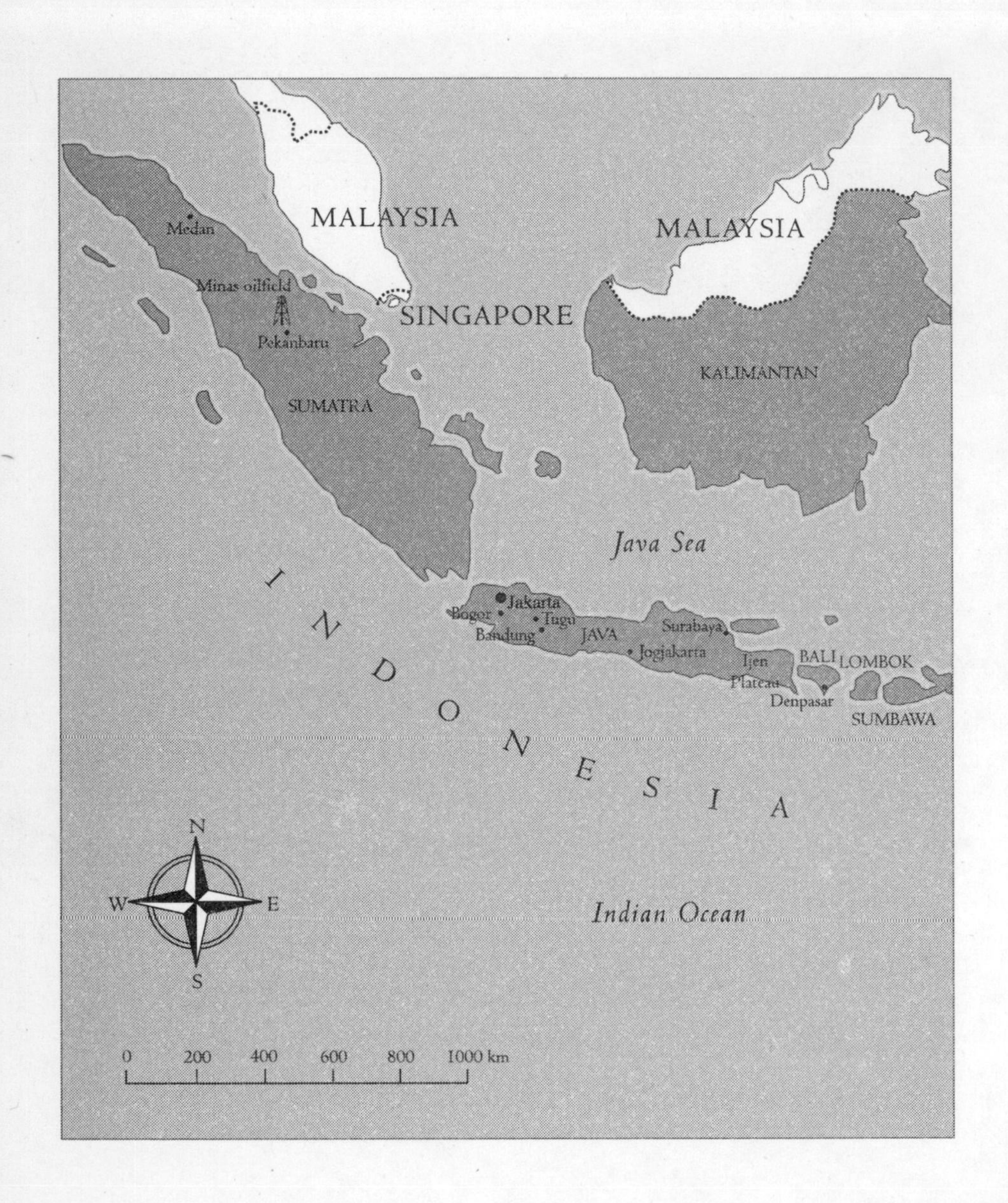
MALAYSIA
MALAYSIA
Medan
Minas oilfield
Pekanbaru
SINGAPORE
KALIMANTAN
SUMATRA
Java Sea
INDONESIA
Jakarta
Bogor
Tugu
Bandung
JAVA
Surabaya
Jogjakarta
Ijen Plateau
BALI
LOMBOK
Denpasar
SUMBAWA
Indian Ocean
N
W
E
S
0
200
400
600
800
1000 km

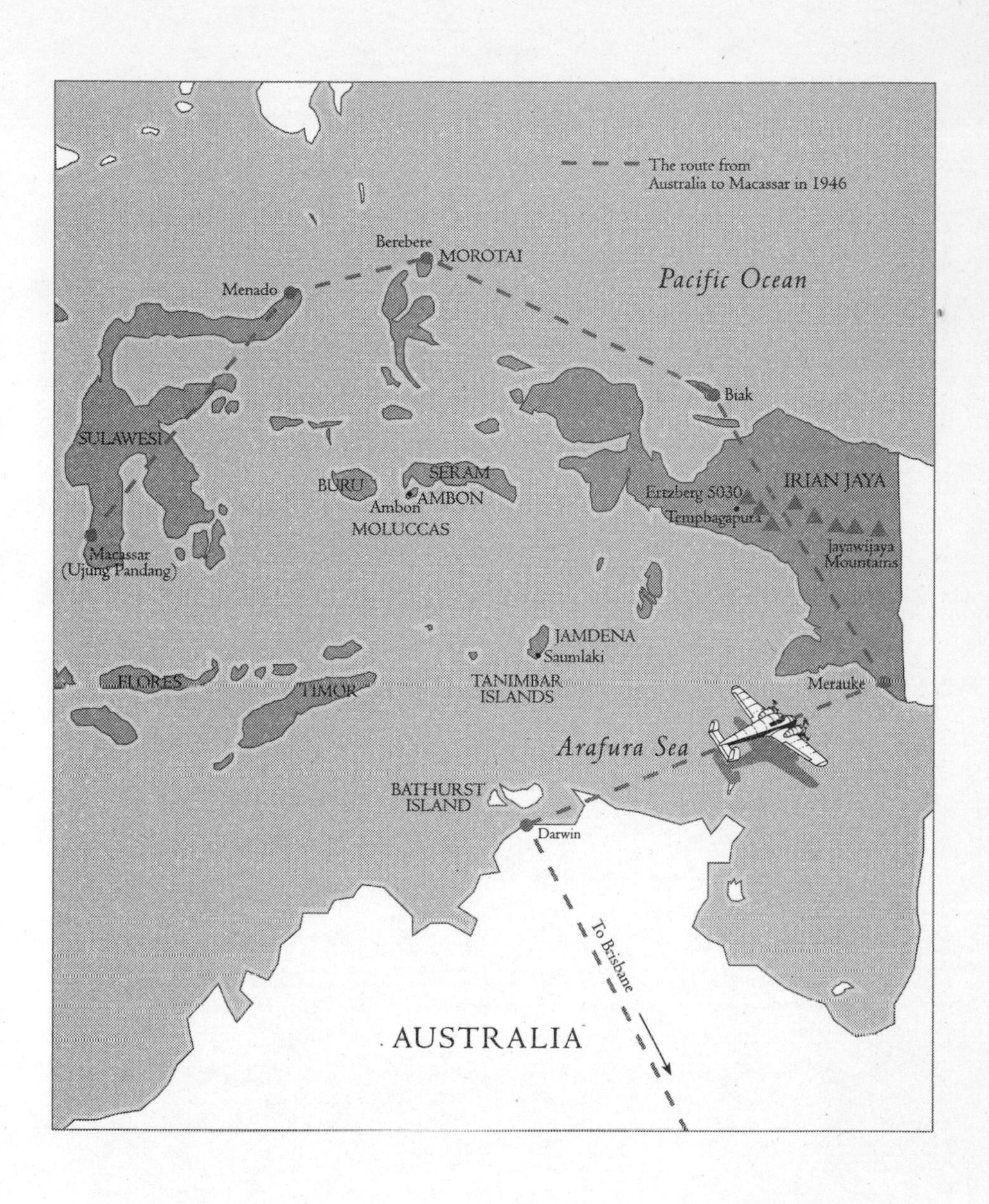

The route from Australia to Macassar in 1946
Berebere
MOROTAI
Pacific Ocean
Menado
Biak
SULAWESI
BURU
SERAM
AMBON
Ambon
MOLUCCAS
IRIAN JAYA
Ertzberg 5030
Tembagapura
Jayawijaya Mountains
Macassar (Ujung Pandang)
JAMDENA
Saumlaki
TANIMBAR ISLANDS
FLORES
TIMOR
Merauke
Arafura Sea
BATHURST ISLAND
Darwin
To Brisbane
AUSTRALIA

one

My father drove me to Essendon Airport. I sat beside him in silence, unable to tell him how excited I was, how much I had looked forward to this moment. The sun had not yet risen and the road was empty, forlorn in the pre-dawn gloom. The rows of brick terraces on Mount Alexander Road were still shrouded in darkness, lit up just briefly by the headlights of my father's car as we drove past. My father looked straight ahead, his face a mask covering his suffering. I knew how hard this drive to the airport was for him. While this was what I had longed for since I had met Julius, it was also something I had dreaded.

This point in our lives had been coming for almost five years. It had been coming since that day in May 1942, when Julius had opened the front gate to our house in Ascot Vale and, through the window of the front room, I had seen him walking up the path towards our front door. Something had happened to me at that moment. Something had stirred in me so that by the time I opened the front door and looked at Julius standing there in his blue airforce uniform, smiling, his startlingly white teeth set off against his dark handsome face, I knew somehow that my life was about to change. Just how it would change was beyond my knowing at that moment. I simply felt a powerful attraction to this soldier from the Dutch East Indies that I had never experienced before.

Not that I was a flighty schoolgirl, bowled over by the first man she'd met. I was twenty-five years old, a mature professional woman at a time when most women did not pursue careers, but set out, from adolescence, to find the man of their dreams, settle down and raise a family. That had not been my chosen path. I had studied to become a dentist – the only woman in the dentistry faculty at Melbourne University at the time – and I had worked hard to achieve my goal.

My parents had made many financial sacrifices in order for me to go to university. My father was a policeman with a passionate interest in the world of books and ideas; a man whose dreams of a higher education had been thwarted by the circumstances of his family. He'd wanted me to have the opportunities that had been denied him. My mother and father, despite their modest means, had given me something available to very few girls of my social and economic class. My father, especially, was a sort of feminist long before feminism came on the scene. He'd believed that girls should be educated; that they should have careers and make something of their lives. And that's what I had done.

Yet from the day Julius came into my life, I knew that my future would be different. I would not end up a dentist with a practice in some nice middle-class Melbourne home, living out the Australian suburban dream. The truth is, that dream had never much appealed to me. I had always felt that I wanted more, though I had no idea what that meant – what shape the more would take. But from the moment I laid eyes on Julius, the shape of my future life began to form in my mind. Although it was hazy at first, and confusing, I knew within days that my destiny lay with this man. Looking back, I think my mother and father knew it too.

I don't suppose that either of my parents were thrilled by the course my life took after I met Julius, but they said nothing to me about it. We never talked about it, my parents and I. We didn't talk about it when Julius and I first met, nor when our love started to grow. It was never once discussed through the years of the war, when I could never be sure where Julius was or whether he was safe; nor after the war, when Julius and I were married. We didn't even talk about it when it was clear that some day soon I would leave my parents, my city and my country for a new life in a place which, to most Australians, was just part of that threatening and unknown mass of islands to the north – a place teeming with people who looked upon the great, almost empty continent to the south with envy and hostility.

For a professional woman like me to give up her comfortable career and her home for the love of an Asian man was almost unheard of in Australia in the 1940s. Yet, as my father drove to the airport on that April morning in 1947, he did so in silence. I too did not speak, not so much because I had nothing to say, but because I feared that if I spoke, I would dissolve into a teary mess. Strangely, I can't recall much about our farewell, except that it was done in silence, but for my sobbing, which my father did not acknowledge. I had never flown before – never been out of Victoria for that matter – but I can remember nothing of my first flight, which took me from Melbourne to Sydney, where the plane re-fuelled before we clambered on board again for the flight to Brisbane.

I stayed the night in Brisbane, my first night in a hotel. It seems strange today that a thirty-year-old professional woman had never spent a night in a hotel room before, but the world was a different place fifty years ago. Fifty years on, the past is a foreign country, as the writer L.P. Hartley says in the first sentence of his novel, *The Go Between.*

On reflection, I guess my life before Julius was a sheltered one, but not particularly so for the times. Few young men or women left home before they married, and those who did brought shame on their families. It never crossed my mind to leave home, nor would such a thought have crossed the minds of my brothers, Cliff and Russell. Cliff was eighteen months younger than me, and Russell six years younger. Both stayed at home until they married. They returned to our house in Ascot Vale at the end of 1945, having both spent three hellish years in New Guinea during the war. There was never any doubt that when they returned to Australia, they would come home to Anne Street. And they did. I remember Russell's homecoming. He walked into the house, looking gaunt and tired. His legs and feet were covered in tropical sores. My father cut off Russell's boots and gently peeled off his rotting socks. He lovingly bathed Russell's feet and legs in warm, slightly salty water.

I hardly slept that first night away from home in Brisbane. My mind was full of images: of my father's silence, my mother's tears, Julius, the dental hospital and Melbourne – the city of my birth and childhood, and my early adult years. I was leaving all that behind, and what lay ahead was a great unknown. All I knew was that a revolution was in progress in Indonesia – or rather the Dutch East Indies as it was called then – and that the country was in turmoil. And I knew that Julius, whatever happened, would be an active player in that revolution, and that its outcome would shape our lives.

After 400 years of Dutch colonial rule, the majority of the people of the Indonesian archipelago – made up of some 16 000 islands – wanted independence. The Dutch were more than reluctant to leave, though they must have known, at least those with any sense of history, that the colonial era was ending. Sooner or later, one way or another, independence for

Indonesia was inevitable. The centre of the revolution was in Java, where the young nationalist leader, Sukarno, in the final months of the war, had declared independence and had set up the Republic of Indonesia. Most of the fighting between the Dutch troops, shipped back to Java at war's end, and Sukarno's Republican soldiers was centred around Jogjakarta in central Java.

Julius, however, was based in Macassar (now called Ujung Pandang). This was – and still is – the capital of the island of Sulawesi – the largest of the dozens of islands that formed the territory that the Dutch had designated East Indonesia. Julius had left the Dutch East Indies army, in which he had risen to the rank of captain, to become a minister in the regional government of East Indonesia. This government was a Dutch creation, designed to offer Indonesians in the area a form of limited self-government. Sukarno's Republicans fiercely rejected such offers, and many of them considered those who served in the East Indonesian government traitors to the revolutionary cause.

Julius saw it differently. He was a nationalist and a firm believer in Indonesian independence, but he was convinced that independence could only be won from the Dutch by a combination of military and political action. For the peoples of East Indonesia, armed struggle against the Dutch was out of the question. Unlike the Republicans, who had acquired weapons from the retreating Japanese on Java, the East Indonesians had no arms. East Indonesia had been liberated by Australian troops, and the Australians had promptly thrown all Japanese military hardware into the sea.

Julius had joined the East Indonesian government convinced that this would be his way of playing his part in the independence movement. What's more, he was sick of war, sick of the killing and the suffering that war brought. No-one could accuse him of being a coward. He had won the Dutch equivalent of the Victoria Cross, one of only three soldiers to win this highest of military awards. He had risked his life many times as a member of the Z Specials, an Allied force that undertook dangerous commando sabotage actions and intelligence missions behind Japanese lines in Asia. He had ended the war in hospital in Melbourne, his nerves shot to pieces, his nights filled with terrible nightmares and bouts of breathlessness. Julius wanted independence, but he wanted to achieve it without bloodshed, if possible.

All of this and more filled my mind as I lay in bed in my Brisbane hotel room. Every couple of minutes, I looked at the clock beside my bed and wondered at how slowly the time was passing. Finally, at 4.30 a.m. the alarm went off. I quickly showered and went down to the lobby where a Dutch consular official was waiting for me to take me to the military airport on the outskirts of Brisbane. It had taken months to arrange this trip. There were no commercial flights to the East Indies. It was only because I was the wife of a minister in the East Indonesian government that Julius had been able to organise my passage.

The plane in which I was to travel to Darwin and then on to Indonesia was not a passenger aircraft. In fact, I was to be its only passenger. It was an old armed forces DC3 cargo plane – or a Dakota, as its American makers, the Douglas Company called it. The DC3 had formed the backbone of the Allied airforce throughout the war, transporting troops and equipment across the globe. Even now, a half century later, scores of them still fly transport missions in many countries. Soon after the war, when the Australian prime minister, Ben Chifley, set up TAA, the first aircraft in the fleet was a veteran war service DC3 which had been lovingly converted into a passenger plane.

Mine had not been converted. Still painted camouflage green, it had no interior padding or seats. Instead, there were a score of fold-up aluminium bottom-rests lined up against the plane's bare walls. Here you sat until rough weather bounced you off. Nor was there any airconditioning. Each perspex window had a hole in the middle to let in air. When it got too cold, you could close it up with an ordinary bath plug.

Although the plane was owned by the Dutch, its three-man crew were all former Australian Airforce men. Full of fun and good humour, they later became our friends in Indonesia. As the plane took off for Darwin, I looked at the enormous drums of fuel and the stacks of parcels stored opposite me, and wondered whether the ropes which kept them in place would hold. Unlike the jet aircraft of today, the DC3 flew at a fairly low altitude. It took us all day to get to Darwin, and through the window, with the plug removed, I thought I could smell the warm air of the outback we were crossing. I had never seen anything like it before. I loved the Victorian bush, but the vast red heart of Australia was a new and thrilling experience for me, and I was lost in wonder at the sight below.

It wasn't until the following day, after another sleepless night – this time in a tiny army barracks room at the small military airport outside Darwin – that it truly hit me: I was leaving Australia. Though I would surely visit my home from time to time, I knew I would never live there again. It had been a hot and humid night in Darwin, the likes of which I'd never experienced before. I wondered whether Indonesia would be like this, this heat and closeness that was almost suffocating. The Northern Territory itself was like a foreign country to me, with its ochre earth and stunted vegetation. Later in my life, the smell of the tropics would become a comforting one, because it signalled that I was at home; but on that night, it was disconcerting.

After only half-an-hour's flying time out of Darwin, we crossed the Australian coastline and my heart skipped a beat. The coastline was a dizzying array of blues – light and dark and all shades in between. Astern, I could see Bathurst and Melville Islands. I was leaving home with a vengeance now, and it was both thrilling and heartbreaking. But not for a moment did I doubt that I had made the right decision. Whatever happened, I would never regret my love for Julius nor my choice to be with him, in his country, which was not my country, but which in time I would grow to love.

Well, perhaps just the slightest sliver of doubt about what I was doing sneaked into my mind when, an hour out of Darwin, the dark clouds rolled in to blot out the view, the thunder started and the lightning flashed. We had flown into a tropical storm of unimaginable ferocity. It felt as though the earth itself would disintegrate before this terrifying assault. The thunder was so close and so deafening it drowned out the roar of the engines. The lightning cracked like a whip around the plane, and it seemed that I could reach out of the window and touch it. Time and again, I was thrown out of my seat towards the centre of the plane which dipped and rose like a cork on a boiling sea. The ropes which held the fuel containers and the stack of parcels quickly loosened, and before long, ten-gallon drums were rolling around the floor. I was all alone, a terrified young woman in a cocktail shaker filled with flying parcels and fuel drums, being flung all over the Arafura Sea.

Then, as quickly as it had started, the storm abated. The skies cleared and below us I could see the deep blue of the ocean. Bill Tilden, the radio operator, stepped out of the cockpit into the body of the plane and slouched against the bulkhead. He was eating an apple and he grinned at me between bites. I had, by then, resumed my seat and combed my hair.

'How are ya?' he asked. 'We'll be landing in Merauke soon. Now there's a tropical paradise for you.'

As I soon discovered, Merauke – near the southern sea-coast of West Irian – borders one of the largest and most desolate swamps in the world. Inland from the town lay the Dutch internment camp, *Tanah Merah* – Red Earth – where Indonesian freedom fighters had been imprisoned before the war. Many of them had died there, ravaged by malaria and dysentery, martyrs to the cause of Indonesian independence. I had met some of the men who had survived. They had been sent to Australia by the Dutch just before the Japanese overran the Dutch East Indies, and had been interned in Cowra, with Japanese prisoners of war. It was only by accident that the Australian government had discovered that these men were not enemies, but simply Indonesian nationalists, and released them. However, none had survived their barbaric internment without permanent damage to their health.

During the war, Merauke had been bombed by the Japanese. As our plane bumped along the rough, pot-holed runway, I could see the abandoned and run-down army huts in which we would spend the night. The heat and humidity descended on me the minute I stepped from the plane in my form-hugging, calf-length, dark blue skirt, my white blouse and my navy cardigan. I felt as if I had suddenly been immersed in a hot bath. My hut was a furnace, but I had to keep the windows shut or become a meal for Merauke's malaria-carrying mosquitoes and its fierce swarms of sandflies. I didn't know it at the time, but Julius had also been in Merauke during the war on a mission. He had stayed in these same huts and been bitten by these same mosquitoes and sandflies. The knowledge may have given me some comfort as I lay there in the hot darkness, exhausted and dispirited, anxious for the journey to end.

The following morning, we escaped Merauke and flew to Biak, an island which lies across the mouth of Geelvink Bay, at the neck of the 'bird's head' which so distinctly shapes the western end of New Guinea. Biak had been 'discovered' by Dutch sailors in the seventeenth century, but had long been a trading post for the gorgeous plumes and skins of the island's birds of paradise, prized throughout Asia.

Despite its colourful past, Biak was anything but romantic on that April morning in 1947. Two years earlier, in May 1945, the Allied Supreme Commander, General Douglas MacArthur, had landed on Biak with his forces, driving out the Japanese invaders and commencing his 'island-hopping' campaign northwards towards Japan. Biak had been ravaged by the fighting. Its once rich coconut plantations were now nothing but rows of charred and leafless stumps. Ruined buildings were everywhere, and around the airport – which was little more than an old tin shack – lay the burnt-out remains of Japanese fighter planes, silent and forlorn monuments to the awfulness of war.

I have a happier memory of returning to Biak with Julius, some twenty years later, on our way to the world's largest gold and copper mine in Freeport, with which Julius had become involved. Together, we climbed the mountain beside the mine and stood on its glacier – the only glacier in whole of the tropics. It was a sight like no other I had ever experienced, a vista of ancient mountains covered by untouched, tropical rainforests, as primeval as anything I have ever seen in my life.

My first visit to Biak, however, was marked by yet another sleepless night spent in an army hut near the airport. Early the next morning, I walked back to the plane and found that I was no longer the aircraft's sole passenger. There were perhaps two dozen people crammed into the cabin, some sitting on the makeshift aluminium seats, others standing and holding on to straps, like those found in Melbourne trams. They were Indian traders, Dutch East Indies soldiers and Chinese merchants, all travelling to Macassar for business. Suddenly the plane was alive with activity, with the chattering of voices and the clanging of different languages forced to cohabit within a confined space. I felt I had finally arrived at the starting point of my new Indonesian life.

Not only did the plane now have other passengers, but it had a stewardess with whom I was to form a lasting friendship. Tuska Donskoi was a plump, friendly, confident woman whose parents were Russian Jews – merchants who had settled in Java in the early part of the century. They lived in Jogjakarta – where Tuska was born – but later moved to Jakarta at the beginning of 1948. Some hours later, when the plane passed through another, smaller, tropical storm, and many of those passengers who'd been standing were tossed into the laps of those who were seated, Tuska smiled calmly and in her thick Dutch accent said: 'So nice and cosy inside, no? Much better than outside in the storm I think.'

I was so tired that I started to laugh hysterically. Tuska was only mildly surprised. She had seen this sort of reaction from bone-weary, frightened passengers before. She patted my head and told me that soon it would all be over. This just made me laugh even harder.

We stopped one last time to re-fuel, at Menado, on the northern tip of Sulawesi. At last, Julius and I were on the same island, and within hours, we would see each other again for the first time since our marriage six months ago. In truth, the months had gone by so slowly that it seemed as though I had not seen him for years. As the plane headed south, I could see lush, green, rolling hills and bright blue lakes. I could even see black-and-white cows grazing in paddocks. It looked almost like the landscape of the home I had just left, and there was something reassuring about it, familiar and comforting.

I tried to picture my husband's face: his dark, kind eyes, his broad smile, his bright white teeth. I tried to picture him standing there at the airport in Macassar, straight-backed and proud in his uniform, impatiently scanning the skies for the plane that would bring me to him. The journey had taken four days, but in a sense, I had been travelling towards this day for almost five long years. It had been a remarkable journey and I wondered what the future would bring.

two

Most mornings, Julius and I are awake by six. Jakarta is best experienced early in the morning, before the heat and the humidity become unbearable and the only respite available is an afternoon rest in the coolest room of the house. We don our dressing gowns and sit on the terrace where we are served coffee. We sit on old rattan chairs beneath whirling fans, placed strategically on the large wooden beams that support the tiled roof. The terrace runs along the length of the house, a distance of perhaps 30 metres, and then continues around at a right angle adjacent to the laundries and work rooms. In this way, it surrounds the tropical garden in which hang dozens of large birdcages, home to every conceivable Indonesian bird species. Early in the morning and at dusk, the singing of the birds is soothing and beautiful, and if we close our eyes, it is as if we are in the jungle somewhere, in Sumatra, say, or Irian Jaya.

We have lived in this house for almost twenty years. It is in a quiet, leafy part of Jakarta, not too far from the office of the family company where Julius still works every morning, despite the fact that our two sons have now taken over its day-to-day running. When we purchased the land, we also bought two blocks nearby for our sons and their families. They now live within walking distance of us, which means we have almost daily contact with our five grandchildren. I look at them sometimes and it strikes me that the Indonesia in which they are growing up is a different world from the one I first encountered when I landed in Macassar to join Julius in April 1947.

When I arrived, Indonesia was in the throes of a revolution that cost many lives and caused a great deal of suffering. The country had just gone through the horrors of Japanese occupation and it had been looted. Anything of worth had been shipped to Japan. When I arrived, Indonesia was still a Dutch colony – backward, economically weak and, while there was no famine as existed in parts of Africa and on the Indian subcontinent, a country of widespread poverty.

My grandchildren are growing up in an Indonesia full of economic opportunities. They come from a family that can give them everything they need to get ahead in their lives. And not only that. For them – and for my sons too – there is no question of divided loyalties. There is no question that they are anything but Indonesians. Their fate and future will mirror the fate and future of this country of almost 200 million people living on 16 000 islands in an archipelago flung across an area larger than the Australian continent.

I have often felt that, despite having lived in Indonesia for fifty years, I am still an outsider. My roots, in a sense, remain in Australia where my parents and my brothers are buried. Australia was where I grew up, where I was educated, and where I came to love the bush and the national ethos – the one captured in the stories of Henry Lawson, Steele Rudd and Banjo Paterson. Sometimes I am aware of the fact that, unlike Julius and my sons, I am neither wholly Australian nor wholly Indonesian. I do not feel like that all the time. Most of the time, I simply love Indonesia and its people.

Asked what am I – an Australian or an Indonesian – I almost invariably say that I am an Indonesian. And I mean it. I have lived here for almost two-thirds of my life. My sons were born and raised here. It is here, in Indonesia, that my husband built his career, where he became a prominent member and leader of the business community, and where our family is respected and seen as a role model of what can be achieved with hard work, determination, and sound moral and ethical principles.

Sometimes, in the morning, after we have had our coffee, after we have showered and breakfasted, and when Julius is working in his office, I sit in my chair beside the garden and, while the birds make their beautiful racket, I look around at this home of ours – at the dozens of artefacts, paintings and statues we have accumulated during our years of travelling around the islands of Indonesia – and I have to metaphorically pinch myself and ask: is this really me? Is this my life? Is this what the fates had in store for Jean Walters? Who could have imagined that Jean Walters, the daughter of a humble Aussie cop, would end up living this life, with Indonesian children and with grandchildren for whom Australia represents only an exciting holiday destination in a country nothing like their own?

Most mornings, over our coffee – which comes from the plantations of central Java and which is, in my view, the best coffee in the world – Julius and I chat for a while about the day ahead. We are both in our early eighties. We have lived together for half a century. We have been in love for fifty-five years. I look at Julius and he looks hardly any different from the way he looked that night he came to our home in Ascot Vale. His hair is still a shiny black, his skin is still smooth and unwrinkled, his back is straight and proud, and his movements as graceful as they always were. I look at him and I wonder: can it really be fifty-five years since we met? Some mornings, it feels like we met just last week, or perhaps a couple of weeks ago at most. Julius is both familiar, like a limb of my own body without which I could not function properly, and exotic – an overwhelmingly attractive stranger to whom I am drawn by a powerful, irresistible force.

In his eighties, Julius remains a man of almost ferocious energy and drive. There is still so much to be done and still too few hours in the day in which to do it. Each day, he spends a couple of hours in the office at home dictating letters to his secretary, or making phone calls to New York or London, where he speaks with brokers or the senior executives of the branch offices of our insurance company, which is a publicly listed company but one in which our family is the biggest stockholder. Sometimes, he needs to call the senior management of Texaco and Chevron, the two American oil companies that jointly own Caltex Indonesia, Asia's biggest oil producer. These calls are often made in the middle of the night. I lie in bed and hear Julius talking to his old friends in the oil business, and there is a youthfulness about his voice, an urgency, that is both startling and gratifying. Julius ran Caltex Indonesia for close to fifteen years. He was the company's first indigenous head. Even now, he is on the board of commissioners of Caltex Indonesia and regularly travels to the company's oilfields in Sumatra.

We always have lunch together, seated opposite each other at the round teak table in the dining room. Lunch is always a cooked meal, consisting of two or three dishes – a fish curry perhaps, some stir-fried mixed vegetables and, if Julius is really lucky, a thick soup of tripe in coconut milk, the sight of which always brings a smile to his face. This is followed by a platter of tropical fruit for dessert. Our cook has been with us for close to thirty years. She has become one of the family and I am as fond of her as I would be of a beloved aunt. Indeed, most of the people who work for us – the gardeners, the security staff, the household staff – have been with us for many years. They have been my companions and friends. They have eased my loneliness when Julius has been away on business, and they have taught me much about Indonesia that I otherwise would never have known.

After lunch, we retire to the bedroom, which is air-conditioned – only the bedrooms in the house have airconditioning because both Julius and I like the heat and humidity of the tropics – and we rest for an hour or two. Sometimes, Julius has nightmares during these afternoon rests. He relives some of his wartime experiences, which come back to him so vividly that he cries out in anguish. It is as if some of the things that happened to him fifty or more years ago are happening to him now, as he sleeps. At these times, I reach across and stroke his face and hands, touch his eyes and tell him that everything is all right, that I am here beside him, as I have always been these many years.

Sometimes, when I cannot sleep in the afternoon, I get out of bed, making sure that I do not wake Julius, and go out to the terrace, to sit by the garden and watch my beloved birds. They are silent in the afternoon, knocked out by the heat and the humidity, and by the stillness of the day. I look around me and think of my father and mother, of my brothers and of my colleagues with whom I worked in the dental hospital in Spring Street. I think too of my student days at Melbourne University, days which I often feel were the happiest and most carefree of my life.

At these times, I wonder what might have been had I not met Julius. The young men with whom I studied dentistry were like brothers to me. There was never more to our relationship than friendship. After we graduated, I loved the hospital life, I never wanted to go into private practice and, had Julius not come along, I would have probably gone on to do post-graduate work in Australia or perhaps even overseas, in Canada.

In those days, to be twenty-six and unattached was tantamount to being an old maid. This did not concern me for I enjoyed my life. What I didn't want was a sedate existence out in the suburbs. My male colleagues who did interest me were the Jewish refugees who had managed to escape from Europe before the Nazis had taken over. There was something about them, about what they had been through, that made them different – more worldly I suppose.

I sit looking at the garden as Julius sleeps in our bedroom, and I think back to our early lives. What a mystery, I reflect, that fate brought two people like us together.

three

Julius and I were born in the same year, 1916, six months apart. Our year of birth was about the only thing our childhoods had in common. I was born at home, in the front room of a small weatherboard house in Anne Street, East Brunswick, a working-class area in inner-city Melbourne. Across the other side of the world, Australian soldiers fighting for the British Empire had just been withdrawn from Gallipoli. Those who had survived the fearful carnage were then sent, a few weeks later, to France where many of them would perish in the trenches at the battle of the Somme.

My father was close to thirty by then – too old to be sent to the European battlefields. In the bitter Australian conscription debates that followed the slaughter at Gallipoli, he was on the side of those who opposed conscription, though he was not a Catholic and therefore not in the thrall of Archbishop Mannix, the primate of Melbourne's Catholics, who led the anti-conscription campaign. My father simply did not think that Australian boys should be forced to fight in a war that had nothing to do with Australia.

I can still remember the house in Anne Street. It had an outdoor wooden toilet beside which stood the laundry with its wood-fired copper for boiling clothes. There was a bath in the laundry, equipped with a chip bath-heater, which resembled a miniature steam engine and was fuelled with woodchips from our stack of firewood. Most of all, I remember that the house always smelt of my mother's cooking – of soups made with lamb shanks and barley, of steak-and-kidney pie, of Irish stew and of my favourite dessert, suet pudding, which was served with golden syrup and large dobs of whipped cream.

I was the first child. Cliff was eighteen months younger and then there was a few years' gap to Russell. There is no doubt that I loved my brothers, but the truth is that we were not particularly close. I was a studious child, particularly attached to my father who imbued in me a love of books and learning. My brothers loved sport and had absolutely no interest in reading or school work.

My father grew up on a small dairy farm outside Wangaratta, in Victoria's north-east. His family was practically a caricature of the battling small land-holders who featured in the stories of Henry Lawson and in Steele Rudd's *On Our Selection*. The farm, which was little more than scrub when my father's family moved there, barely kept the family in food let alone the other necessities of life. The work was back-breaking and long, often starting before dawn and finishing after sunset.

My father hated his life on the farm. He was a sensitive child who loved books and poetry. He was desperate to continue at school and dreamt of going to university one day, but his father was adamant that his son did not need an education and that his life was on the land. My father left school at the end of grade eight, when he was thirteen, but he remained bitterly determined to leave the farm as soon as he could. That chance came in 1909, when George Walters was sworn in as a foot constable in the Victorian police.

It was while out on patrol on a summer's day in 1914 that George Walters met Olive Ward on the banks of the Yarra River, in the gardens beside Prince's Bridge. In pre-war Melbourne, it was fashionable for smart young people to promenade in the city, the girls twirling an elegant parasol if it was sunny, the boys in straw boaters worn at a rakish angle.

Olive Ward was very much a member of this smart set. A city girl, she was the daughter of a well-to-do merchant, an importer of German sewing machines, which he sold through a dozen shops that he owned in inner-city Melbourne. On Saturday nights, my maternal grandfather would don his Salvation Army uniform and conduct meetings in a draughty hall near Russell Street, where he gave the drunks a bob each if they sat through his sermon. Years later, I can remember my grandfather visiting us on Sunday afternoons in Anne Street, having been driven there in his limousine by his full-time chauffeur who wore a smart grey uniform and a black, peaked cap. What the other residents of working-class Anne Street made of such grandeur is not all that hard to imagine.

Olive Ward and George Walters married in 1915 and I, their first child, was born the next year. It was a happy marriage as far as I could tell. My father simply adored my mother, and had done from the day he met her. When I consider my relationship with Julius, I sometimes wonder whether love at first sight is in the Walters family genes.

No doubt my mother loved my father too, because she gave up a life of upper middle-class wellbeing for something materially much less comfortable. My father earned two pounds a week, which was a reasonable salary for a working man, but it meant that my mother had to sew all our clothes – including our pyjamas – and buy cheaper cuts of meat and cheaper vegetables than she had been used to at home. She never complained. There was always laughter in our house. On Sunday nights, my father's police friends, as well as some of my aunts and uncles, would congregate in our lounge room for tea, after which we would gather around the piano and sing some of that era's popular songs – mostly tunes my father and mother had heard at Saturday afternoon matinées at the Tivoli, Melbourne's best vaudeville theatre.

Sometimes, as a special treat, my parents would take me along to these matinées. A trip to town was an occasion. Men always wore suits and homburgs and women wore their finest dresses, gloves and hats. Children were spruced up in their Sunday best. We always travelled by tram. The men sat in the outside sections on slatted wooden seats, while the women sat inside, away from the draughts and the cigarette smoke.

The Melbourne of my childhood was a city of few cars and virtually no high-rises. It was full of elegant, often imposing Victorian buildings built with fortunes amassed during the nineteenth century gold rushes. It was a conservative city, heavily influenced by its British heritage, from its architecture to its food. Sometimes my mother took me to town to go to Myer's, Melbourne's only department store, where she would buy me a new pair of shoes. Later she would take me to the Lattice Tea Rooms in Collins Street where the specialty of house was mince pies. I preferred their little cream cakes that were called 'monkeys' for reasons that were never clear to me. The place was always crammed with people at morning and afternoon tea times. My mother often said that for a lot of people, going to the Lattice Tea Rooms was like taking a trip back to the old country, England.

My father loved vaudeville. During his police shifts, he would sometimes go backstage at the Tivoli and watch the show from beside the stage, pretending to be on the look-out for law-breakers or drunks behaving offensively. He got to know many of the chorus girls who I thought were the most beautiful-looking girls in the world. I quite liked a comedian called George Wallace who was extremely popular and who produced full houses whenever he featured on the Tivoli's bill. But then one day my father told me that Wallace was a terrible man who treated the chorus girls very badly. I assume that, in today's language, he sexually harassed them, though I was never supplied with the specific details of his unacceptable behaviour. After that, I still laughed at Wallace's rather lewd jokes, but did so quietly, so as not to upset my father.

Not that my father was a man easily shocked by a lewd joke. He was, after all, a cop, based in those days in working-class Collingwood, not exactly Melbourne's most salubrious suburb. Gang fights were commonplace and I can recall my father coming home some nights looking a little the worse for wear and describing a particularly nasty brawl he and his colleagues had had with some of the petty criminals in the area.

Later, my father was transferred to the vice squad which was mainly involved in the detection of illegal drug use, gambling and prostitution. In those days, drug-takers were usually opium-users who congregated in dim and smoky dens in the narrow maze of lanes and alleyways behind Chinatown. The Chinese were the only 'foreigners' in Melbourne at that time, and they kept mostly to themselves. Melbourne's Chinatown, which spread across a couple of city blocks, consisted mainly of restaurants, several Confucian temples, some illegal gambling rooms, and rows upon rows of small terrace houses where the Chinese lived.

We hardly ever went to Chinatown when I was a child, but during the war, after I had met Julius, we often went because Julius loved Chinese food. He thought the food in

Chinatown better than the best Chinese food he had eaten in his home town of Surabaya, which had a far larger Chinese population than Melbourne.

My father had a soft spot for the Chinese. His systematic raids on the opium dens were never violent.

'Who does this place belong to?' he'd ask.

The busted Chinese would have a quick discussion and then one of them would step forward to take the blame. Their arrangement was that they would take it in turns to be arrested and serve some time in jail.

The brothels were mainly to be found in the lanes off Little Lonsdale Street, not all that far from Chinatown. They were usually small shopfronts with a light above the entrance and the proprietor's name discreetly engraved on a small brass plate on the door. Sometimes, when I was out with my father doing the week's shopping in nearby Carlton, he would be greeted by amiable, heavily made-up ladies who were also doing their shopping. One time, when I was perhaps ten years old, I can remember meeting a woman in a bright red dress, wearing the most startlingly red lipstick I had ever seen.

'Hello, Constable Walters,' she called out. 'Is that your little girl? How are you, love?'

'I'm fine, thank you,' I answered, wondering how my father knew this exotic woman.

'Who was that, Dad?' I asked as soon as she had gone.

'That's Mrs Stella Collins,' he replied. 'She runs a shop.'

'What does she sell?' I asked.

'Oh . . . I think it's lollies . . . yes, lollies,' he said.

Years later, when I was at Melbourne University, I walked down Little Lonsdale Street with a group of students on the way to the dental hospital. One them pointed to a shopfront covered in bright red tiles and said, 'That's a famous brothel. I think it's known as The Blood-house.' I looked at the brass plate on the door. It said 'Proprietor: S. Collins'.

Vaudeville was not my father's greatest love. More than anything, he loved reading. In his spare time, he haunted Melbourne's second-hand bookshops of which there were many in the inter-war years. Sometimes he took me along on these trips. I loved to hear him talk about his favourite writers and poets – Henry Lawson and Banjo Paterson, of course, but also Wordsworth, Tennyson, Byron and, his favourite, Adam Lindsay Gordon. Often on Saturday mornings he would sit in an armchair in the front room, with me seated on the floor by his legs, and tell me stories of his country childhood, or read a Henry Lawson story or a Banjo Paterson poem to me.

My father's dream of an education had been thwarted, but he was determined that I would get a chance to do what had been denied him. Of course, he would have been thrilled had his sons also shown an interest in pursuing their education, but they both left school at fifteen to work for our maternal grandfather in his sewing machine shops. It is hard to exaggerate just how unusual my father's determination was that I should have a good education and, if I was good enough academically, to go on to university. Hardly any working-class child went to university. A tertiary education was for the children of the upper middle classes or the upper class, because only their parents could afford to pay the fees. The children of working-class parents usually left school after year eight and, if they were lucky, found work as apprentices in trades like plumbing and carpentry. The rest toiled away at unskilled jobs.

Even girls with well-to-do parents rarely went on to tertiary education and, if they did, it was mostly to teachers colleges and nursing schools. Few women studied science-based courses like medicine or dentistry. Girls were not expected to take their studies too seriously. What they were expected to take seriously was finding a husband and settling down to have children. They were expected to be wives, mothers, homemakers. If a few girls from wealthy backgrounds studied medicine or dentistry, there were none from working-class homes. Or at least there were none until I came along.

I do not take credit for this. My father may have been just a humble policeman but he was, in many ways, a man whose thinking was ahead of his time. He believed in the equality of the sexes, an idea that in the Melbourne of the 1920s was considered rather radical. Women, he often said to me, should have the same opportunities as men. Every career choice should be open to them, including the sciences, medicine and dentistry. He was determined that I should have every opportunity, and to that end I was enrolled at Methodist Ladies College after I completed grade six at the local East Brunswick primary school.

MLC, as the college was known, was one of Melbourne's best private schools for girls. Situated in the upper middle-class suburb of Kew, I had to travel an hour by tram each morning from Ascot Vale to get there and an hour after school to get back home. The girls wore navy blue dresses with white collars in summer and pleated wool skirts with a white blouse in winter. The navy blue school blazer with the school badge on the pocket was always worn outside of the school, as were navy gloves.

MLC had its share of aristocrats. I can remember Betty and Nola Nicholas, whose family had made millions of pounds from Aspro – the most popular brand of aspirin on the Australian market – being picked up from school in a limousine. While I waited for the tram, I would watch, fascinated, as their chauffeur tucked a rug around Betty and Nola's knees. I was not jealous – just very curious.

From his small wage, my father paid for my tuition at MLC. It was a small fortune for my family and I tried to pay my parents back for the sacrifices they made on my behalf by studying hard. When, in my final year at school, I received marks good enough to get me into medicine, my parents were overjoyed. To pay for my university course, my mother set up a sideline business at home, knitting pullovers, socks and cardigans on a knitting machine she purchased with the family's savings.

We were lucky. The Great Depression had devastated the lives of hundreds of thousands of Australians. My father, secure in his police employment, even though his wages were cut, was still able to provide for the family and even managed to help the destitute who would come to our back door seeking food or small change. While I was aware that many people were suffering, my life was not greatly changed by the Depression. I went to school each day and did my homework at night. Some Saturday nights, I would accompany my mother to the Salvation Army hall to hear my grandfather preach, and on Sunday nights we continued to have friends and family over for tea and a sing-along. Looking back, I think the Depression had a profound effect on my father, as it did on most people of his generation. It certainly made my father a supporter of the Labor Party and I remember how thrilled he was when Robert Menzies lost the general election in 1941.

By then I was in the final year of my dental course at Melbourne University, having switched from medicine to dentistry after my first year. I did so because dentistry was a five-year course while medicine was six, and I did not want to burden my parents with extra costs for my education for any longer than was absolutely necessary. My university years were, in some ways, the happiest of my life. They were carefree years of social outings and developing friendships, yet they were also years of hard study and learning. I was always aware that I was a working-class girl who had been given a chance in life open to few, if any, girls of my background, and I was determined to do well. Even when the war in Europe broke out in 1939, my life remained more or less unaffected. Each day, I would catch the tram to the city and then walk to the dental hospital where lectures and practical classes were held. Each evening, I would travel back home by tram to help my mother prepare the evening meal. There was no thought in those days that it was dangerous for young women to travel on trams alone after dark or walk home from the tram stop. It is not just a form of nostalgia to say that those were safer and simpler times.

Sometimes, I would go out with university friends after tea. Most of my friends were boys from the dental course. I had few girlfriends, basically because I lived most of my life in a male world. I do recall feeling that I was missing out on something – although being the only girl gave me a cachet I otherwise would not have had. While none of the boys interested me much romantically, I enjoyed being the centre of attention.

One of our favourite meeting places was Acland Street in St Kilda, an inner-city, bay-side suburb that boasted lovely Victorian mansions, built with money made on the goldfields or in the land boom of the 1880s. It had grown a little seedy over the years, but that was part of its charm. Acland

Street was a unique street in Melbourne, with its continental coffee houses and cake shops run, for the most part, by Jewish refugees from Europe. For someone whose idea of coffee had always been a cup of hot water with coffee and chicory essence in it, the espresso coffee I drank in the Acland Street cafés made me feel daringly cosmopolitan. When I come back to Melbourne now on visits, it is hard to imagine the Melbourne of my university years. It was such an insular, monocultural city in the 1930s – more British, I'd say, than cities in Britain itself.

Acland Street was important in my life not just because I drank espresso coffee there for the first time. It was in Acland Street that I first encountered people from a culture very different to my own. These were people who had suffered from racism and who had been forced to leave the countries of their birth to make new lives on the other side of the world. The middle-European Jews who frequented Acland Street fascinated me. They seemed so cultured, so well read, so complex compared to the Australians I knew who, for the most part, weren't much interested in anything but football and horse-racing and an hour or two in the pub each afternoon. I loved to listen to their conversations, and it was through them that I came to understand that Nazism was a terrible evil that had to be fought and that, if left unchecked, would touch all of humanity – even Australians, for whom the conflict in Europe seemed a distant one, unrelated to our lives.

Later, after I had graduated and was working at the dental hospital in Spring Street, I met Jewish refugees, mostly from Germany, who had been lucky enough to escape the country before the war started. These men had trained as dentists in Europe but were being asked to re-train in Australia. Some of them were already middle-aged, but despite the turmoil their lives must have been in, they seemed grateful for the chance offered them by Australia to build new lives. They were funny and lively people who did not hide their sadness, but who nevertheless were full of an endearing zest for life. I liked being around them.

I also enjoyed my work at the dental hospital and I am sure I would have stayed there had I not met Julius. I was there for five years, three of them as registrar. I loved the large hall we worked in, crammed together in a way that would be totally unacceptable today. I liked the fact that I had to work hard and that opportunities were open to me that otherwise wouldn't have been had it not been for the war. As soon as my male university colleagues graduated, they joined up and, within months, they were sent off to the Middle East or North Africa. But the war in Europe did not affect our lives all that much. It wasn't until the Japanese attacked Pearl Harbor and began their march through Asia that Australians felt threatened.

Cliff had not joined up when the war in Europe broke out in the 1939. Instead he and Russell worked for our grandfather, though it was soon obvious that they would never make great businessmen, certainly not selling sewing machines. The sewing machine business simply did not suit their temperaments. They liked a drink and a yarn at the pub, none of which made Grandfather Ward, with his Salvation Army background, particularly happy. When the war in the Pacific started, first Cliff and later Russell came home and told Dad that they were going to enlist. I don't think my father said much when they told him. He probably reckoned that it was inevitable that his boys would eventually go off to fight in the war. But Dad had memories of the first war and the dreadful carnage that came with it. This war, he thought, would be no different. His boys had to go and fight, but he accepted their decision to join the army with something approaching dread.

My mother, like so many other mothers, cried – though not in front of her sons. In front of them, she put on a brave face. She said the war would be over before we knew it and the boys would be home within months, if not weeks. But her face told another story altogether. Only after I had children of my own did I truly understand what it must have been like for my mother – for all mothers – to send her sons off to fight in a war, not knowing whether they would survive. But Julius went to war with no mother to send him off.

four

Julius was born in Surabaya on the northern coast of east Java. His parents moved there from Ambon just before he was born in 1916. Surabaya was – and remains today – the major port city of the Indonesian archipelago, and is the second largest city in Java behind Jakarta. Julius's father worked as a security guard in an asphalt plant owned by Shell, but was known locally for his expertise in traditional herbal medicine. After he finished work at the Shell plant, Julius's father would dispense herbal remedies from his home to a range of clients who included the local Dutch civil servants and businesspeople.

Julius's mother died when her son was ten. Julius remembers her as a beautiful woman who wore colourful sarongs and had immaculately groomed, long black hair. His mother's death affected Julius deeply. It signalled the end of his family life, for his father was a remote and distant parent who, while he cared for Julius and was concerned that he have a good education, could not give him the love he needed and had received in such abundance from his mother. It was his mother's death, more than any other event of his childhood, that formed Julius's character. He developed a self-sufficiency and a drive to succeed that has stayed with him all his life. Like so many children who lose a parent early, Julius entered the adult world while still young, for he had to fend for himself in a way that inevitably meant an end to his childhood.

Julius was a slight, dark-skinned boy, much darker than the average Javanese, and he was always conscious of his Melanesian roots. His ancestors had come from the Moluccas, known universally as the Spice Islands, where the soil is just right for the growing of cloves and cinnamon and nutmeg. He lived with his father in a *kampong*, a small village, on the edge of the city where the communal life provided some compensation for the loss of his mother.

Surabaya was the principal business centre of the Dutch East Indies, and through its port passed most of the colony's imports and exports. The city was surrounded by plantations of tea, coffee, sugar, rubber and tobacco; the city's wealthy families – and there were many of them – lived in beautiful colonial homes with high ceilings and lush gardens. The local women wore sarongs and the men white pants and high-collared white jackets with large-brimmed straw hats.

Julius was not an ethnic Javanese, but having been born in

Surabaya and having grown up there, he was immersed in Javanese culture – a culture that dates back thousands of years and has survived until today, despite centuries of foreign domination. The Javanese are quiet people who respect their elders and who have a strong belief in hierarchy and authority. In general, they do not show emotion – a characteristic, I must say, that Julius does not possess. When they are angry, Javanese always remain polite and many people from the West misinterpret this politeness for humility. This veil of politeness can create difficulties for outsiders like me, because you never know what a Javanese is truly thinking. What you must learn to do is to read people properly, a skill that took me years to acquire.

From very early in his life, Julius was aware of the fact that Indonesians did not control their own destiny, and that in many ways their fate rested in the hands of the Dutch colonists. The Dutch were not all that interested in educating Indonesian children and by the time Julius reached school age, only a small proportion of Indonesian youngsters made it past third grade. The only Indonesian children who managed to get into Dutch schools were the sons and daughters of local dignitaries.

Because of his standing as a herbalist, even amongst the Dutch, Julius's father managed to get both his sons – Julius had a brother two years younger than him – into a good Dutch elementary school. The school was a heady world for a child from the *kampong* and it was to have a huge influence on Julius who grew to love the Dutch language and culture. Slowly, Julius learnt to adopt western ways, something his father wanted for him but which alienated parent from child. On one occasion, father and son were invited to lunch by the school's minister, whose American wife had taken a liking to Julius. To begin the meal, she served them a typical American salad. Later, on their way home after lunch, Julius's father muttered: 'How is it possible that my son is being fed grass and other uncooked vegetables as if he is a goat?'

Despite the difficulties of bridging two cultures, Dutch and Javanese, Julius was already trying to come to grips with a third. While still a young boy, he began taking a bus across Surabaya to a night school that offered English classes. Having looked at a map of the world and seen that the British Empire stretched across half the globe, Julius had decided that English would be an asset no matter what he did later in his life. Most of the students at the night school were of Chinese descent, and it was from them that Julius developed his passion for business, for trading, and for what he still calls 'making a guilder'.

By the time he was twelve, Julius could speak English fluently – as well as Dutch, Malay, German and Javanese. He had learnt to live across cultures – the Dutch and the Javanese – and, from his Chinese friends at the English school, he had learnt the importance of persistence and hard work. His father gave him his daily tram fare but Julius would walk part of the way and save a penny each day. After several weeks, he had enough money to set up a lottery at his school. The prize was a pen which Julius purchased with his saved pennies. He made sure he sold enough tickets to more than pay for the pen and made a tidy profit.

Julius was always on the look-out for business opportunities. Shortly after his successful lottery, he noticed that the women of Surabaya had to struggle to carry their heavy bags of rice home from the markets – often dragging the sacks, which carried up to a month's supply of rice, onto buses and trolley trams. Julius promptly decided to offer a door-to-door rice delivery service. He purchased rice from the wholesalers and every day after school delivered it, in an ox cart he had hired, to the women in his district. The rice delivery business made him enough money to live on through his high school years.

Julius did not go on to tertiary education. Instead, at eighteen, he left the rice delivery business behind him and branched out into selling textiles and housewares door-to-door on commission. A bicycle fitted with a large basket on the handlebars was his main mode of transport. Within a year, Julius had built himself a mini-empire, trading in textiles and housewares imported from Europe, as well as books and cosmetics. A fleet of small trucks was now delivering Julius Tahija merchandise. Julius had learnt to trade, and trading was the economic lifeblood not only of Java, but of all the islands of the Indonesian archipelago. Indonesians have been traders for as long as there have been records – though for much of that time, Indonesian trade was dominated by its colonial masters, first from Asia and later from Europe.

Of course, there were other things in Julius's life than work. He was a big fan of American westerns – he still is – and every Saturday afternoon, he would head off with his friends to the local soccer oval where an oil company had set up a large screen and charged only a penny for admission. The films were not subtitled, but that wasn't important: it was clear who were the goodies and who were the baddies and that's all that really mattered. Even today, if asked, Julius would undoubtedly say that John Wayne was the greatest actor of all time.

But even more than American westerns, Julius loved *wayang,* which means 'people puppets'. In the West, puppets are largely used to entertain children, but in Java the *wayang* is a form of epic theatre. Every story is about love and power, and each performance has ogres, demons, poetry, humour and music.

Shortly after we moved from Macassar to Jakarta in 1948, I saw my first *wayang*. The performance started at around nine in the evening and lasted until sunrise. I did not last that long, but Julius did. He sat there until morning, in front of the screen, behind which the puppeteer worked his magic: telling his story and moving the shadowy figures of his puppets on a large, back-lit sheet. This is all that most of the audience ever see of the dozens of puppets, made from the stretched, dried skin of a female water buffalo and then painted with great attention to detail.

One of Julius's fondest childhood memories is of attending *wayang* with his friends from the *kampong* – his Dutch school friends were not interested. He has often spoken fondly of the adventures they shared as the *wayang* went on through the night. When they became restless, they would go for a walk and perhaps buy some food from the hawkers who sold cooked rice, peanuts, coconut, sweets and a noodle called *bami*. They would flirt with girls and burn sticks of incense. But mostly they sat there for hours, transfixed by the tales the puppeteer spun with consummate skill.

In 1937, when he was twenty-one, Julius decided to join the Dutch East Indies army. I have never been sure why he did this, but no doubt the fact that his father had been a soldier must have had something to do with it. As with most things in his life, Julius carefully weighed the pros and cons before joining the armed forces. He loved his business life, but was concerned that he had seen nothing of the world but Surabaya. The army offered him the opportunity of seeing more of Indonesia – there was no thought of travelling overseas – and, over time, of making contacts that would help him develop his business interests, some of which he hoped he could continue even while he served in the military. Julius did not know, of course, that he would never live in Surabaya again, that he would not see his father for nearly eight years, and that the knowledge of English he had developed so early in his life would eventually lead him to Australia and to me.

Julius did his military training in west Java before he was sent to Aceh, in northern Sumatra, where he joined an elite corp of Acehnese jungle fighters. The Acehnese were renowned for their fighting qualities and their courage. They were a proud and independent people from whom Julius learnt a lot. This was a new world for Julius. Over the next four years he learnt to fight, using a curved sword that was so sharp it could cut through the trunk of a banana tree three times while the tree was still standing. He learnt how to read broken leaves for signs of animals and people; he learnt how to set traps; to use bamboo as a weapon; to recognise edible vegetables; and to get water from rattan vines. Above all, he learnt how to survive in the jungle, a skill that would save his life on some of his secret missions during the war.

The outbreak of war in Europe did not affect the East Indies. It seemed a long way away from the jungles of Aceh where Julius was based. It was not until the Japanese attacked Pearl Harbor on 7 December 1941 that Julius's life changed dramatically. The Dutch government-in-exile declared war on Japan and sent troops to bolster the British forces in Singapore. To no avail. Singapore fell in mid-February and the Japanese began their march down the Malayan Peninsula. On 2 March 1942, the Dutch surrendered to the Japanese in the East Indies.

Three weeks before the surrender, Julius had been chosen to lead an escort of East Indies soldiers on the ship taking Japanese internees to Australia. By then, he was a sergeant and one of the few indigenous soldiers who could speak English. Before they could return, Java fell to the Japanese and the ship on which they were travelling turned back to Fremantle. Julius's only memento from home was a pocket watch that his uncle had given him when he left Surabaya for his military training in west Java.

Thinking he would be back in Indonesia within weeks, Julius had taken no other mementos with him when he sailed. No photographs of his childhood and none of his parents survived the Japanese occupation. When he finally went back to Surabaya four years later, after the war, his father – who had been interned by the Japanese – was sick and dying.

Those weeks Julius spent in Fremantle were lonely ones. He knew no-one in Australia and very little about the country. He had spent all his years in Surabaya and though his English was quite good, Fremantle was a small town unused to the presence of strangers. Most of the time, Julius stayed in the barracks to which he was assigned, wondering what was happening to his younger brother and his father back home. Terrible stories were filtering back to Australia of Japanese atrocities, but Julius had no way of communicating with his family and friends in Indonesia. When he was told by his Dutch military commanders that he was to go to

Melbourne, where he would be given new duties, Julius wondered whether the food there would be any better than the army rations of bully beef and over-cooked boiled vegetables he had been living on in Fremantle.

By the time Julius arrived in Melbourne, Japanese bombers had attacked Darwin, killing 240 people. By then, General MacArthur had arrived in Australia to take command of the Allied troops and the Australian prime minister, John Curtin, had won the battle with Winston Churchill to get Australian divisions back from the Middle East to defend the country from what many considered an imminent Japanese invasion. Apart from sending Australian troops to New Guinea and the Solomon Islands to protect the island route to the Australian mainland, Allied troops were also sent to the Indonesian islands for what was vaguely described as intelligence-gathering missions.

Three weeks after we first met, Julius was sent on such a mission. Of course, at that stage, neither of us knew what lay in store.

five

The dental hospital in Spring Street, Melbourne, was an old, two-storey Victorian building which, in the autumn of 1942, had its large wooden windows covered in black cloth in case of enemy air raids. Having graduated from the dental school at Melbourne University a year previously – the only woman graduate in a class of twenty-four, and one of only a handful of women to have studied dentistry in Melbourne – I was virtually the only one of my graduating class working at the hospital. The only other was a young Italian boy, Mario Ballini, who could not join the Australian forces, even if he wanted to, because Italy was one of the Axis powers and therefore at war with Australia. Despite the fact that Mario had come to Australia when he was a child, he was considered a potential enemy alien.

Mario had a hard time of it. Professor Amies, the head of dentistry, treated him with contempt, often referring to him as the enemy and alluding to the supposed cowardice of the Italian troops, then fighting Australian soldiers in the African desert. I liked Mario a lot. I was as patriotic as anyone in the hospital, but I felt that my former classmate did not deserve the jibes directed at him by our boss or, for that matter, the insults whispered behind his back by many of the staff.

After the war, Professor Amies actually apologised to Mario for the way he had treated him, confessing that he had always thought Mario would make a first-class dentist. And Mario did go on to build himself a very successful practice. At the time, I felt sorry for Mario; but, in truth, I was more concerned with how the war effort was going, and whatever his feelings, I fervently hoped that the Australian troops in Africa would win a great victory against the Italians.

It was not just my former classmates who were off fighting the war in Europe and in Asia. My brothers, Cliff and Russell, had enlisted shortly after the Japanese attack on Pearl Harbor in 1941, and both of them had been shipped to New Guinea at the beginning of 1942. Like thousands of other parents, my mother and father lived in dread of receiving that awful telegram from the military informing them of the death of one of their children. Such telegrams had arrived for neighbours and friends. The pain they caused is indescribable. Often parents suffered silently, behind closed doors, so as not to upset others whose sons were still alive but in mortal danger. My father, who at the time was in charge of Melbourne's vice squad, would spend most evenings sitting in front of our radio, desperate for news of the war. He was not a man who spoke easily of his feelings, but the pain of having two sons in danger was permanently etched upon his broad, handsome face.

My brothers wrote intermittently, and then, only short notes that conveyed nothing of the horrors they were going through. It was not their way to talk about their fears and hopes. Their letters, which arrived perhaps once every three months, simply told us that they were alive and unharmed. Each short note always had a joke at the end for my parents.

From time to time my mother would send them parcels made up of several pairs of woollen socks knitted by friends and relatives – their contribution to the war effort – and several sets of warm underwear. Of course, these gifts were of no use to them in the tropics, but so insular were our lives that it never dawned on us that such clothing was inappropriate for men sweating it out in the jungles of New Guinea. There was, however, one item in those parcels that my brothers did appreciate. Mum would hollow out a loaf of white bread and carefully, lovingly, place a bottle of beer inside. This was her special contribution to the war effort of her sons.

It is difficult to convey the mood in Melbourne during those autumn months of 1942. The Nazis had conquered much of Europe and seemed to be well on their way to occupying Russia. Our finest troops and almost all our naval and air forces were across the other side of globe, stationed in

Britain or in North Africa and the Middle East. Meanwhile, the Japanese had begun their relentless march through Asia. Singapore, once considered impregnable, had fallen almost without a whimper. So too had much of Southeast Asia, and by the beginning of 1942, the Dutch had abandoned the East Indies to the Japanese. In New Guinea, Rabaul and Lae had been taken. It seemed that nothing could stop Japan's progress towards an Australia that felt defenceless and alone.

There were some things, because of wartime censorship, that we did not know. We did not know of the Japanese air attacks on Darwin, which had killed hundreds of people. We did not know that Japanese submarines had fired on Sydney and Newcastle. And we did not know that the Japanese were flying reconnaissance missions over Melbourne.

The people of Melbourne, those of us left in the city – soldiers waiting to be shipped out, women and children, men too old or infirm to fight – spoke of hardly anything but the war and how it was going. We knew, from the news coverage of Japan's bloody ten-year rampage through China in the 1930s, what the Japanese Imperial forces were capable of. There had been horrifying stories in our newspapers about the hundreds of thousands of Chinese civilians – men, women and children – who had been tortured and murdered in the rape of Nanking alone. It was frightening to know that some of the regiments involved in the war crimes committed in Nanking were deployed for Japan's assault on the south-west Pacific.

Given all our fears, most Australians welcomed the presence of American troops in the country. There were people – mostly Australian soldiers – who resented their wealth and their success with the local girls, but they were a minority. Our spirits rose when we learnt, in April 1942, that the supreme command of the Allied war effort in the south-west Pacific had been placed in the hands of the US commander in the region, General Douglas MacArthur.

The black curtains that covered the dental hospital's windows were in response to a general order for all Melbourne buildings to be blacked out after dark in case of Japanese air raids. Windows were shuttered each night and black curtains, sewn by thousands of women, were drawn over the panes of every suburban house. Lights were dimmed, and the lawns in public parks, school grounds and even the backyards of homes were scarred by the zigzag lines of narrow trenches. We were supposed to crouch in these when the bombs began to fall.

My father had dug such a trench in the backyard of our rambling, red-brick, Edwardian home, which we had bought in 1941 and which, despite the war, my father was renovating with the help of friends and neighbours. Each afternoon, around dusk, he would check the trench to make sure the walls had not caved in, then he would go inside and draw the black curtains my mother had sewn for every window of the house. He would switch off every light, bar the one in the front room. There he would sit in an armchair beside the radio and listen, for hours, in silent concentration, to the news from the front.

Despite the danger Australia was in and despite our fears and our obsession with the war, life in Melbourne went on. Each morning, I caught the tram that ran along Mount Alexander Road to the city. I would get off at Bourke Street, and then walk the four blocks to Spring Street to the dental hospital. Each day, I would put on my white coat and line up my instruments beside the dental chair in the large, high-ceilinged hall on the second floor where we worked, perhaps two dozen of us.

In truth, I loved the work. Then, as now, the dental hospital was there for Melbourne's poorer citizens, those who could not afford private dental treatment. I was in charge of 'locals' – extractions done mainly under local anaesthetic. Within a few weeks of my starting at the hospital, I could not begin to count the number of teeth I had removed. This was long before Melbourne's water supply was fluoridated, and it was quite normal for young children to need virtually every tooth in their jaw removed as a result of decay. More often than not, the adults who came to the hospital were white with pain as a result of toothache, and in terms of treatment, all I could do was remove the tooth or teeth that were causing such agony.

I quickly became expert at extractions, which are less a matter of brute strength than of good timing and expert positioning of the forceps. While the armed forces had their own dental facilities, most of the merchant seaman who visited Melbourne came to the dental hospital for treatment.

Most were surprised and disconcerted to find that their dentist was a petite, young, blonde woman who was only a little over five foot tall.

One burly Yugoslav seaman simply refused to believe that I was a dentist. No woman, he cried, would ever put a pair of pliers in his mouth! After a while, when it finally dawned on him that he could either let me deal with his toothache or take it back to sea with him, he relented. Moments after I had removed the troublesome tooth, he suggested that a beautiful young woman in wartime should do more than just peer into the mouths of seamen. She should, he said, experience romance, love, adventure – before it was too late. He would be delighted, if I was agreeable, to provide all of this. I politely declined, but assured him that the next time he was in Melbourne I would be happy to peer into his mouth again if it proved necessary.

On weekends, I helped my father work on the house, along with his friends. One of them, whose home we visited frequently, lived in North Melbourne, close to Camp Pell, a sprawling, makeshift military depot made up of endless rows of corrugated iron huts which covered much of Royal Park. Camp Pell was a transit camp for soldiers from various Allied countries, including some detachments of Indonesian troops from the Dutch East Indies army who had escaped the country before the arrival of the Japanese. They were small, dark-skinned men of slight build who, when given leave, could been seen wandering around the city in small groups looking a little lost and bewildered. Unlike some other soldiers, they were never drunk or obstreperous. I can recall neighbours of ours commenting on their good manners, despite the fact that they spoke virtually no English. We had no idea how they had ended up in Australia or indeed where they had come from.

One detachment, I later learnt, had been escorting Japanese civilians from the Dutch East Indies to Australia for wartime internment. Having unloaded their prisoners at Fremantle, the ship they were travelling on returned to Java. But before they could berth, the Dutch surrendered and the Japanese occupation of the East Indies began. The ship quickly turned around and headed back to Fremantle, from where the soldiers on board were sent to Melbourne by the Dutch military commanders in Australia. Strangers in a strange country far from home, unsure what was happening to their loved ones now living under Japanese occupation, the soldiers were left, more or less, to their own devices.

While American soldiers were welcomed into many homes, as were Australian soldiers from other states who were based in Melbourne, many of the locals who lived near Camp Pell saw the Indonesians as a strange and exotic group of men with whom they had nothing in common. My father's friend did not see it that way. Harry Anderson was an old policeman, a gruff, straight-talking man who beneath his grumpy exterior had a kind and generous heart. He befriended some of the Indonesians, especially a young sergeant who spoke English well. He was, according to Harry, 'a smart little bloke'.

Harry asked my mother to invite some of the Indonesians home for tea, and she immediately agreed. These men were fighting the same war as her sons, and she was prepared to do whatever she could to make their stay in Melbourne comfortable. Essential foods were rationed so that our forces and the Americans could be adequately supplied. For butter, tea, sugar and meat, you had to hand over coupons to the shopkeepers. Nevertheless, we managed to feed several groups of Indonesian soldiers. We communicated in a sort of sign language and there was much laughter around the dinner table as we fumbled to make ourselves understood. Looking back, the cold meats and salads we served them must have been strange and exotic fare for these men, whose diets would have consisted mainly of rice, vegetables and salted dried fish.

One day, Harry's 'smart little bloke' telephoned my mother to thank her for her kindness to his men. In turn, Mum invited the sergeant to tea the following Saturday, at 6.30 p.m.

Saturday, 18 May 1942, was one of those gorgeous, early winter, Melbourne days, with pale blue skies and just enough warmth in the sun to take the chill off the crisp, still air. Mum and I went to the Victoria Market, which was only a short tram ride away from our house. The market was a collection of large tin sheds inside which were dozens of fruit and vegetable stalls. There were also sheds full of clothing, and a large red-brick building at one end of the market that, in normal times, housed dozens of butcher shops and delicatessens selling exotic items like salami and continental cheeses that could be found in few places elsewhere. Most of the butchers were closed because of wartime rationing, and the shelves of the delicatessens were almost empty. Still, the market was a lovely place in which to spend a couple of hours.

We bought lettuce and tomatoes and onions for the salad we were going to make, and managed to scrape together enough coupons to buy some ham and corned beef. For dessert, we bought oranges, pears and apples which I would chop up for a fruit salad. It seems absurd that almost fifty-five years later I can clearly recall such trivia, but then again, this was to be a life-changing day. Of course I didn't know that as I stood cutting up fruit in our newly renovated kitchen with its white-painted wooden cupboards and gleaming stainless steel sink – a real luxury in 1942 – while Mum laid out the cold meats on our Sunday-best meat platter and chopped up the salad vegetables.

At six, we set the dining table which, when it wasn't used for eating, was a billiards table. There would be only the four of us for dinner – my mother, my father, the Indonesian sergeant and me. Having set the table, I went to my room, where I changed into a navy knit-suit that I felt complimented my slim figure and blonde hair. Did I have some premonition about Julius? It is impossible, looking back, to know, because that day is now invested with so much retrospective meaning – each moment special and preserved forever in my memory.

After I'd dressed, Dad lit the fire in the front room. We all sat beside it, more or less in silence – and in semi-darkness – waiting for our guest to arrive. The house wasn't the same without Cliff and Russell. It felt empty and forlorn. Mum missed her sons terribly. You could see it on her face and hear it in her voice whenever we spoke about the war – which was a lot of the time – and you could feel it when she hovered around Dad's chair as he listened to the war news on the radio. Dad suffered too, but more silently than Mum. Both of them clung to me more than they ever had in the past. In a way, I was their only child, and though I was twenty-six years old, I was very close to them too.

At six-thirty, I heard the front gate creak open, a signal that our guest had arrived. I pulled aside the blackout curtain on the window beside the fireplace, and saw a slim man wearing a blue airforce uniform close the gate and turn around slowly before making his way up the path towards the front door. In the dim light of the blacked out streetlamp, I could see that he was dark-skinned, had shiny black hair and very white teeth. I ran to the door and opened it before he could ring the bell. He smiled and removed his cap.

'Hello, I am Sergeant Julius Tahija,' he said, pronouncing it as Ta-heer. 'You can't be Mrs Walters, so I must assume you are her daughter. I'm very pleased to meet you.'

He held out his hand. I noticed how slim his fingers were, how long and graceful. His skin was the colour of dark chocolate. His fingernails were pink and well looked after. I put my hand in his.

'Yes, I am her daughter,' I said. 'My name is Jean and I am very pleased that you could come, Sergeant Tahija.'

'Please,' he said, 'call me Julius.'

'Well then I'm glad you could come, Julius,' I said.

Did he hold my hand for a moment longer than was proper? Did I feel a slight trembling of my fingers as he wrapped them in his palm? Did these things happen, and is that why I suddenly felt as if a small electric charge had passed through my body?

Mum and Dad were standing behind me, but for several moments I was oblivious to their presence. Something passed between us at the moment we met, some sort of recognition of each other that was conscious, but that didn't come from thought but from somewhere else. Were I not a rationalist, I would say that our souls collided at the front door of that house in Ascot Vale fifty-five years ago.

I do not know to this day whether either of my parents realised what was happening when Julius and I first met. I do know that for the rest of the evening, I was a little dazed. Julius and Dad talked a lot about the war and about what might happen with the Dutch in the East Indies after the war ended. My father said that the time when the nations of Europe could rule countries on the other side of the world was virtually gone. I could see that Julius was impressed by his knowledge of the world and his anti-colonialism, but all the time, Julius kept his eyes on me, and I returned his stare, even though I felt my mother watching us. Once, in the kitchen, she asked me what I thought of Julius. I blushed and said he seemed like a nice young man. My mother smiled, but said nothing more.

Even now, the immediacy of my attraction to Julius seems remarkable. I was a mature young woman who had gone out with several men, though none of these relationships had been serious. Certainly none of these young men had stirred my heart the way Julius did that night. In fact, there had been times when I doubted that I would ever meet a man with whom I would fall in love. This was not something that caused me great sadness. I was not pining for a knight in shining armour to come along and take me away. I liked my life. I liked my work. I thought that some time in the future, it might be nice to get married and perhaps even have a family, but if the right man did not come along, I felt I would be quite happy to remain single.

How was it then that moments after I'd met him, I knew that Julius would be in my life for a long time? There was nothing rational about it, and not for a second that night did I stop to reflect on the difficulties I might face. We were in the middle of a terrible war. My brothers were away and we feared that they might never come back. This man for whom I felt such an instant attraction was a soldier from a country about which I knew nothing. He was an Asian. Most likely, he would soon be sent overseas to fight the Japanese. It was a form of madness to get involved with such a man at such a time. But madness or no, I knew that night that I would love Julius for the rest of my life. I knew that he knew it too.

six

When Julius left our house on that first night we met, I walked him to the front gate. The taxi that was to take him back to Camp Pell was already there waiting. Walking beside him, it felt almost as if we were touching, as if the distance between us didn't exist. He did not touch me, nor did I expect him to. Mum and Dad stood at the front door waving goodbye and I wondered whether they were watching us, whether they had caught any sign of what Julius and I were feeling. Actually, I wasn't certain what Julius was feeling. I only knew that his presence next to me was so powerful that I wasn't sure I could cope if he put his hand out to bid me farewell. As it was, he didn't. He just smiled and said, 'Goodnight, I hope to see you again'. Then he stepped quickly into the taxi and was gone.

I don't think I slept very well that night. I think I lay in bed wondering what had come over me. I think I tried to tell myself that nothing would come of this, that he would never call and that I would never see him again. But all of this was unconvincing. When Julius called the next evening I was thrilled, but not really surprised. Actually, he spoke to my mother. He asked her whether she would mind if he took me out for dinner.

'When?' Mum asked.

'Perhaps tomorrow night, Mrs Walters, if you don't mind. I'll have Jean home early. By nine-thirty at the latest. Probably before then,' Julius replied.

You might think that at twenty-six I could have handled the arranging of dinner with Julius myself, and in normal circumstances that's exactly what would have happened. Even in 1942, young men did not need parents' permission to take a young woman out to dinner. Julius, unsure of the local customs, had decided to play it safe. My mother, for her part, seemed to enjoy the experience immensely.

'Well, as long as she's home by nine-thirty, that should be fine,' she said with as straight a face as she could manage.

The next day Julius picked me up at six-thirty sharp. I'd had just enough time to change out of my dental hospital clothes into the same blue knitted skirt and jacket I had worn when Julius came to dinner. Julius told me I looked beautiful. In the back seat of the taxi we sat close together, but not so close that we were touching. We said nothing. I looked out of the window at the darkened streets. They were virtually empty but for the occasional tram that rattled past out of the gloom. Julius held his army cap in his hands and looked straight ahead. There was a tremendous sort of electricity between us, a physical attraction that was very powerful and a little disconcerting. I'd never felt anything like this before.

Julius told me years later that in the taxi on the way to the restaurant, he had wondered what he was doing. He had always been someone who planned things carefully, who was level-headed and rational about the decisions he made regarding his life. Here he was, cut off from his home, likely to be sent away to fight the Japanese, unsure of how long he would be away or even whether he would survive, and he was already contemplating a commitment to a woman he had met only once and about whom he knew next to nothing.

I knew nothing about Julius either, and I knew even less about the East Indies than he knew about Australia. Julius, whose knowledge of Australia had been picked up during his school years in Surabaya, knew the country was very large and that it was mostly desert. He knew that it had far more sheep than people and that Australians ate lamb for breakfast, lunch and tea.

We were strangers from very different cultures who, superficially, had nothing in common. Yet the attraction we felt for each other was so powerful that it overrode all our doubts. I knew that, almost inevitably, Julius's stay in Melbourne would be a short one. Soon he would be shipped off somewhere and in all probability I would never see him again. But, as I reasoned to myself at the time, what was the point of thinking about the future when the future was so clouded, when we weren't even sure that the future would exist. They were desperate times in which to fall in love, but when one did, one often loved desperately.

We had dinner that night at the Eastern Café on the corner of Russell Street and Little Bourke Street in Chinatown. It was a large barn of a place with Chinese lanterns hanging from the black ceilings and chipped laminex tables and chairs. The windows, because of the blackout, were all shuttered and the room was suffused with a dull red light. There were perhaps a dozen or so people in the restaurant when we arrived, scattered around the edges of the room. For the first of what were to be many times like this, everyone turned and stared at us as we entered. There was no open hostility in this – not as far as I could tell anyway – just puzzled curiosity at the sight of a white Australian woman on the arm of an Asian man. I have no doubt that Australia was a racist country in those days and, in some ways, I think it still is. But in 1942, with the country at war with Japan and people's worst fears of invasion on the verge of being realised, racism was probably at its peak.

Julius was far less sensitive to the stares we received than I. In Surabaya, intermarriage between the Dutch colonists and the local people was relatively commonplace. Whilst the Dutch did little to ensure that indigenous Indonesians received a proper education, and senior civil service posts were all reserved for Dutchmen, Julius had gone to a Dutch school and had never felt inferior. He had certainly never thought that a love affair across the races was somehow taboo.

Interracial love affairs were far less common in Australia and I have no doubt that many people found such relationships distasteful. I think that because Julius was so clearly a proud man, unlikely to take abuse lightly from anyone, he was only confronted by racist remarks in Australia on one or two occasions. Once, in another Chinese restaurant when we were out with my mother, a man refused to pay his bill. The Chinese proprietor was pleading with him, but to no avail. Julius stood up from his seat and walked over to the man. He advised him quietly to pay.

'What's it got to do with you?' the man shouted. 'Anyway, you're not even a white man, you black bastard.'

Julius took the man by the arm. 'You don't want any trouble, I'm sure. Pay the bill now and leave. Please.'

The man paid and left.

More often, colleagues and acquaintances of mine would say things that made it clear they disapproved of my relationship with Julius. The head of the dental hospital, Professor Amies, once asked me about Julius in a tone that was expressly designed to convey his distaste.

'How did you meet that chap from Asia?' he asked.

'Oh, we invited him home for tea,' I said sweetly.

'For tea?' he echoed, as if this was the most unusual thing he had ever heard.

Once, in the dental hospital's common room, one of the nurses, after asking me about Julius, said: 'I can't imagine having black hands on my body'. There was an embarrassed silence at this crude remark, but no-one said anything – including myself. I was shocked into speechlessness.

None of this mattered, not at the beginning and not later. After we were married, *The Herald* reported on our relationship in a short article headlined, 'Black Hero Returns for White Wife'. My parents were more shocked by this than I was. I'd grown accustomed to the ignorant reactions my relationship with Julius sometimes provoked.

Julius and I did not discuss racism that night at the Eastern Café. Julius ordered a delicious meal of chilli prawns, roast duck and stir-fried vegetables, and we talked about ourselves the way people do when they first meet and are attracted to each other. Julius told me about his childhood, and about the death of his mother and how it had affected him. He described Surabaya for me so that I could imagine the city in which he'd grown up. He told me of his early business career, of his Dutch education, and of his training in jungle fighting and survival. He also told me about the men who'd come with him on the ship to Australia: men from all parts of Indonesia, simple men who were brave soldiers but who were confused by the war and what was happening to them. I loved to hear him talk. I loved the stories he told.

I too told stories of my childhood, and we spoke of how different my upbringing was from his. At some stage his hand must have reached across the table and taken mine because, in one of those awkward moments of silence, I became aware that his fingers were caressing mine and that I was enjoying it immensely. In the taxi on the way home, Julius kissed me for the first time. I can still remember that kiss because, at that moment, I knew that this would not be just a casual fling, but a serious relationship. The war was always in the background, a blanket on my dreams, but I knew then that war or no war we were a couple and that, God willing, we would make a life together after the war.

Julius kissed me again at the front gate of our house. I watched as he climbed into the taxi and headed off, back to Camp Pell. I wondered how long we would have together before he was sent away. I hoped that it would be long enough for us to get to know each other better. And I hoped that he would not be sent too far away – to somewhere out of Australia, somewhere dangerous.

Mum and Dad were in the front room, waiting for me. They tried hard not to look concerned, but they didn't quite manage it. They asked me how the evening had gone. I told them the food was delicious and said that the four of us should go out to dinner sometime. My mother suggested that it might be best if Julius came home again for tea. She would call and invite him.

I slept fitfully that night and there is every possibility that my extractions the next day weren't quite up to the high standards I'd set for myself. The next night, Julius and I met at the dental hospital and walked around Melbourne for a couple of hours. It was enough just to be with each other, holding hands. I could not bring myself to ask him for how long he would be based in Melbourne; and he didn't want to tell me that within a few weeks he'd be sent to Canberra for training and then on to Cairns for a special mission.

Later that week, Julius came to our house for tea again. My father sat next to him and, as on the previous occasion, they talked about Indonesia and about the overthrow of colonialism. Julius said that Indonesia would be the United States of Asia one day. They seemed to get on well, but that didn't mean my father wanted our relationship to be anything more than platonic. Mum said almost nothing. She was worried about my brothers and now she was worried about me – about what would happen if this relationship became really serious. She never said a word to me about the concerns I knew she had. She didn't once talk to me about Julius – not even when it became clear that I was deeply in love with him. Nor did my father. He treated Julius with great kindness, but he kept his distance. I guess he hoped our relationship would not last. I believe my parents both hoped for this, not because they were racist or bigoted, but because I was their only daughter and they didn't want me leaving them to live in Indonesia.

I saw Julius every day. Sometimes, we would go for a walk. At other times, he would come to the dental hospital after I'd finished work and we would snatch a couple of hours together in the empty hall filled with dental chairs. On weekends, we often went to the zoo – one of Julius's favourite places – where we'd wander through the animal enclosures and then sit on a bench near the lion's enclosure and talk. I'm not sure now what we talked about, but I know we didn't talk about the future. There was no point.

Perhaps other couples might have considered getting married straight away; perhaps they might even have considered having a child so that, whatever happened, something would remain of the relationship. I thought about it, but decided it would be too difficult. What if Julius was sent away on a mission from which he never returned? I would be left with a child who would have no access to a heritage of which he was so visibly a part, in an Australia which would make his life hard. On one occasion, Julius told me I would look lovely in white. That was the only time he ever hinted that we might get married one day. The rest of the time, we lived in the present. It was enough that we enjoyed being with one another, holding each other, talking and just being quiet together. I only slept a couple of hours a night. So did Julius. The rest of the time we spent together.

Late at night, Julius would come to our house and stay with me until dawn when he had to go back to his barracks. For all our happiness, I felt a deep underlying sadness. When Julius left me to return to camp, I'd lie in bed and cry myself to sleep. I could not stand the thought that, any day now, Julius would be sent away. I went to the dental hospital each day red-eyed and tired. Work gave me some respite from my depression. With most of the male dentists away in the armed forces, I was frantically busy. I had no time to think about Julius and about what I would do when he left. But I started to make mistakes. In those days, dentists made up their own local anaesthetic, and I was so tired and preoccupied that on one frightening occasion I mixed up the wrong percentages. Luckily, I realised my mistake before some poor soul was injected with it. This sort of thing had never happened to me before.

Finally, the inevitable occurred and Julius came to the dental hospital and told me he'd be leaving Melbourne in two days' time.

'Where are you going?' I asked. Although I had been expecting this to happen, I began to cry.

'I don't know, darling, I don't know,' he said, putting on a brave face and smiling at my tears. 'Even when I know, I won't be able to tell you.'

'But I won't be able to stand it Julius. Not knowing where you are. Or what's happening to you. How will I cope?'

Julius just held me and said that we'd be together again soon.

Our last two days together passed in a blur and then suddenly Julius was gone. We'd said goodbye at my home, in the middle of the night, desperate to have a few more moments with each other. I stood at the window of the front room and watched him leave. He closed the gate, then turned around and waved. There was a big smile on his face and I cried even more. I was terrified that we might never see each other again.

seven

Julius had told me to write to him care of the army headquarters in Melbourne, from where my letters would be forwarded to him wherever he was sent. I wrote every day, sometimes twice a day. They were desperate letters and, in a way, I am glad that few of them reached Julius because he had enough to contend with without my sadness. He did call me from Canberra where he was based for two weeks before being sent to Darwin. He sounded relaxed and hopeful. He led me to think that he would staying in Australia, that he would be safe, and that he would be returning to Melbourne soon. But after Julius reached Darwin, I didn't hear from him again for seven weeks. When I did hear, it was ominous news. His last communication was a cable sent to the dental hospital. It said: 'Please stop writing. Keep smiling. Julius.'

In Melbourne, the mood was grim. Each day, the newspapers published lists of those who had died. Telegrams were arriving at the homes of neighbours informing them of the deaths of loved ones. My father and mother were desperately worried about Cliff and Russell. The Japanese had landed in New Guinea and it seemed that nothing could stop their march towards Australia. I was worried about my brothers and I was frantic about Julius, not knowing where he was or what was happening to him. I ignored his instruction and continued to write every day, hoping that my letters would somehow get to him. They didn't. Nor did I receive the letters he sent to me. And when he was eventually sent away from Darwin on what was essentially a suicide mission, there was no opportunity for him to write, and certainly no chance of him receiving news from me.

During those frightening months of early 1942, when the Japanese seemed invincible, it seemed inevitable that Australia would be invaded. In desperation, teams of Allied soldiers were sent on secret missions to the small islands of Indonesia that lay like stepping stones off the Australian coastline. The size of these teams varied from ten men to a thousand. They were transported to the islands in small, virtually unarmed boats from Darwin. Their job was supposedly to gather intelligence on the Japanese, but in reality they were futile attempts at resistance. The men were equipped with only the lightest of weapons and limited rations. There were no plans to support them if they got into trouble and no plans to re-supply them if something unexpected happened on the islands to which they were sent.

In the biggest of these secret Allied actions, over a thousand Australian soldiers known as the Gull Force were sent to defend the island of Ambon. These men were expected to sacrifice themselves in order to try to prevent the Japanese from taking over the island. They had no hope. With no means to evacuate Ambon and with no hope of reinforcements, the Australians were soon overrun by a far larger Japanese force. More than half the Australian soldiers died in the attack. The rest were taken prisoner. Many of them died or were killed by their Japanese captors before the war was over.

Despite this, Allied commanders continued to parcel out small numbers of troops to any island that might serve as a springboard for a Japanese invasion of Australia. In Darwin, Julius and his team of Indonesian soldiers were told that they would be part of these secret missions. They spent three weeks in Darwin undertaking special training in guerrilla warfare and then, in early July 1942, they sailed to Indonesia as part of a convoy of three small groups of men. The boats which carried them were old, fragile, rickety wooden vessels that seemed certain to sink in any sizeable storm. They were no more than thirty foot long and were armed only with small deck guns. Julius commanded a troop of thirteen other Indonesian soldiers on board one of these boats.

Once at sea, Julius opened the envelope that contained his orders. He was to sail for the island of Jamdena in the Tanimbar archipelago, which lay 300 miles north of Darwin. He was to berth at the village of Saumlaki, and from there gather as much intelligence as possible. It wasn't even clear whether there were any Japanese on Jamdena. If there were, Julius and his men would simply be massacred.

It took three days for the boat to reach Saumlaki. The sea was often so rough that everyone was seasick, including the boat's captain, an old Australian sailor who told Julius the mission was a form of madness. The soldiers, when they weren't sick, ate Australian army rations of bully beef, biscuits, powdered egg and beer. They especially enjoyed the beer.

When the boat finally arrived at Saumlaki, it was early morning. From the deck, Julius could see a pier about one-third of a mile long, which extended out across the coral reef that surrounded the island. At the end of the pier were several bamboo buildings with thatched roofs. Beyond that lay thick jungle. The pier was deserted. As they disembarked, Julius fired several shots in the air but nothing happened. Then people began to emerge from the jungle. When they saw that Julius was waving a Dutch flag, they rushed forward to greet the soldiers. At the same time, the captain returned to the boat, waved to Julius, backed his vessel away from the pier and sailed for the horizon.

Julius decided that only by digging trenches at the end of the pier and positioning themselves there would he and his men be able to withstand the Japanese in the likely event of an attack. But to dig the trenches in just a couple of days would require at least a hundred men, and so Julius marched off to speak to the Dutch civil servant in charge. He was conducting his daily routine as if he had never heard of the war. Julius informed him that martial law was now in effect and called a village meeting. Soon all the men in the village were digging. Two days later, there were trenches covering every possible sight of the pier, including one which had been dug into a twenty-foot cliff that overlooked the wharf. The trenches were a gamble. The Dutch military manual advised that trenches should be positioned under cover of vegetation. But Julius, guessing that the Japanese were well aware of this instruction, ordered they be dug right on the beach. If the Japanese arrived in daylight, the trenches would be clearly visible and their warships would blast Julius and his handful of soldiers away within seconds. Julius prayed that the Japanese would arrive at night, which would give him and his men a slim chance of survival.

Julius's band was armed with jungle carbines, an old Lewis light machine-gun (a relic of World War I) and thirteen new American Tommy guns. They had only enough ammunition to last a very short time.

As the days passed, Julius and his men took it in turns to watch the pier around the clock. The majority of the villagers were on their side, and shortly after Julius's arrival they revealed that a few of the locals were in fact spies for the Japanese. Julius rounded these men up and questioned them. He told them they faced a simple choice: tell the truth and he would spare their lives; lie and he would kill them on the spot. They confessed everything, including how they'd been recruited by the Japanese and how their job was to report on Allied movements in the Tanimbar islands. They were then locked away in a wooden hut that served as the Saumlaki jail.

The waiting was agony. Julius wrote me letters which he knew he would never send. I seemed to belong to another world – a world that he might never be part of again. The radio they had brought with them no longer worked, and they were completely cut off. Then, at 11.00 p.m. on 29 July, the inevitable happened. Julius was asleep in his hut by the pier – dreaming, he told me later, of me and of his home in Surabaya – when he was shaken awake by the sentry on guard. Two Japanese warships had just entered Saumlaki Bay.

Julius walked to the pier and made his way to the water's edge. In the moonlight, he could see the Japanese flag flying from the two ships. He could also see hundreds of troops in full combat gear climbing over the ships' railings into landing craft. He turned and walked slowly back to the end of the pier, keeping his movements unhurried so as not to attract attention. He assembled his men and they climbed into their positions in the trenches. He told them to hold their fire until he gave them a signal.

The Japanese clearly thought that Saumlaki was unprotected and that the local villagers were asleep. Their landing craft reached the pier and they began to unload their guns and their supplies. Then they assembled and began to march down the long pier. They held their weapons upright, as though marching in parade.

When the Japanese were within firing range, Julius ordered his men to open fire. Scores of Japanese fell during the first few minutes of fierce fighting. Julius had been trained for this, but it was his first action and nothing had prepared him for the noise, the screaming and the fear. The Japanese were trapped. They could not jump off the pier into the water because they were wearing full battle gear and so would almost certainly drown. Instead they retreated back to their boats, sustaining heavy casualties as they ran back along the pier. Within minutes, the big guns on the warships came alive. The shells flew over the heads of Julius and his men and landed in the jungle behind them. Searchlights played on the trees at their back. Shrapnel chopped through the vegetation.

The Japanese troops began to move forward again along the pier, using their dead as cover. Julius and his men continued to fire and eventually repelled this second assault. All the while the big guns kept firing – this time with more accuracy. Then the Japanese tried to land along a broader stretch of the pier. Julius and his men were ready for them and pushed them back. Suddenly, the guns on the warships fell silent. The searchlights went out and only the moonlight lit up the scene of battle.

There was no way, once daylight came, that Julius and his men could withstand another Japanese attack. It was time, as they had planned, to fall back into the jungle. Julius gathered together the local village and Dutch officials who would certainly be killed by the Japanese if left behind. He burnt all of the group's military documents and then ordered his men to destroy the town's petroleum dump. As they raced into the jungle, the petroleum dump went up and the Japanese gunners immediately opened fire. Shells exploded all around as they escaped into the jungle.

Julius led his men through the jungle towards the opposite coast. His greatest fear was that, on seeing their retreat, the Japanese would quickly land and try to cut off their route to the sea. When they reached the ocean, villagers provided them with small handmade boats which they used to continue their journey along the coastline. They dumped most of their weapons en route because they were out of ammunition. Stopping at a village on the far end of the island, they discovered that the Japanese had just been there and had offered a reward of 1000 guilders for anyone who delivered Julius to them. Instead, the villagers gave Julius and his men a boat on which they could return to Australia.

It was midmorning when the small wooden boat carrying Julius, his remaining six troops and the civilians they were protecting headed out to sea. Julius's patrol had been on the island for two weeks and they were fast running out of supplies. They had no compass and Julius navigated by the stars, following the Southern Cross. Their rations consisted of sweet potato, small tins of fresh water and several coconuts. For the next five days, they ate tiny amounts and allowed themselves only the smallest amounts of water. They spent the daylight hours scanning the sea for any sign of a Japanese ship. After sundown they would relax a bit, but they had to remain silent because Japanese submarines came up at night to get air and noise carries a long way over water. They were virtually defenceless and had no idea of when or if help would come.

On the morning of their fifth day at sea, an Australian plane flew over them. They spread out their Dutch flag and the pilot tilted his wings to say he had seen them. Several hours later, they landed on Bathurst Island where local Aborigines took them to the Aboriginal mission. There they were fed and given clean clothes. The next day, they were flown by military aircraft to Darwin. Getting off the plane, Julius looked inside his breast pocket and realised that he had left his only photograph of me beside the stretcher bed in his hut in Saumlaki.

In Darwin, Julius also learnt what had happened to the other two boats that had left at the same time as his patrol had set sail for Saumlaki. One had gone to the Tual islands. They had found no Japanese but had decided to settle in and wait. A few nights later, the Japanese landed and captured the entire group. Their commanding officer was taken to Ambon where he was beheaded. The second boat had sailed for the Dobo islands, but on seeing that the Japanese were already there, had turned back. On their safe return, their commander, an Australian officer, was court-martialled for dereliction of duty.

Within hours of landing in Darwin, Julius called me at home. I had not heard from him for almost two months.

eight

A few days later, Julius cabled me that he was coming to Melbourne to brief his commanding officers at Camp Pell. I had no idea what Julius had been through but I knew from the sound of his voice during our earlier phone conversation that it had been traumatic. He'd sounded so tired and sad. Back home, we were aware that the war was still in the balance despite the fact that the Americans had joined the struggle. What we didn't know, because of wartime censorship, was that the Japanese had bombed Darwin in February, killing 240 people and injuring another 150. Had we been told, we would have been devastated because we would have taken these raids to be the first steps on the road to invasion. Recent experience had shown us that no country had been able to withstand the Japanese for very long.

Julius's cable informed me that he was arriving at Spencer Street railway station in three days' time. While he'd been away, I'd sent him a letter a day care of army headquarters in Darwin. He had not received a single one. I'd been busy at the dental hospital, trying desperately to lose myself in my work. But most nights I'd hardly slept for more than an hour or two. I'd lost weight because anxiety had killed my appetite, and my clothes looked as if they were made for a bigger woman. Even my white dentist's coat looked like it belonged to someone else. There was no-one I could talk to about what I was going through. My parents were deeply worried about my brothers who were both in New Guinea, waiting for what we all thought was a certain Japanese invasion, and I could not bring myself to add to their troubles by telling them of my fears for Julius. Nor was there anyone at work who would understand my predicament. Some of my colleagues had already made it very clear that they disapproved of our relationship and I knew I would receive little sympathy. So I kept my feelings to myself and poured my heart out to Julius in dozens of letters which were never read.

I took the morning off work the day Julius was due to arrive. It was late August and very cold. The sun was just coming up when I left home to catch the tram to the station and the streetlights were still on. They cast a pale yellow light that made the streetscape seem even gloomier. A few middle-aged men carrying kitbags were waiting at the tram stop. Melbourne was not a particularly happy place, but my heart was thumping with excitement and joy at the thought of seeing Julius again.

At the station I waited anxiously behind a steel mesh barrier on the platform where Julius's train was due. All around me were middle-aged couples desperate to see their sons again, women like me waiting for their boyfriends or husbands, and soldiers waiting to take the men away to their barracks as soon as they arrived. We all waited in silence. Some people marched up and down the platform, but I stood still, staring down the empty tracks, wondering what Julius would look like, how he would greet me, what he would say. I knew that he had seen action for the first time, and I knew such experiences changed people.

The train finally pulled into the station, half-an-hour late. Hundreds of men poured out of the carriages. At first, all I saw were Australian and American soldiers looking haggard and tired after their long journey. Then, in the distance, I saw a group of Indonesian soldiers alight. Amongst them was Julius. He looked older and thinner. As he came closer, I saw that his eyes were bloodshot from lack of sleep and stress. I wanted to rush up to him, but the steel barrier lay between us. We stood there and he touched my hand through the wire and smiled. He looked like he had been through a major trauma.

'Hello darling,' he said quietly. 'I can't tell you how good it is to be here.'

We barely had time to say anything more than those first few words of greeting. Instead, we embraced for a second or two outside the station, where a bus was waiting to take

Julius to Camp Pell. As it was, we could not speak further because the officer escorting Julius back to camp had ordered him not to talk to anyone before he was debriefed. I watched the bus depart, then walked to my tram stop in a daze and went to work. I'm not sure how I made it through the day nor can I remember the patients I treated that afternoon. Chances are, they did not receive my undivided attention.

That evening I waited by the phone, but it didn't ring. Julius's debriefing would take two days, and during that time he was not allowed to have contact with anyone outside the camp. I later learnt that Tokyo radio had boasted that the Japanese capture of the Dobo, Tual and Tanimbar archipelagoes was the last stepping stone for the invasion of Australia. The radio report went on to say that the only resistance the Japanese forces had encountered had been at Saumlaki, where a fierce Allied defence had caused severe casualties.

The next day, Melbourne's newspapers published reports of what had happened at Saumlaki. I had to learn what Julius had been through in the press. The newspapers called Julius a hero: a black sergeant from the East Indies who, with a handful of men, had withstood a large Japanese invasion force and inflicted massive casualties. It was just the sort of story Australians needed to read, for we were desperate for some stirring news. But I was furious – not at Julius of course, but at the Dutch commanding officers who had sent him and his men to certain death. From that day on, I disliked the Dutch intensely. I became a firm supporter of

Indonesian independence, convinced that the Dutch, like every other colonial power, treated the people under their rule with contempt. It was during this time, too, that Julius began to believe that Indonesian independence was not only right but inevitable after the war.

When the doorbell finally rang at seven-thirty that night I rushed to open the door, leaving my parents standing in the kitchen. I pushed Julius outside and closed the door behind us. We hugged each other properly, alone, for the first time in almost two months. I was crying. Julius stroked my hair. All I wanted was to stay like this.

Later, we sat together, Julius, my parents and I, in the front room and Julius described what had happened at Saumlaki. He spoke calmly and quietly, yet there was great emotion in his voice – not anger, but pain and anguish. Several of his men had been captured by the Japanese in the jungle outside the village and there was no way of knowing what had happened to them. While he was being lauded as a hero, all Julius could think of was his captured colleagues and the fact that he had killed men who must have had wives and children and families. He knew it had had to be done, but he was clearly disturbed and distressed. I could see my parents were proud of Julius, but I knew that they were also thinking of Cliff and Russell in New Guinea and wondering whether their sons too would have to face what Julius had been through.

After my parents went to bed, Julius stayed with me until dawn. Getting ready for work that morning, I thought about how unsettled everything was. I had no idea how long Julius would be able to stay in Melbourne before he was sent off on another mission. What if it were another Saumlaki? How many times could he go through that sort of experience and survive? Everything was unsure except our love for each other and our desire to be together. The prospect of that lay somewhere in a clouded and uncertain future.

In the end, Julius stayed in Melbourne for a week. After three days at Camp Pell, he was granted four days' leave and I suggested he stay at our home. My parents accepted this without argument. They may have wondered just how serious my relationship with Julius was and where it might lead, but once again they never said anything to either of us.

When the Allied command announced that Julius was to receive the *Militaire Willems Orde* – the Dutch equivalent of the Victoria Cross or the US Congressional Medal – for his bravery at Saumlaki, the Melbourne newspapers reported it at length. Julius was the only Indonesian to receive this medal, of which only two were awarded during the war. The award ceremony was held at Camp Pell and I was there with my mother and an aunt who was particularly fond of Julius. The governor of Victoria was there too, as were a number of Allied generals, including the commander of the East Indies armed forces in Australia. When the Dutch ambassador, Baron van Aerssen, pinned the medal on Julius's tunic, six warplanes roared overhead in salute.

Despite all this pomp and ceremony, I remained angry

with the Dutch who had originally nominated Julius for his award believing it would be posthumous. I was concerned that they had more suicide missions in store for Julius, who had been promoted to Lieutenant.

'The colonels who plan these missions are living in exclusive hotels,' I said to Julius the night before he was due to leave Melbourne. 'They run around with women. They have marvellous cars and lots of money, and they want you to go off and risk your life again. I can't bear it.'

'Yes you can,' he replied. 'I need you to.'

We said our goodbyes at home, late at night, and then on a fine cold morning early in September, Julius left for Cairns. A few days later he called me, a short, tense call, during which he told me that he would not be calling again for some time and that he could not tell me what he was doing.

I only found out later what had awaited Julius in Cairns. On arrival, he'd been told that his next mission would be to Timor on another intelligence-gathering mission – which, in reality, meant sitting around and waiting for the Japanese to attack again. Days before he and his men were due to leave, Julius was approached by an American officer who told him about a secret division, the Z special unit, which operated behind enemy lines. The officer invited Julius to join. He agreed and a transfer was organised. A few days later, the ship carrying his former comrades left Cairns for Timor. Within hours of heading out to sea, it was attacked by a Japanese warplane and sank. All on board died.

Julius spent weeks at the Z Experimental Station, a secret camp about a mile inland from Cairns. Every day, Allied instructors conducted courses on weapons, navigation, infiltration, silent killing, booby traps and time bomb deployment. Practice missions took the men into the wilds of northern Australia for weeks at a time. Some men couldn't cope and were sent back down south; others died in the desert. One afternoon, Julius's unit was practising landings on the coast near Cairns. Each man had a canister of liquid shark repellent tied to his feet. The repellent was meant to discharge slowly in the water. Suddenly there was a scream and within seconds the water was red with blood. Julius scrambled ashore. The man who had been attacked was never found.

Later Julius told me that, of all the hardships he went through during training, the most difficult to cope with was the food he had to eat. He hated the bully beef and boiled vegetables that made up standard Australian army rations. Whenever possible, he exchanged his rations for a handful of rice, which he and the other Indonesian soldiers in the unit cooked with wild chillies they found growing in the outback.

Then the missions started. Julius once described them to me as straightforward and simple. His unit would approach an occupied island at night by submarine. The submarine would surface and Julius's unit, consisting of about six or seven men under his command, would climb aboard a rubber dinghy and row to within about a mile of the island. They would anchor and swim ashore. They would then gather intelligence about the deployment of Japanese troops on the island and, when possible, train local guerrillas. They would also bury food, medicine and radios in isolated places. Allied airmen on missions throughout the Pacific would have maps which detailed where the Z Specials had been. If they were forced to eject from their aircraft, they would try and do so close to these spots where supplies had been left.

Most of Julius's missions lasted a few weeks, during which period the men rarely slept more than an hour at a time. Although Julius and his men were in uniform, they would have been executed by the Japanese if captured. They would also have been tortured. As a consequence, they carried 'death lollies', colourless cyanide pills that would kill them instantly, which they were ordered to take if the situation became hopeless. There were many near-death experiences. After each mission, the units would return to the Z Experimental Station near Cairns. Some units never returned. The soldiers were wary of making friends in case these friendships were brought to an end by death or capture.

Sometimes, between missions, Julius would be allowed to come south to Melbourne for a few days. He stayed at our home, but he never spoke to me in any detail about what he was doing. He was sworn to secrecy. We would spend our short time together wandering around Melbourne or sitting in silence on the grass in the Botanical Gardens, just holding each other. We spent most nights together, awake, talking and hugging, afraid of wasting a precious hour together by sleeping. Every now and then, Julius would fall asleep and he would have nightmares, his dreams full of the killings at Saumlaki. These nightmares continue until today, at times as intense and as disturbing as they were fifty years ago.

nine

The next two years were agony for Julius and me. I did not see him for months on end and when I did, it was only for a few days. While he could not tell me exactly what he was doing, Julius told me enough for me to know that his life was constantly in grave danger. That thought was unbearable. All my life I had been waiting for this man and this terrifying war could, at any time, take him from me. I was torn between wanting to marry him straightaway, no matter what the consequences, and knowing that such a marriage would only put more pressure on both of us and on my parents. More than anything, I wanted to be with him all the time – something that was clearly not possible.

During the times Julius was away, I was constantly depressed. My only consolation lay in writing to him every day care of army headquarters and hoping that somehow my letters would get through. Some, miraculously, did. All these letters to Julius have since been lost, bar one – the first letter I wrote to him after he left for Darwin, before the mission to Saumlaki. I re-read this letter from time to time. It's as if it had been written by another person and yet it brings back the most vivid memories.

Dental Hospital
193 Spring Street
Melbourne
7.7.42

Dear Julius,

I have only time to write a short letter. I am writing from a crowded room where I cannot concentrate. Julius, you have been gone only a fortnight, but it seems like a year. I miss you more every day. When I think of you, I feel terribly depressed. I cannot weep. I just feel hopeless.

Every night I read the war news with such care and when I see that Timor, Salamaua, Lae and those other islands are being continually bombed and that you may soon be there yourself – well, can you blame me for feeling like that?

But I love you and trust you and pray that you may be safe and that perhaps soon, I may see you again.

By the way, I bought several Dutch books, but it is so difficult to learn a language by one's self. There are so many things that crop up and one has no means of finding out.

I have also been given some important research work to do. It means many months of hard work with very little time during the day and that is what I want. Otherwise, I think of you at all sorts of queer times and it makes me too unhappy, wondering if you are safe or whether you are in danger.

Write to me when ever the opportunity offers itself or send me telegrams because these are the only links between us now. I shall say goodbye now and pray you may return safely.

Love, Jean

P.S. Reading this over, it seems a mournful sort of letter but every Tuesday I think it is just a week or just a fortnight etc. etc. since Julius left and it makes me sad.

I also have the handful of letters which I received from Julius during this time. I have kept these letters for fifty-five years. Most of them are on thin yellowing paper and, being hastily written, are hard to read. But every now and then, I take them down from their special spot above my desk in our Melbourne flat and read them again.

Lieutenant J. Tahija
Box 349
Cairns
10.5.43

My darling,

I am writing this letter for I have such a lot of thoughts going through my head. The weather is very good and at night, rather cold. It is raining at present. I wish I could have you here to keep me warm. Darling, my longing for you is sometimes too much to bear.

Today is a very remarkable day. It was on 10 May 1927 that my mother died. Since then, I haven't got any love from any person. I was just a ship sailing without a destination, until I met you one year ago. Darling, I am glad I did meet you for you make the world different for me. I wish I could this afternoon be by my mother's tomb and put some lovely flowers on it. I know now, and realise what does it mean when you lose your mother just at the time that you really need her. I realise now what I have missed.

Darling, if our children are cheeky to me I might not punish them, but if they do that towards you (their mother) I will give them a good lecture about what a mother means for her children. Darling, how lovely would it be when we can sit down on our verandah and look at our children playing in a well-kept garden.

Darling, look after yourself and keep always in mind that Julius wants you to be his wife and the mother of his children.

Julius

Throughout this time I continued to work hard at the dental hospital, sometimes twelve hours a day. The work kept me sane. But fewer and fewer of my younger male colleagues remained. Even my boss, Professor Amies, joined the forces and was sent off to North Africa. Only Mario Ballini remained. He was miserable, feeling that he had been singled out for particularly harsh treatment by the authorities.

Increasingly, the patients at the dental hospital were merchant seaman on leave and I met men from countries I had barely heard of. Most of them were involved in dangerous work, their boats constantly in peril of attack from either Japanese or German warships. They were in Melbourne on leave and what they wanted was to have a good time before they were sent back to sea. I received countless invitations, all of which I knocked back. They couldn't argue, because mostly they were sitting in my dentist's chair, open-mouthed and at my mercy.

By now, the Americans had arrived in Melbourne in force, and many young women – including some of the nurses at the dental hospital – thought snaring an American serviceman might be a great prize. The Americans were well dressed, well fed and had lots of money. I can remember them roaming the streets of Melbourne, many holding bunches of flowers for the new sweethearts they had just met. My heart, of course, was elsewhere. But who could truly understand my love for this Indonesian soldier?

On one of his visits to Melbourne in between missions, Julius bought a battered old car so that we could enjoy trips to the countryside together. He loved the bush in Victoria, particularly around the Grampians, where we would climb the mountains and have picnics near waterfalls and rock pools. Julius also loved the Dandenongs, the hills outside Melbourne, where we would walk through the forests and then sit on a blanket in the afternoon just quietly holding each other.

Even with his life constantly endangered, Julius made sure to save a certain amount of money each month from his Dutch army salary of about twenty-five pounds a week – an enormous wage for the times. I looked after the banking, making sure that the money he sent me each month was saved. Despite the future being desperately bleak, Julius continued to plan for a life after the war had ended. He used to say that if he did not survive, at least I would have some money with which to make things easier.

At some stage – I can't remember when – we talked about what would happen to us once the war was over. We assumed that we would marry and that I would go with Julius to live in Indonesia. That was where his future lay – if he had one – and I was prepared to fit in with that. Julius had dreams for his country and plans for the role he would play. Sometimes, he would let himself tell me about them and I found his hopes and aspirations thrilling. I wanted nothing more than to share them with him and to make them come true.

Lieutenant J. Tahija
Box 349
Cairns
11.5.43

My dear darling,

I haven't got a letter from you for almost five days. I expect to get two tomorrow. The mail is coming very irregularly these days.

Darling, the last two nights were awful ones. I couldn't sleep at all. I was awake the whole night. My thoughts were with you my darling. Jean, never in my life I have had such a feeling before. It is terrible darling. That is the reason why I want to work hard and so keep my mind occupied. I know that a lot depends on my job. Realising this, I do my best to concentrate all my attention on the work. But darling, these thoughts come up all the time when I stop working.

Darling dear, it is now exactly a year since I met you first. I will never forget how this happened. I see myself standing in the front room taking off my overcoat while you were standing in front of me. The light was shining on you. I could see your lovely face. Darling, it is wonderful what can happen in a year of a human life. The past year has changed your life and mine completely. It has been a successful one.

It has also put us, especially you, in a very difficult position. Darling, bear in mind that I will do my best to be worth your love. You mean more to me than anything in this world. I do this for you. I must prove to you that I am worth to be your husband, and so when the time comes, when we marry, you could say, 'Dad and Mum don't worry, I am in safe hands.' Your parents have to like me.

As you said in your letter, our marriage will be rather unusual, but we will prove to them how wrong the ideas of a lot of people are. I know that you would do anything to help me. That's what makes me feel so sure and safe. Darling, so would I do anything to assure you and our children a good future.

It is good that your salary has increased to fifty pounds a month. Mine has gone up too. At present I get about 106 pounds a month and that will go up to 112 pounds. I can save at least half of that.

Darling, take great and great care of yourself, for you mean very much for me and I love you more than anything else in this world.

Julius

Only in his letters did Julius talk about marriage and children and about our future together. When we were together for those brief periods in Melbourne, we lived for the next hour or the next day and Julius would resolutely put his troubles behind him. These troubles included bad news from home. Julius's father had been interned by the Japanese and had become gravely ill. Through his intelligence work, Julius knew of the harsh treatment the Japanese occupying forces were meting out to the Indonesian people. To make matters worse, the Japanese had put a price on Julius's head after Saumlaki and he was constantly worried that they might make the connection between him and his family in Indonesia.

At the time, Julius told me none of this. Nor did he speak of his fears of what might happen in Indonesia when the war ended. If the Japanese won the war, Julius could never go back home. With his Dutch education and his military service, he could go to Holland, but in 1943 the Netherlands was occupied by Nazi Germany, and it was no certain thing that the Germans would be defeated in Europe. Julius was cut off from home, unsure of the future and in constant danger during his secret missions. But he said nothing about all this. He couldn't even tell me what he was doing in Cairns.

The only way I knew that Julius had been sent out of Australia was that suddenly there would be no letters for weeks on end. These were the worst times. I would stand at the mailbox each day waiting anxiously for the mailman. When nothing arrived from Julius, I was devastated. When I did get a letter, my depression would lift, at least for a moment or two, even when they touched on the dangers which he was exposed to.

Lieutenant J. Tahija
Box 349
Cairns
12.7.43

My lovely and dearest darling,

I received tonight your telegram wishing me all the best with my birthday. Thanks a lot. Darling, it is a pity that I have failed twice in trying to celebrate my birthday in Melbourne.

Today, it is just one year ago when I arrived at Saumlaki. Darling, I am glad that I am again in Australia. I really don't mind to go through dangers etc. but nobody can say that it is enjoyable. Still, if I have to do such things, I would do it with pleasure for I know I am doing something good.

I know you don't like these ideas, but I also know that you support me because you know it is my duty to do these things. It is these qualities that I admire so much in you. Darling, I am really happy. Happy, for I know I am doing these things for somebody who really loves me and for somebody who it is really worth living for and to work and struggle for. I love you so much dear darling Jean!

Julius

It is hard to imagine what Julius's life must have been like during those three years of the war that he spent in the Z special unit. Even today, he refuses to talk in detail about the missions he was sent on, primarily because they bring back memories and these memories inevitably turn into nightmares. Most of these nightmares are about people dying, both colleagues and Japanese soldiers who were killed by his unit. Julius suffered terribly during those years, but he never once despaired. He developed a fatalism about his future that sometimes frightened me. 'If I survive, then it was meant to be', he would say. But each time he came to Melbourne, he looked older and thinner than the last time I had seen him. He looked like a man who had been through something unutterably traumatic. We would feed him up, my mother and I, on lamb roasts which he loved, and make frequent visits to Chinatown where he ate hungrily.

In recent years, Julius has re-established contact with several Z Special veterans and has twice attended reunions of the Z Specials. In 1994, he came to Melbourne to march in the Anzac Day parade, and later attended a special dinner with his wartime colleagues. He had tears in his eyes when he returned to our hotel room. Then in 1997, he flew to Sydney for another Anzac Day march and another reunion. Julius has also funded a small monument on Bathurst Island which recognises the Aboriginal people who helped him and his men after they landed there following their mission in Saumlaki.

ten

In 1944, the tide of war turned, both in the Pacific and in Europe. The Japanese were in retreat and the Allied forces under General MacArthur were reclaiming the Pacific, country by country, island by island. In Europe, the Allies had landed at Normandy and had begun their major campaign against the Germans in western Europe. At the same time, the German army was in retreat in Russia where the siege of Leningrad had been broken. In fact, towards the end of 1944, Russian troops had driven the Germans out of most of eastern Europe and were marching towards Berlin.

For Julius, this meant that Holland soon would be liberated and his hope that the Dutch royal family could return to the Netherlands would be fulfilled. He was unsure, however, about what the Dutch would do in the East Indies when the Pacific war ended. Would they understand, he wondered, that things could never be as they were before the Japanese occupation?

Julius's letters started to look more and more to our own personal future and that of his country. He was increasingly focusing beyond the war to what he thought would be a troubled peace for him and for Indonesia.

Lieutenant J. Tahija
GPO Brisbane
8.30 a.m.

My dearest darling,

As you see, I am writing this letter early in the morning, straight after breakfast. I am still at the same place and waiting for the next move.

I don't know what is wrong with me lately, but for the last three days, I feel very tired although I am not working particularly hard. I feel restless too. There are so many things we have to be patient with. Darling, I think that after the war you have to get me settled. It seems sometimes difficult for me to sit down and relax for a while. Gosh darling, sometimes I think and long so much for you that I can get very restless if I haven't got something to occupy my mind.

I often think that it probably would be impossible to create a permanent peace or one lasting more than thirty years or so in this world. There is only one good thing of this war. I would not have met you without it. We have been through so many pleasant and unpleasant events that we know now what we do mean to each other. We have learnt to respect and appreciate each other. In the future, when we marry and settle down, it will not only be love that shall make us happy, but also the mutual respect, appreciation, and the knowledge that we can and will survive if things become a bit tough in our lives.

I am thinking all the time about what is happening in my country and what will happen there after the war.

Your Julius

But the war was not yet over and Julius was still involved in dangerous missions on Japanese-held islands – missions that, without him knowing it, were pushing him towards a breakdown. Three months before the war ended, Julius was on a submarine with his commando unit heading for one of the Indonesian islands when he collapsed one morning and could not get out of his bunk. He was disoriented, shaking, and had great difficulty breathing. He stayed in his bunk that day and felt better the next morning, although the submarine's captain told Julius that he needed treatment and that he should take no part in this mission. Julius ignored the advice and completed the mission with his men. When he arrived back in Cairns he collapsed again, and this time he did not recover the next day. Julius was transferred to Melbourne and admitted to hospital in Heidelberg.

I did not know of his illness until I was contacted by one of his fellow soldiers some days later. Stunned by the news, I left work in a daze, unsure even of which train to catch to get to the hospital. Somehow I made it there, only to find that Julius could receive no visitors that day. I was told that he was suffering from shock, that he was in a critical condition, and that there was a new treatment they planned to give him.

As the news sank in, I realised that there had been signs for several months that Julius was unwell. On his recent visit to Melbourne I'd noticed that he'd become jittery, unable to sit still, his nights always interrupted by nightmares. He was more absent-minded than he had been in the past and often he would forget what he was saying in the middle of a sentence. But I was shocked by his hospitalisation and bitter when I thought about what he had been through. The end of the war was now in sight, we could start planning our future, and yet the doctors were saying that Julius was dangerously ill. Whatever happened, he should never again be allowed to go on dangerous missions, I was told. The stress would almost certainly kill him.

For the next six weeks Julius was injected with insulin every day as part of his treatment. The dosage was so high that he would drift off into unconsciousness for several hours. It was an entirely experimental treatment and insulin was later found to be a totally inappropriate drug for people in his condition. Some soldiers actually died from the dosages they received.

Each day after work I would visit the hospital and wait for Julius to wake up from the insulin-induced coma he was in. Then I would sit with him into the night. Although Julius gradually started to sleep, he would still wake up every night unable to breathe. He would have to get out of bed and stretch out his arms to catch his breath. As the weeks passed, however, he suffered fewer and fewer episodes of breathlessness. I saw the sparkle return to his eyes, and his mind became sharper. He seemed to remember things he had forgotten, things from the recent past and from his childhood.

It was while Julius was in hospital that my brothers returned home from New Guinea. After years of waiting and worrying, their homecoming marked a joyous time in Asçot Vale. Once again I kept my fears for Julius to myself, not wanting to intrude on my parents' happiness. Mum came to the hospital with me to see Julius a couple of times, but I never told her how ill he was or my anxieties about the treatment he was receiving.

Julius was released from hospital ten days before the war ended. He came home with me to Ascot Vale, weak and tired, but his nights were no longer interrupted by nightmares or breathlessness. We all knew the war would soon end, even before the bombs were dropped on Hiroshima and Nagasaki. While we were horrified at the destruction wrought by nuclear weapons, we felt at the time that if those bombs shortened the war and saved the lives of Allied soldiers, then the Americans were right to drop them.

The day the war ended was sunny and warm in Melbourne. As soon as we heard the news, we rushed outside. The streets were full of our neighbours hugging each other. It was hard to believe that at last there would be no more fighting. There would be no more sitting at the radio at night anxiously listening to the war news, hoping for signs that things were improving. There would be no more waiting for the dreaded knock on the door and the delivery of the telegram that told you your loved one was not ever coming home. We hugged each other and we hugged our neighbours and we hugged any stranger who happened to be passing by.

That night, there was a fireworks display at Albert Park lake near the city. Tens of thousands of people came, a large, joyous crowd celebrating peace. People sat in family groups on blankets on the grass. There were thousands of soldiers in uniform and children waving Australian flags. I went with Julius and Mum. For the first time in years, we could be unashamedly happy. And we were. But, at the back of my mind, the question lurked: What happens now?

Two days after the Japanese surrender, Indonesia's Republicans under Sukarno declared independence. With their headquarters in Jogjakarta, in central Java, the Republic's guerrilla fighters had been armed by the Japanese, who knew the war was lost but who wanted to create as many problems as possible for the returning Dutch. This declaration of independence excited and frightened Julius at the same time. Indonesian independence was inevitable, he thought, and Sukarno was a national hero who had fought for freedom even before the war. But Julius had mixed feelings about the Republican determination to fight rather than negotiate with the Dutch if they returned. Julius was sick of fighting and sick of war. He hoped there might be some way of convincing the Dutch that their days of colonialism were over. With the declaration of independence, however, he knew that fighting was inevitable. What would that mean for his future? And for us?

I knew that Julius would have to go away again soon, back to Cairns to help the East Indies army pack up and load the ships that would take them and their supplies back to the Indonesian archipelago. He would have to go back to his home without me, back to what we quickly realised would be a dangerous situation. Already, fierce fighting had broken out between the Republicans and the Dutch and British troops that had landed in Java to supervise the Japanese surrender. We did not know how much time we would have together before Julius had to leave, and we had no idea how long it would be before we saw each other again. So we spent as much time as we could together in the few days we had left. I continued to work at the dental hospital, but every spare minute I had was spent with Julius. Again, we hardly slept, determined as we were to make up for time already lost and time we would lose in the future.

Julius returned to Cairns two weeks after the war finished. He was there for three weeks before his ship sailed for

Indonesia. I wrote to him every day and he wrote back whenever he could. I still have the last letter he wrote to me before he left Australia.

Lieutenant J. Tahija
Box 911M
GPO Cairns
Wednesday
26.8.45

My dearest darling,

This is my last letter from Australia, as I am going on board in a couple of hours and will be leaving tomorrow morning. Unfortunately, I have booked a call to you for tonight, but I will now not be able to make that call. I am sad too darling, but keep your chin up. We both shall see that things get done satisfactorily.

Please look after yourself darling. Do it for my sake, as I am away to work and settle things for your and my future. Gosh, I feel alone and miss you so much.

Darling angel, try to take things easy and be careful.

Love from Julius

I was not to see Julius again for more than a year. Indonesia was in turmoil. Sukarno's Republican fighters were battling the Allied troops that had taken over after the Japanese surrender. Guerrilla units were also operating in Jakarta and on other Indonesian islands, but their main stronghold was in central Java. In a sense, this struggle ran the risk of becoming a civil war because 80 per cent of soldiers in the Dutch East Indies army were indigenous Indonesians. Many Indonesians were nationalists who wanted the Dutch to leave, but they were not all Republicans. The Republicans had set up a full government complete with a cabinet and ministers. What they wanted was an immediate transfer of sovereignty from Holland to a government headed by Sukarno, the father of the Indonesian independence movement.

By the time Julius arrived in Jakarta on 15 October 1945, he had been promoted to the rank of captain. He had had no real contact with Indonesia for four years. Nor had he any idea what had happened to his father or younger brother, although he had heard that his father was gravely ill. Indeed, both his father and brother had been imprisoned during the war and his father died in Surabaya several months after Julius returned to home. Although Julius managed to see him several days before he died, his father was so ill that he did not recognise his eldest son.

Julius was now a senior officer in the Dutch East Indies army and was considered by many Republicans to be on the enemy side. Several days after he arrived in Jakarta, he was driving a Dutch army jeep when suddenly bullets started flying all around him. He managed to avoid being hit, but at that moment, Julius understood that a revolution was truly under way.

Julius stayed in the army, convinced that he could best advance the cause of independence by working with the Dutch. He spent his first few months back home travelling to the Moluccas, Sulawesi and Ambon to record eyewitness accounts of Japanese war crimes. Most involved the mistreatment of prisoners of war and the Allies later used this information during war crimes trials. In Ambon, Julius found some of the men who'd been with him at Saumlaki and who had been taken prisoner by the Japanese. The Japanese, perhaps out of respect for their bravery, had given these men favourable treatment throughout the war.

Up until the time of Japan's surrender to the Allies, there had been about a quarter of a million Japanese military personnel in Indonesia. The Japanese army had controlled Java and Sumatra and had trained a large force of Indonesians which they planned to use, if possible, to fight the Allies. These men became the core of the Republic's fighting units.

After the surrender, Allied command decided that all the Japanese forces in the Indonesian islands east of Java would surrender to the Australian armed forces. The Japanese on Java and Sumatra, however, were to surrender to British troops. The Australians and the British were to remain in Indonesia only long enough to disarm and repatriate the Japanese, before returning control to the Dutch.

The Australians moved quickly, disarming the Japanese and throwing the weapons they captured into the sea. Any remaining Japanese were turned over to the returning Dutch soldiers and administrators. By Christmas 1945, the Australians had completed their mission. In contrast, the British arrived in Indonesia months after the war had ended and remained in the coastal areas of Java and Sumatra. They made no effort to control the interior of Java where the Republicans were based. This left the Japanese commanders free to turn their arms over to the Republicans who were eager to fight the returning Dutch. In February 1946, when the Dutch returned to Java in force, they faced an armed independence movement in Java, but little armed resistance on the eastern islands of Indonesia.

Three months after he returned to Indonesia, Julius was appointed aide-de-camp to General Simon Spoor, the chief of staff of the Dutch East Indies army. Julius was the first Indonesian to hold the post and he considered it an honour. He knew, however, that the Dutch would use his appointment to demonstrate their new sensitivity to the changed political climate in the East Indies. It was not an easy time for Julius. Many of his fellow Indonesian officers in the Dutch East Indies army had decided to leave and join the Republicans. They came to say goodbye to Julius. Some urged him to leave and join the guerilla forces. Julius was a war hero who commanded the loyalty of many of the soldiers in the East Indies army. If he had ordered them to do so, thousands would have left and joined the Republicans.

Julius was torn. The United Nations was pressing the Dutch to exercise restraint in their actions against the Republicans, and for a while the fighting stopped. But Julius knew that this lull in the fighting would not last. He told General Spoor that, if it came to it, he would refuse to order his men to shoot at their own people and that he was going to open a dialogue with the Republicans. Spoor understood. He too was convinced that the Dutch would have to grant Indonesia independence, but he was a professional soldier, loyal to the Netherlands government. He asked Julius to be discreet.

Julius met with the Republic's prime minister, Sutan Sjahrir, several times to discuss the independence struggle. Sjahrir, with whom Julius remained on good terms for years after independence, did not try to talk Julius into joining the Republicans. Instead, he told him that he must do what he thought was right. In the end, Julius decided he could best serve the independence movement by entering politics. Indonesia, he thought, could best achieve independence through negotiations and diplomacy. Fighting the Dutch should be only a last resort, when everything else had failed. Julius wanted, if it was possible, an independent Indonesia that maintained close links with Holland. What sickened him was the thought of more violence and, particularly, the thought of Indonesians killing Indonesians.

Early in 1946, Julius began training at the Ministry of Finance in Jakarta for a political role in the regional government of East Indonesia. He had decided to leave the army and throw himself into the political process. Soon after, he was appointed as a delegate to the Malino conference in Sulawesi, held to prepare a blueprint for a new form of government in Indonesia based on a federal system similar to Australia's. The Republicans were opposed to a federation: Sukarno wanted a strong central government that could unite the hundreds of different ethnic groups which spread across Indonesia's 16 000 islands. A federation, he argued, would never work: Indonesia would simply be torn apart by ethnic strife. So while Julius worked with the Dutch on the creation of a United States of Indonesia which would exercise self-government under Dutch sovereignty, Sukarno and his Republicans continued their armed struggle in Java and Sumatra.

This struggle received widespread – if sensational – coverage in Australian newspapers. Australian trade unions put bans on the movement of Dutch goods to Indonesia. Wharfies refused to load Dutch ships and in virtually every Australian capital city, university students organised street demonstrations against Dutch rule in Indonesia. There were horror stories in the newspapers of people who supported the Republicans being killed by the Dutch in central Java and even in Jakarta. Republican guerrilla units attacked Dutch soldiers and police in towns throughout Java, killing scores of people.

I had, by this time, become a staunch supporter of Indonesian independence, probably more radical in my views than Julius. He had suffered so much under the Dutch that I had come to dislike them intensely. I thought the Indonesian people would be better off running their own affairs. Early on, I was a supporter of the Republicans because I believed the Dutch would never leave Indonesia unless they were forced to do so.

I had started to read as much as I could about the East Indies and the more I read, the more certain I was that independence could not come quickly enough. I also started to take Indonesian lessons in preparation for the time when I would join Julius, though I had no idea of when that might be. I did not even know when we would have a chance to get married. Towards the end of 1945 and in the early months of 1946, I attended meetings of Republican supporters in Melbourne. While I stopped attending these meetings after a while, I remained in contact with several people I met during this time. Two in particular were to come in and out of my life for years to come. They were women who, like me, had fallen in love with Indonesians and had become caught up in the Indonesian revolution.

We did not share the same hopes and aspirations, nor did we agree on what should happen in Indonesia. The three of us were different in virtually every way and, as a result, our lives went in very different directions. But these two women, in their own ways, touched me deeply. Their stories are not the same, but they are remarkable. Both women suffered immensely for their love. Both women became deeply committed to the Indonesian cause, though for one of them that commitment was lifelong, while for the other it was cut cruelly short by tragic circumstances and by the unthinking actions of Australian officials.

eleven

I met Molly Warner shortly after the war ended when I went to an Indonesian independence meeting at the Melbourne Trades Hall that Molly had actually organised. Molly was a short, plain-looking woman with mousy brown hair. But once she started speaking, you could not help but be struck by her energy and cheerfulness. She was the most determined and committed young woman I had ever met.

It was clear to me right from the start that Molly would, if asked, give her life for the Indonesian revolution. When I met her, she had already fallen in love with Bondan, a veteran Indonesian nationalist who had spent nine years interned by the Dutch at Boven Digul, a notorious internment camp in central Irian Jaya where the inmates were exposed to malaria, dysentery and other tropical diseases.

In 1943, Bondan escaped from Boven Digul with a group of sixteen prisoners. They made their way through the jungle to Merauke, near the border of Australian New Guinea, where they were re-captured by Dutch soldiers. The Dutch gave them a choice: they could go to Australia and help in the war effort against the Japanese, or they could return to Boven Digul. Bondan and his men chose to go to Australia. But the Dutch had no intention of enlisting Bondan and his men in the war effort. Instead, these veteran Indonesian nationalists were transported to Australia as prisoners of war and placed in a prison camp at Cowra in New South Wales. Two of Bondan's fellow prisoners died there of exposure.

It was only four months later, upon learning that these men were not Japanese sympathisers but nationalists fighting for Indonesian independence, that the Australian government ordered their release. Bondan went to Queensland where he worked for the Australian army. At the same time, he set up a committee of Indonesian nationalists in Australia to lobby for Indonesian independence when the war ended. Within days of Sukarno's declaration of independence in Java, Bondan's committee was organising protest rallies against the Dutch in every major Australian city.

Molly Warner was at this time a journalist with sympathies for the Indonesian independence movement. But it wasn't until she met Bondan in Brisbane, where she had travelled for a protest rally towards the end of 1945, that she became truly committed to the Republican cause. Her commitment to Indonesia, from that time on, remained fierce and unwavering.

When she met Bondan, Molly was twenty-five. He was in his mid-forties and ill with malaria after his years of internment. But he was a passionate and charismatic man who had virtually sacrificed his life for the independence movement. Molly married him a year after they met and in November 1947 left for Indonesia with Bondan and their six-week-old baby.

I saw Molly several times in Melbourne. She knew, of course, that Julius was an officer in the Dutch East Indies army and that, while he was in favour of independence, he did not believe that armed struggle was necessarily the best way to go. But she treated me with great warmth and had a lot of affection for Julius. No doubt Molly was more radical than me, and certainly more radical than Julius. She hated the Dutch and believed any collaboration with them was futile and counterproductive. While I am not sure whether she was a member of the Australian Communist Party, she was clearly a communist sympathiser. She knew that Julius was a strong anti-communist, a believer in free enterprise and a supporter of a federal political system for Indonesia. Yet we never argued, not in Melbourne, nor later when we met in Jogjakarta and then in Jakarta.

Molly, Bondan and their baby went to Jogjakarta immediately upon their arrival in Indonesia. This was around the same time that I arrived in Macassar to join Julius. I knew that Molly and her family had settled in Jogjakarta which, at the time, was the epicentre of the Indonesian revolution, with constant battles between Republican guerrillas and Dutch troops. On his return, Bondan, like so many of the veteran nationalists who had been interned by the Dutch in Irian Jaya and who had later been sent to Australia, found that a new generation of nationalists under Sukarno were in control and that there was virtually no role for him. His health too had been broken, and although he had survived the years of internment with his spirit intact, Bondan relied increasingly on Molly's energy and drive to keep on going.

Molly wrote pamphlets for the Republicans and did English language broadcasts for the Republican radio station. Jogjakarta was a city devastated first by the Japanese and now by revolution and the Dutch blockade of the city. Its streets were full of beggars, and apart from rice, there was little fresh food. Every night, bullets would echo around the streets and guerrilla units came out of the jungle to attack Dutch military and police positions.

Some years later, in 1948, Julius and I went to see Molly and her family in Jogjakarta. They lived in a small room in a house teeming with people on the city's edge. I remember being shocked by how much Bondan had aged. He was in despair, out of work and out of favour with the revolutionaries. But Molly was indefatigable. She taught English in a local Chinese school in order to earn enough money to feed her husband and her child. At the same time, she worked tirelessly for the Republican cause. She was as cheerful as she had been in Melbourne despite the difficult conditions in which she lived. Nothing could cause this charismatic young Australian woman to lose heart or abandon the Indonesian cause.

Molly and her family moved to Jakarta in 1950, shortly after the Dutch finally granted Indonesia independence. She worked for the Ministry of Information, translating speeches by Sukarno and other Indonesian politicians into English. The family often made do with only the barest necessities, even after independence. But Molly had no interest in material possessions or in creature comforts and her spirits never flagged. She attracted all sorts of young idealists, many of them naive and ignorant about what was happening in Indonesia. Their house was constantly overflowing with visitors, some of them students from Australia who wanted to help the new nation of Indonesia in whatever way they could. Molly made them all feel welcome, made them feel as if they had a role to play in the great Indonesian struggle for nationhood.

Molly Bondan became a heroine to many Indonesians. She endured much for her beliefs and her commitment to Indonesia. She could have led a comfortable and peaceful life in Australia, but instead opted for a life of hardship in her adopted country, the country she had come to love with such passion. While we were not exactly friends, I saw Molly from time to time and enjoyed her company. I disagreed with her politics which, in the 1950s and early 1960s, saw her ever more closely allied to the Indonesian Communist Party, but I admired her integrity and her courage.

Later, after the attempted communist coup in 1965 and

the great blood-letting that followed, when tens of thousands of people suspected of being communist sympathisers were killed, Molly Bondan was treated with respect and kindness by President Suharto. She had, by then, grown disillusioned with the Sukarno government. As she told Julius before the coup, most of the politicians she knew were interested only in feathering their own nests, and had betrayed the revolution by becoming greedy. President Suharto gave Molly a house in which to live and a small pension to live on. I did not see her much after the coup. Bondan died in 1981, and Molly disappeared from public view in the last years of her life. She died while I was overseas in January 1990.

Unlike Molly Bondan, Jean Edgar never made it to Indonesia. Jean was a pretty redhead, a Melbourne girl with a social conscience who attended pro-Indonesian independence meetings at the Metropole Hotel in Bourke Street. That's where I met her and that's where she met Jack Zakaria.

Indonesians – unless they are Christians like Julius – do not have first names. Zakaria was called Jack by Australian friends and the name stuck. Like Bondan, he was a veteran Indonesian nationalist who had been interned by the Dutch at Boven Digul for almost a decade before being sent to Australia as a prisoner of war. Jack was imprisoned and then released from Cowra at the same time as Bondan.

Jean Edgar fell in love with Zakaria and they were married shortly after the war ended. Unlike Bondan, Zakaria was not particularly active in the independence movement. It seemed that, after the years of suffering in detention, all Zakaria wanted was to start a new life in Australia with Jean. That's what she wanted too. Jean did not have the drive and energy that propelled Molly to the centre of the Indonesian revolution. Jean was in favour of Indonesian independence and she attended rallies and marches, but what she wanted most was for her and Zakaria to be together. She would have followed him to Indonesia if that was what he wanted, but she was equally happy to stay in Australia with him.

Shortly after their marriage, Jean became pregnant. Her mother, however, disapproved of their relationship and reported Zakaria to the Australian immigration authorities. Zakaria, who had been working on the Melbourne wharves, was deported immediately.

Jean was heartbroken. She tried desperately to join Zakaria in Indonesia, but it was Australian government policy at that time to refuse exit visas for Australian women who had married Indonesians except in exceptional circumstances. There was a revolution going on, and the Australian government felt the country was unsafe for girls like Jean.

Jack Zakaria ended up in Jogjakarta where he found that his years in internment counted for little. He had no role to play in the revolution that was now taking place and lived in great poverty in a small room in the slums, where his health deteriorated and where he was reduced to despair. Jean, meanwhile, gave birth to a girl in 1946. She continued to try and join her husband, but permission was always denied her. Eventually she gave up and went to live in Queensland with her child.

In April 1948, I came back to Australia from Macassar to visit my family and called Jean who, at the time, was still in Melbourne. Was there anything I could do for her? Jean told me she had a parcel she would like me to deliver to Zakaria. We met for lunch. I felt overwhelmingly sad for her. She no longer looked like the optimistic, bright young girl I had first met at the Metropole Hotel. Jean had clearly suffered a lot. She could not live with her mother, whom she felt had betrayed her, yet having a small child made independence difficult.

I told Jean that I would do my best to deliver her parcel to Zakaria. There was not much more that we could say to each other. Our lives had taken dramatically different paths. My marriage to Julius had taken me to Macassar, far away from the centre of the Indonesian revolution. We lived in a nice house and we travelled all over East Indonesia. Julius had become a prominent politician who was clearly going to play a role in post-independence Indonesia. He had gone through many hardships, but he had persevered and survived. We were not sure what the future held in store for us, but we knew we had a future together.

Things were different for Jean. Her relationship with Jack Zakaria had left her alone, with a baby and with a great deal of bitterness towards her mother and the Australian government. I did not see Jean again after that lunch. When I returned to Melbourne again late in 1948, I was told she had moved interstate and had married again. She had left her daughter with the child's grandmother.

I delivered Jean's parcel to Jack Zakaria two months after she gave it to me, in June 1948. Julius had a conference to go to in Jogjakarta and I went with him, on board a United Nations plane with other Indonesian and UN officials, including Tom Critchley, the Australian diplomat who was to play a key role in negotiations for Indonesian independence.

It was a spooky flight, and not without a measure of danger. Air travel in Indonesia was risky. Some flights vanished forever into jungle-smothered valleys; others arrived sporting fresh bullet holes. The Republicans had shot down several Dutch aircraft approaching Jogjakarta. I went along because I wanted to deliver Zakaria's parcel.

The nearer we got to Jogjakarta, the more the tension rose. Nervous, I looked towards my neighbour in the next seat. She was Sybil Bayer, a UN secretary, and she smiled when she caught my glance. 'Have a sip,' she said, and from her handbag produced the most welcome flask of brandy I ever saw.

Jogjakarta shocked me. There was enormous poverty everywhere and people were literally dressed in rags. They rode around on bicycles with no tyres. There were hundreds of young men on the streets who had decided that they would not cut their hair until the revolution was won. They looked like they were starving. Thousands of beggars filled the streets, and whole families sat in doorways with their hands outstretched for help. The shops were virtually empty. There was simply nothing to buy – not food, not clothing and not medicines.

Julius had an uncle in Jogjakarta who ran an orphanage for children who had lost their parents either during the war or in the revolution. He had met us at the airport and had taken us to stay with him at the orphanage where he struggled each day to feed the children in his care.

Oom Bram, as the uncle was called, was so poor that Julius and I went out to find a restaurant where we might eat without imposing two extra mouths upon his slender resources. At last we located a dim Chinese place where they offered us pigeon and rice. By the time it was served, the doorway was filled with starving people dressed in rags, watching in complete silence.

'I can't eat,' I said to Julius.

'Nor me,' he said. 'I couldn't swallow a mouthful.'

We sent for more rice and, with our meal, gave it to these people, and went on our way.

Shortly after we arrived in Jogjakarta, Julius and I decided to find Zakaria to deliver Jean's parcel. It took us all day. We had Zakaria's postal address but this proved not to be his home address. We wandered the streets where we were both appalled all over again by the deprivation we saw.

Oom Bram had warned us that the streets of Jogjakarta were dangerous at night, but it was well and truly dark before we found Zakaria. There was no street lighting and almost every house was in darkness. It was hot and humid. Eventually, we found the house where Zakaria lived. A woman opened the door and showed us to Zakaria's room. We knocked and waited. We could hear someone scrambling around inside. Eventually the door opened gingerly. Zakaria was obviously relieved when he saw us standing there. He must have thought we were the authorities, come to take him away. He looked terrible, dressed in a dirty white singlet and a sarong.

Zakaria was pleased to see us, but ashamed of the condition of his room which was bare but for a small single bed, a chair and a battered box that he used for a table. Here was a man who had sacrificed much of his life for the independence movement, who had suffered unimaginable hardships during his internment, and who, as reward for his efforts, had been more or less discarded. He had lost his wife and child and had no real hope of ever seeing them again.

He had no future and he knew it, though as we sat and talked Zakaria hid his feelings, like a true Javanese. He was calm and quietly spoken. He asked about Jean and I told him what I could, without saying too much, for what was the point of telling him how upset she was and how hurt she had been by everything that had happened? When he opened Jean's parcel and saw that she had sent him some shoes his baby daughter had worn and a few of her little clothes, Zakaria's body shook slightly, but that was all. He thanked us for coming.

I did not see him again. Zakaria died soon after our visit. He had been weakened by malaria and the other diseases he had suffered from during his internment by the Dutch, and though he was only in his early 50s, he had looked like a frail old man when we saw him. I wrote to Jean about our meeting with Zakaria but I never received a reply. In fact, I never heard from Jean again.

In 1995 a letter arrived at our home in Jakarta from a young Australian woman who wrote that her name was Naraya and that she was Jack Zakaria's daughter. I couldn't believe it. The letter described how Jean had led a miserable life in Queensland and had died in the 1960s. Naraya had gone through her mother's belongings after she died and had found a letter mentioning Jean Tahija. It was the letter I had sent Jean after we visited Zakaria. Naraya, through some Indonesian friends, tracked me down to Jakarta. She wanted to know whether I could tell her anything about her father. She knew nothing about him. She wanted to find his relatives – who, of course, were her relatives too. She had no-one left in Australia except for her son who was in his early twenties.

Naraya eventually traced some of Zakaria's relatives and then came to Indonesia in 1996 to meet them. She was met at the airport in Jakarta by Zakaria's brother and sister who took her back to their home in Sumatra where she met uncles, aunts and cousins she had never known. She was deliriously happy.

Naraya was studying for a Ph.D. at Monash University in Melbourne so she had to return to Australia within a few weeks. But she came back to Indonesia a couple of months later and had dinner at our house with her son. Seeing her brought back all the memories I had of Zakaria and Jean. We talked a lot about that time. Naraya told me that her mother had refused to talk about her father and she certainly could not talk about him with her grandmother or great-grandmother when she was growing up. There had always been this big gap in her life which now, for the first time, was being filled. How wonderful, I thought, that after all the suffering of her parents, Naraya now had an extended Indonesian family that loved her and made her feel welcome, made her feel that she really was Zakaria's daughter.

We have not been in touch for some time now. Naraya went back to Melbourne to complete her degree. She then went to Brunei to teach on a two-year contract. I am sure that she will come back to Indonesia and we shall see each other again.

I often think about her, and about Jean and Zakaria. Jean had a tragic life and so did Zakaria. They were victims, I suppose, of the times in which they lived. Zakaria's spirit and health had been broken by the Dutch. Jean's hopes for the future were dashed by her mother and by unthinking, unfeeling Australian bureaucrats. Their story however does not have an entirely unhappy ending. Naraya, I am sure, will one day write a book about her parents. She has, after many years, reclaimed her Indonesian heritage.

twelve

I cannot remember when we made the decision, but some time towards the middle of 1946 Julius and I agreed to get married in Melbourne as soon as he could organise some leave and come to Australia. We could wait no longer, even if it meant that Julius would go back to Indonesia without me after our wedding. He was adamant that he would not take me back to an Indonesia in which there was still heavy fighting. Nor would he take me back until he knew where his future lay.

Over the last four years, Julius had worked his way from a sergeant in the Dutch East Indies army to a point where he was about to become the youngest cabinet member of the proposed new government of East Indonesia. After the conference at Sulawesi, where he had given a major speech on his vision for a federation for Indonesia, Julius had become a key player in Indonesian politics. He travelled extensively throughout the archipelago, taking part in countless conferences between the Dutch, the Republicans, and the local politicians representing the islands of East Indonesia. While he was criticised by some Republicans for co-operating with the Dutch, he never wavered in his belief that independence could be achieved through political activity. Above all, Julius wanted to avoid unnecessary bloodshed. As he remarked in a letter to me at the time:

> There are so many people who are opportunists. If it is suitable to them, they will be very pro-Dutch. But if it is better for them to be pro-Republic, they will be pro-Republic. People like this we can do without. I can say for myself that the Dutch know I am first of all an Indonesian and that if I see they are going the wrong direction, I will resist. They also know that I am on this side only because I know I can serve the interests of my people, especially of the outer islands, here where I am now. The Dutch also know I have close contact with the leaders of the Republic.
>
> The Republic leaders realise that I serve the Indonesian people best at the place where I am now. I have a position and a reputation which is prominent. These leaders of the Republic also know that I agree with many of their principles. I want Indonesians to govern themselves and be independent as soon as possible . . .
>
> I would like you to tell me what you think. I think that for the sake of our future, I should stay here for a while, although I can't wait to see you. To wait another three months seems a long time, but in the long run, I think that it would be better to do so. But you must decide what I

> should do darling. Your happiness and feelings come first. I will withdraw tomorrow if you think it is better for us that I come down to Australia.

As so often happened in our subsequent life together, I told Julius that his work had to come first, that what was happening in Indonesia was more important than my impatience to see him. I missed him terribly. I was still busy at the dental hospital and I had begun to take Dutch and Indonesian lessons from a rather boorish Dutchman who thought that the Indonesians were charming children who would never be able to rule themselves. He was, of course, totally opposed to Indonesian independence and more interested in criticising the Sukarno-led Republicans than in teaching me Indonesian. I persisted, despite his reluctance and my dislike of him. I was determined go to Indonesia with at least a smattering of Dutch and Indonesian. Every Thursday, after I finished work at the dental hospital, I caught the tram to his home in Kew. I still had not discussed the future with my parents. I suppose they were still hoping that I would not marry Julius and that I would stay in Australia. This was a forlorn hope and I imagine that, in their hearts, they knew it too.

By the time Julius arrived in Melbourne at the beginning of November 1946, he had been elected to the East Indonesian parliament as a representative of the Moluccas and had been appointed Minister for Information. I hadn't seen him for thirteen months. Though he had quit the army, he was wearing his khaki captain's uniform when he arrived at our house in Ascot Vale. He looked marvellous. We embraced outside the front door while Mum and Dad stood in the hallway watching. They knew what was coming.

We had dinner together, a tense, silent dinner. Everyone was very nervous. My brothers were still in the army and had been sent to Queensland, so the four us sat at the kitchen table just picking at the roast lamb my mother had cooked. Julius was so tense that even he left his favourite dish almost untouched. I was so pleased to see him, to sit beside him, that I forgot about eating.

Julius looked as striking as ever in his uniform, so handsome. I wanted to hold him, to make up for all the time we'd spent apart. Instead, I sat at the table in silence, just staring at him. I had rehearsed the scene to come many times in my head. I had imagined my parents' response to the announcement that Julius and I were to marry. I had imagined the look on their faces when I told them that I would live with him in Indonesia. They knew, without me ever saying anything specific, that my commitment to Julius was unswerving. They had seen my anxiety during the war when Julius was away; had seen me grow ever thinner, unable to eat because of the danger he was in. They knew that many people, including some of our extended family, disapproved of my love for him, and that many people were outraged at the thought of a woman like me marrying an Asian.

I do not believe my parents were concerned about my marrying Julius because he was an Indonesian. On the contrary, they genuinely liked and respected him. For more than five years, he had been a regular visitor to their home. They had welcomed him without reservation. Dad loved talking to Julius about politics and the state of the world. Mum loved cooking for him because he ate her food with such gusto. Julius had become friendly with Cliff and Russell. He had even lived with us while he was recovering from his breakdown towards the end of the war.

But my parents were conservative people and, for the times, my marrying Julius was unconventional to say the least. They also hated the fact that I would be leaving them and going so far away. It took at least four days to fly from Melbourne to Jakarta and it was an expensive, difficult and sometimes dangerous trip. Mail from Indonesia to Australia hardly ever arrived. Indonesia's phone lines were ancient, and making calls to Australia was impossible. What's more, the country was in the middle of violent upheavals. The prospect of their daughter living there in such circumstances must have filled my parents with dread.

After dinner, we all retreated to the front room and sat in four armchairs facing the open fire. Dad and Julius read the afternoon paper. Julius was so nervous that he read his bit of it upside down. Mum and I sat quietly, looking at the flames, waiting for one of the men to say something. I had decided that Julius should do all the talking because I knew that if I tried to speak, I'd break down and cry. Julius was taking his time. His hands trembled as he held the paper the wrong way up. It struck me that this man, who was so brave in battle, was a quivering mess in our lounge room as he waited for the right moment to speak up. Eventually he did, his voice as timid as I had ever heard it.

'I'd like your permission to marry Jean,' he said, looking at Dad as he spoke. No-one said anything for a long while. My father's face seemed to be full of pain. Mum shuffled in her chair and continued to stare at the fire. There was a lot of emotion in the room. Finally my father responded. 'Well, if that's how it is, that's how it is.'

'I hope you know that I will always love Jean and look after her,' Julius said, his voice a little more confident now. 'I understand how you must feel, your only daughter marrying someone like me and going off to Indonesia. But I will never put her in danger, I promise. I will work hard to make her life comfortable. And I will make sure she comes back to Australia to see you both as often as possible.'

Dad nodded. Mum was crying. Nothing more was said. I wanted to reassure my parents that everything would turn out well, that I would never abandon them, but I was so choked up with emotion that I couldn't talk.

I was heartbroken at the thought of leaving my parents, though I had no doubt that I had to do so. There was no question of Julius staying in Australia and us making a life for ourselves in Melbourne. I had no choice but to leave, but it wasn't easy. I was my father's favourite child. I had achieved what he had only ever been able to dream of achieving. And he had sacrificed much in order to give me the opportunity to do so. Yet here I was, giving all that away. Dad went to bed that night without kissing me goodnight, a rare occurrence. Mum followed him minutes later.

Julius and I sat together in one armchair by the fire, hugging each other. I had not been close to him for so long. During the four years I had loved him, we had spent perhaps two or three months together, but never more than three weeks at a time. When, I wondered, would we finally be able to live together?

Julius and I were married at Wesley Church in Lonsdale Street in Melbourne on 22 November 1946, four and a half years after the night we met. My father did not attend the ceremony. All these years later, I am still not sure why. He told me that he had to attend court that day, but I am fairly sure that he didn't come because it would have been too upsetting for him. Mum came with her sister, Auntie Grace. No friends or colleagues of mine attended our wedding – something that says a lot about how people saw our relationship. Many disapproved, though few ever said anything directly to me. In turn, I did not want people there who were convinced this marriage would be disastrous.

The church was empty but for the four of us and the minister who married us. Julius wore his army uniform and I wore a grey flannel suit. The ceremony only took a few minutes. Julius was so nervous that when the time came for him to repeat the words 'vow and covenant' after the minister, he said 'cow and vovenant'.

There was great happiness and great sadness for both of us that day. After all our years of waiting, we were finally married. But my father was not there, and Julius was sad that his mother couldn't see him and that his father had died before he could meet me. Julius was also leaving the next day to return to Indonesia. Neither of us knew when I would be able to join him there.

After the wedding, Julius and I went to the Victoria Market to buy some clothes for Julius's uncle and for some of his friends in Indonesia. We walked together, hand in hand, though the aisles of the great tin sheds in which hundreds of merchants displayed their goods on old, wooden trestle tables. I was proudly aware of the ring on my finger. I wanted the whole world to know that I was married to the man beside me. I wanted to show the ring to every stranger who walked past.

That afternoon, I helped Mum prepare our wedding dinner – a roast lamb, of course. My brothers were still away. Dad came home from work and came into the kitchen. He looked upset, but he smiled and hugged me. I had tears in my eyes.

There was little celebration that night. One of my aunts came for dinner as well as Dr Wunderly, a delightful old lecturer in dentistry who was probably the only one of my colleagues at the dental hospital who had been totally supportive of my relationship with Julius. Dr Wunderly made a little speech in which he said that he was convinced Julius would play an important role in the development of Indonesia and that we would have a wonderful life there.

The party was over by 10.00 p.m. The next day, Julius caught a plane to Sydney and from there boarded a DC3 that would take him via Darwin to Jakarta. I would not see him again for five months.

thirteen

The five months I spent waiting to join Julius in Indonesia were the slowest months of my life. Most of the time, my parents were glum and silent. I understood, but I became increasingly anxious to get away.

In Indonesia, things were changing fast. Julius spent most of those intervening months travelling. He even went to Holland for three weeks at the beginning of 1947 for a conference with the Dutch on a timetable for independence. The conference was a failure because the Dutch were not interested in setting a timetable. They simply wanted to drag out the process for as long as possible. Their strategy was to promote a system of regional governments where their influence would remain strong. The government of East Indonesia was one of these governments.

Julius understood the Dutch strategy, but held fast to his convictions about how independence could be achieved.

Unlike the Republicans, he also thought that an independent Indonesia should be a federation and that it should maintain close links with Holland. Julius was to later change his mind when there were a series of regional rebellions against the federal government in the early 1950s.

The first three months of 1947 were also spent organising my departure from Australia. It wasn't easy. Julius arranged visas for me, but the Dutch representatives in Australia were reluctant to grant me permission to enter the East Indies. The Australian government too was reluctant to let me go. Julius wrote to me often during those months. Because letters posted in Indonesia hardly ever arrived, he would arrange for his letters to be taken to Australia by Dutch officials or East Indies soldiers travelling to the country, and they would mail them to me. These letters were often a wonderful blend of Julius's personal and public plans and concerns:

> You have to promise me one thing darling. As you know, I do not like dancing. But in my position [as a minister] I shall be forced to do this often. So what I would like you to do is to dance with your husband as often as possible when you are here. I have taken all sorts of lessons, but because I do not like dancing, I just do not get any practice. You wouldn't want people to say that your husband cannot even dance, would you?

Julius was also worried about how I would continue with my work, and about how the move to Indonesia would affect my sense of independence.

> I am sorry to have to tell you that it would probably be difficult for you to work in any other capacity than an honorary one darling. In my position and with my salary, it would be difficult. What you probably could do is work in an honorary capacity at the hospital in Macassar and then have a private practice at the hospital in the afternoon. Don't worry about sending things home and using my money for you are running the show. What is mine is yours, and Dad and Mum are just as dear to me as they are to you.

As he reassured me:

> Darling, I am glad and proud you have your profession. Do you know that in the whole of the Moluccas, with a population of over five million, there is only one dentist? You see how busy you could be. I only hope we can get all necessary instruments for your practice.

At the beginning of April 1947, I finally received permission from the Dutch and Australian governments to join Julius in Indonesia. Five years after we had met, I was about to live with the man I loved. My long wait was not all that unusual. Thousands of young women who married soldiers during the war had to wait years before they could live a normal life with their husbands. What was unusual was that I had married an Asian soldier and that the end of the war did not signal the end of our struggle to be together.

The last few days before I left for Indonesia were hectic and emotionally exhausting. There were farewells at the dental hospital – none of which I particularly enjoyed. I had loved working at the hospital and have no doubt that had Julius not entered my life, I would have had a continuing relationship with the place. I did not, however, love farewells. What's more, there were people at the hospital like old Professor Amies whose hostility to my marriage to Julius was thinly veiled at best.

I spent most of my remaining evenings with my parents. I promised them that I would return to Australia regularly and that when things were calmer in Indonesia, they could come and visit us. There were moments when it really hit me that I was about to leave them and Australia for a new life in a country about which I knew almost nothing. I realised that there were things about Australia that I would always miss. I loved the Australian bush, the look and smell of it, its harshness and size. My father was a boy from the bush and he instilled in me a love of the Australian countryside that has not grown weaker over the years. I would miss Australia terribly and I would, for some time at least, be a stranger in the country in which I was going to live. But I had not the slightest doubt that my destiny, for better or for worse, lay with Julius, and that if I had to, I would give up everything to be with him.

It is not just now, in retrospect, that I say this, having lived with Julius for fifty years. We have lived a life that has been privileged in many ways, a life that has given me two sons and five grandchildren, a life full of history-making drama, filled with achievements and satisfactions for which I thank my lucky stars. But even when my father drove me to the airport that morning in April 1947, his face set in stone to mask his pain, his silence almost unbearable, I had no doubts about what I was doing. Even when my journey to Indonesia turned out to be hard and hazardous, when I felt alone and apprehensive about the place to which I was going, I had no doubts about the choices I had made.

Many strings had been pulled to get me onto that DC3 flight from Darwin to Macassar. There had been cables back and forth from Julius to the Dutch vice-consul in Melbourne, and I went to the consulate several times myself to plead with him to expedite my visa. I can no longer remember his name, but the vice-consul was a balding, middle-aged Dutchman who seemed puzzled by the fact that I was so anxious to travel to the Dutch East Indies when there was a revolution in progress, and even the bare necessities of life were hard to find in the aftermath of the Japanese occupation.

'A young woman like you, Mrs Tahija, should not put herself in danger by travelling to the East Indies at a time like this,' he informed me gravely. 'Why not wait until things settle down a little before you leave Australia?'

Even now, I can recall my deep feelings of frustration at his attitude. Wait a little while? I had waited five years to live with Julius! I had waited through the war; I had even waited after the war had ended, and Julius, having recovered from the nervous breakdown he'd endured towards the war's end, had returned to Indonesia to play his role in the independence movement. I had waited far too long already to wait any longer.

'It may take years for things to settle down,' I told him. 'I can't wait that long. I must join my husband as soon as possible. With your help of course.'

Now, for better or worse, I was about to do just that.

By the time the old DC3 approached Macassar Airport on 21 April 1947, the skies were clear, with no hint of the storm that seemed to have pursued us from Darwin. Macassar is on the southern tip of Sulawesi, on one of the island's four ungainly peninsulas. It is a town with a long and colourful history, and was an important trading port hundreds of years before Australia was settled by Europeans. Its name has become embedded in the English language through the linen or crocheted cloths which Victorian ladies used to spread on the backs of armchairs and which they called antimacassars. The cloths were used to protect the upholstery from macassar hair oil, made from the palm trees that grew around Macassar and favoured by those well-groomed English gentlemen who were determined to give their hair a special sheen.

Not that the hair styles of Victorian gentlemen were uppermost in my mind as we circled Macassar airport before landing. After four days of travel, I felt as if I hadn't had a bath for a year and hadn't slept for about as long. But while I was tired and a little dazed by all that I had experienced since leaving Melbourne, I felt that my whole life had been a kind of preparation for this – for my arrival in Indonesia where my husband of six months was waiting for me. A husband who, after a two-day honeymoon spent at my parents' house, had returned to Macassar unsure of when I would be able to join him.

As the plane came in to land, I could see that the bare, brown-looking area surrounding the runway was covered in very large holes, which turned out to be bomb craters. Hundreds of men in old army uniforms were working with shovels to fill in these craters. They were Japanese troops who had surrendered to the Australians at war's end in August 1945. For almost two years, they had been held in Macassar and its surrounds because there were no ships available for their repatriation to Japan. Tens of thousands of them lived in camps in southern Sulawesi, despised by the local people who had suffered so much at the hands of the occupying forces.

The plane touched down and we bumped along the pock-marked runway. The clearing surrounding the airport buildings had been transformed into a muddy, light brown bog by recent rains. Beyond the airport, I could see scores of coconut trees and, in amongst the trees, bamboo-framed, thatch-roofed huts on stilts. It looked like a scene out of one of those *Road* movies with Bing Crosby, Bob Hope and Dorothy Lamour.

As we came to a halt, there was a sudden rush towards the exits. I did not move. I felt as if I had been travelling for years, and that I had left home a lifetime ago. I sat with my face pressed up against the smudgy perspex of the window, searching the faces of the crowd that waited on the tarmac. Though I'd known Julius for five years, the only clothes I'd seen him in were the blue airforce uniform he had worn when I first met him, or the khaki-coloured Dutch East Indies army uniform he wore when we were married. In my mind, Julius had always been a soldier.

There were no soldiers waiting outside the plane. Instead, I saw a group of men dressed in ill-fitting suits of loud, brown-checked material. They looked like a bunch of bookmakers on their way to the local racetrack. Then I saw Julius. He was one of the bookmakers! The pants of his suit were too short and the jacket was too long. He looked like he'd been out in the rain for some time and his suit had shrunk on him. His eyes scanned the plane's windows, his broad forehead wrinkled with concern and concentration. I tried to wave, but the perspex was so smudged that he couldn't see me.

Down on the ground, the plane was heating up by the second. The white blouse I wore felt like a warm towel clinging to my body. I had saved my favourite navy woollen skirt for this last leg of the trip, but four days of being tossed around in the plane had left it a little the worse for wear. This was not how I'd imagined our reunion – me looking as if I'd been put in a steam bath, fully clothed, for a few days, and Julius dressed as if he were about to fleece a few hapless punters at the local racetrack. (I later learnt that these brown suits were the only civilian attire to be bought in war-ravaged Macassar.)

Tuska Donskoi, the stewardess who had joined the flight in Biak and with whom I'd already formed something of friendship, sat down beside me as we waited for the other passengers to disembark. I must have looked a little deflated because Tuska put her arm around my shoulder and gave me a squeeze. 'Soon you will be with him,' she said. 'And don't worry, you will get used to the heat.' We both laughed.

What I wanted to do when I finally managed to leave the plane was fall into Julius's arms. What I actually did was kiss him on the cheek before being surrounded by the other men in funny suits who, it turned out, worked for my husband. Each of them was touchingly anxious to be introduced to the minister's Australian wife. The introductions completed, Julius took me by the hand and led me to the black Nash limousine which was flying the East Indonesian flag. I had expected none of this – not the welcoming committee nor the limousine with the flag on it – and I had certainly not expected to be treated as if I was minor royalty.

Julius and I sat close together in the back seat of the car. We held hands, our fingers intertwined so tightly they ached. I wound down the window and looked outside. I was so excited I felt almost numb. Julius said nothing, just held my hand and smiled. We drove past clusters of bamboo-framed houses with thatched roofs. Outside them, I could see beautiful brown-skinned women with the most lustrous, long black hair, dressed in cerise-coloured silk sarongs. Babies as brown as chestnuts crawled around at their feet. Naked children ran in and out of the houses, their laughter high-pitched and exuberant.

Behind the houses stood clumps of coconut trees, and beyond the trees lay the lush green growth of the tropics. I had never seen anything like this before. And I had never smelt anything like it either. The odour was of coconut oil and fish, brine and stagnant water. It is a smell that over the years has become so familiar to me, so much a part of my world, that I do not notice it, except when I have been away and it envelops me like a welcoming friend upon my return.

We drove past a dozen or more of these small villages, called *kampong* in Indonesian, and for some absurd reason I thought about my dental hospital colleagues and my university friends. What would they think if they could see me now? Jean Walters, driving through these picture-postcard villages, heading towards her new home, with her husband beside her. Jean Walters, who was determined not to end up in a suburban dental practice somewhere in Melbourne and instead ended up in Indonesia, in the middle of a revolution.

As we drove into the outskirts of Macassar itself, the tropical vistas gave way to a more troubling sight. The small, once neat brick villas where the Dutch had lived had been vandalised during the war, while their former residents had been interned in camps in central Sulawesi. Everything of value had been stripped from the houses – even the fences had been removed and the wrought iron and wood shipped off to Japan. Some of the Dutch who had been interned during the war had come back to their homes, but many had returned to Holland, their health broken by their wartime experiences. Despite the suffering of some of our soldiers, we had been fortunate in Australia that the Japanese had not managed to invade. The people of Macassar, and of the East Indies in general, had not been so lucky. As we drove, I reflected once again on the fact that I had truly led a sheltered existence.

Further into the town, we passed small churches with whitewashed walls and domed mosques. The road we travelled on was lined with tiny, box-like shops from which merchants sold all sorts of household goods, fruit and vegetables, cigarettes and hot food. The streets were shabby and the bitumen road was pot-holed and in a state of disrepair. Everything looked run-down and a little depressed. There had been great privation here and now, with Indonesia in turmoil as a result of the independence struggle, little had been done – nor could be done – to repair the damage.

After returning to the East Indies when the war ended, Julius had been involved in hunting down Japanese soldiers accused of committing war crimes in Indonesia. Some of the stories he heard of what the Japanese had done, especially to women, both Dutch and Indonesian, gave him nightmares for months afterwards. It took him years before he could tell me some of them, and even then he refused to tell me everything.

After about half an hour of driving, during which Julius and I hardly said a word to each other, our car turned into a street that seemed a world away from what I had seen just moments before. It was a wide avenue, lined with cemara, a tropical pine tree. The villas, with their steeply tiled roofs and red-brick walls, looked immaculately kept. There were no signs here of war.

We turned down a driveway beside a house that was set in a garden full of oleander and frangipani. Lined up beside the drive were two men and two women, who peered inside the car for their first glimpse of the minister's wife. They were, Julius informed me, our domestic staff. Domestic staff! I was expecting to be taken to an army camp where we would live in one of those prefabricated buildings – or in one of those igloo-like Quonset huts that look like small airport hangars.

Julius, still holding my hand tightly in his, led me from the car and up three stairs to the front porch. Through the open front door, I could see a large room with a leather sofa and two leather armchairs. There were small rattan tables and a couple of rattan chairs at the side of the room. A fan whirled around on the ceiling. The floor was made of local brown marble and through the doors at the back of room I could see a neat, green garden.

We walked through the front door together, trailed by the

four domestic staff, the driver and a security guard. We stood in the middle of room and, for the first time in six months, we held each other. There was a murmur of voices behind me which reminded us both that we were not alone. We moved apart. Julius smiled and stroked my damp hair. I was dog-tired, unused to the heat and the humidity which was relieved only minimally by the overhead fan. I needed a bath.

The bathroom when I found it was tiled but had no bath. Instead, a sort of upraised well filled with water occupied one corner. Next to it lay a dipper which, I supposed, was used to scoop up water from the well-like structure. How, I wondered, do you bathe in this thing? Tired and a little irritable, I splashed some water on myself, soaped up, and then used the dipper to pour some more tepid water over my body. Within days, I grew to like this method of bathing, but on that first day I wondered whether I would ever get used to these strange ways – not just to the bath, of course, but to having staff, security people and gardeners, and to never really being alone.

Having changed into fresh clothes, Julius and I sat at a small table on the front porch where we were served tea. Despite my efforts to learn some Indonesian before leaving Melbourne, I had not learnt enough to understand more than a word or two of what the middle-aged woman who served our tea and fried bananas said to me. So I nodded, and smiled, and hoped that she could understand that I appreciated what she had prepared for us. She smiled back and I noticed that her teeth were black.

'Don't worry,' said Julius, seeing how startled I was. 'It's from chewing betel nut. That's what happens.'

As a dentist, I did not feel entirely reassured. I knew that betel nut was a mild narcotic that was popular through much of the South Pacific and parts of Asia, and that in the long run it did more than just blacken teeth: it destroyed them.

I looked at the vista that surrounded us, and Julius told me of our neighbours. Across the road from our villa stood an imposing white colonial mansion which had once been the Dutch governor's residence but was now the official residence of Soekawati, the president of East Indonesia. Soekawati was a Balinese prince and his wife a former French dancer who took on many of the ways of Balinese royalty. Each day, she would dress her hair with fresh flowers. All their servants were Balinese, beautiful young girls in brightly coloured sarongs who always wore flowers in their hair – some of them picked, to my chagrin, from our front garden.

The prime minister lived several doors down from us. He too was Balinese royalty. Over the years, Julius and Anak Agung Gde Agung were to become close friends. I could always tell when Julius was on the phone to Agung because they only spoke to each other in Dutch, a hangover from their childhood when both had attended Dutch schools. In the 1960s, when Sukarno's government became heavily influenced by the communists, Agung was jailed for five years for treason. His crime was that he criticised Sukarno's association with the communists. Throughout his time in prison, Julius supported Agung's family.

It was late afternoon by the time we finished our tea. We sat silently on the porch as dusk fell and the clouds started to encroach on what had been a cloudless sky. It was quiet and still and very hot. I had not slept properly for days, yet I was not sleepy. I thought about my parents sitting in our house in Ascot Vale; our house which was no longer my home, and which existed somewhere in another world. I was not unhappy, but I was lost, I suppose, between the life I had left and the life I was just beginning. I'd never been away from home for anything more than a few days before and here I was in Macassar, surrounded by people who spoke a language I could not understand, and whose culture and customs were alien to me. I was not unhappy. How could I be? Julius was there beside me. He looked a bit funny in that loud, brown-checked suit, but it was the same Julius I had fallen in love with virtually at first sight five years ago.

Dinner was served at a round, teak dining table. Julius and I sat opposite each other, a bit embarrassed by the formality of it all. What I really wanted to do was sit beside him, look at him, hold him, and talk about how happy I was that we were together. Instead I waited as one of the young boys brought in a trolley of food from the kitchen and placed the plates of fish and vegetables on the table. Julius ate with relish but, try as I might, I could not swallow more than a few mouthfuls. Now the cook came out of the kitchen and stood with the young man behind my chair. I pushed the fish and the pieces of lettuce and tomato – prepared specially for me, European-style – around my plate.

'Do they have to stand there behind me?' I asked Julius. 'I'd much rather eat without an audience.'

He seemed surprised by this question. 'That's how it is,' he replied. 'It's the custom. They stay around in case you want something. It would be insulting to them if I asked them to go away.'

Over the next months of our new life together, Julius would continue to educate me about local customs and the local culture. I was never to offer pork to anyone, for most people were Muslims for whom pork was a forbidden meat. I was not to use my left hand and, if I had to point, I could use my thumb but never my forefinger, for such pointing was taken as rudeness. I was never to touch anyone's head as that was a sign of disrespect.

'Have some pork,' I joked one day to the ever-present young man who served our meals and who had been studiously watching every mouthful I took. He just smiled and shook his head. But Julius was furious.

'Never do that!' he roared. 'It's not funny.'

Although I grew accustomed to the presence of our staff, I still could not eat. In fact, for the first six weeks in Macassar, I hardly ate at all. I lost weight and Julius became increasingly concerned about what was happening to me. Looking back, I am still not sure what caused my lack of appetite. People coming to the tropics for the first time sometimes lose their appetites as a result of the heat and the humidity. In my case, however, I think I was simply overwhelmed by the changes that were taking place in my life. I loved Julius but for the first time in our relationship, he was at home while I was far away from everything that had defined my life – my parents, my family, my friends, even my work. Fifty years on, living anywhere else but Indonesia is unimaginable to me and I cannot conceive of a life without Indonesian food, which is as varied and as subtle as any cuisine in the world. But during those first weeks in Macassar, I was a stranger in a strange place – just as Julius and his troops had been in Melbourne in 1942.

As night fell that first evening, Julius and I were like two youngsters finally left alone by their parents. Our bedroom was a large room with closed and shuttered windows and white-washed walls. The bed was covered by a large mosquito net. It was so hot that by the time we climbed into it, I was covered in perspiration. The net made it even hotter, but when I kicked it off, Julius gently put it back in place. As he explained, I could either sleep without the net and be eaten by malaria-carrying mosquitoes, or I could lie under the net in the stifling, sleep-denying heat. I chose the net. I lay in Julius's arms and it was wonderful to be in bed with him, in my new home. When he fell asleep, I lay there looking at him in the half-darkness and tried to imagine what our life together would be like.

Julius was no longer the army sergeant who had walked through the front door of my parents' house in the darkest days of the war and into my life. Not only had he emerged from the war a highly decorated soldier, but he had gone on to become a captain in the East Indies army. He left the army to enter politics, and had become the minister for information in the East Indonesian government, having been elected to the regional parliament by the people of Ambon island, his ancestral home. (The Ambonese were mostly Christian and were considered to be the East Indies equivalent of the Nepalese Gurkhas – fierce, brave soldiers who formed the backbone of the Dutch East Indies army.)

Julius, I recognised, was a man who had large personal ambitions, but even larger ones for his country. He was a nationalist, and was determined to play a role in the emerging Indonesian nation. Whatever our life together would be like, our destiny would be inextricably tied to the destiny of Indonesia.

fourteen

As was to be our habit for the next fifty years, Julius and I had coffee together early the next morning, sitting on the front verandah that looked across to the president's palace. Julius told me then that he had to leave me in two days' time because there was a conference in Jakarta he needed to attend. Once again it struck me that I had entered a strange new world – one that was entirely different to the life I had known.

The domestic staff hovered around us, waiting to serve coffee. Little plates of fried banana were set out on the rattan table. Some of the staff had worked for Dutch officials before the war and it was common practice for them to approach on their knees as a mark of their servitude. The older ones still bowed to the waist as they served us. I told Julius that this must stop, that people had to be treated with respect and the old colonial ways had to go. He agreed, and while our staff were puzzled, they accepted our decision. In time, the domestic staff became like members of our family, especially after we moved to Jakarta. Some stayed with us for forty years. In a sense, they were my best friends, the people to whom I was closest and who taught me what I needed to know about Indonesian ways.

It was still relatively cool that first morning, the sky a cloudless, pale blue. But the smell of the tropics was as pungent and striking as it had been the day before. After breakfast, Julius was driven to his office and I was left alone. I wandered through the house, marvelling at the way Julius had gathered together enough furniture to fill it. Most of it was borrowed, but the house was comfortable and clean, and I was a new bride inspecting her first home.

That morning I finally managed to work out how the old Dutch colonial bath worked, ladling tepid water over myself as I stood on the tiled floor thankful for a few minutes' respite from the heat and the humidity. I wrote a letter home and letters to several of my colleagues at the dental hospital, telling them of my trip to Indonesia and of my first impressions of Macassar. None of these letters ever reached their destination.

Julius came home for lunch. I was too overwhelmed to eat, but Julius ate heartily from the selection of dishes that had been placed before us on the dining room table. There was fish curry, pickled vegetables, roast duck, and a thick chicken soup. All this was followed by bowls of tropical fruit including some that I had never seen before.

Later, Indonesian food became a particular passion of mine. For close to fifty years, I kept a massive, old-fashioned office ledger in which I wrote down recipes for dishes from all over Indonesia that Julius and I particularly liked. This ledger, which began its life in Julius's first humble office, is now filled with yellowing, dog-eared pages, but I still refer to it every day when deciding the day's menu with our cook.

One of my fondest memories of our son George's childhood is of us consulting that recipe book together. Today he is kind enough to say that it is 'probably the best selection of Indonesian recipes ever put together', then he adds, with a slight smile, 'organised in a manner which only my mother could understand.'

But on that first day in Macassar, I simply watched Julius eat. He didn't seem to mind. It was as if he was still making up for all those Australian army meals he'd been forced to consume during the war. After lunch, we retired to the bedroom for a rest. This too seemed rather exotic to me, but later it became just a normal part of life in the tropics. I lay on the bed watching Julius sleep, aware of the whirring overhead fan blowing hot air around the stuffy room. How different this was from my routine in Melbourne.

Late that afternoon, Julius and I went for a drive to the outskirts of Macassar, both of us sitting in the back of the black ministerial car with the government flag flying on its bonnet. We drove through suburbs that had once been predominantly Dutch and the houses were large and gracious, with steep, tiled roofs, wide verandahs and large shuttered windows. The once manicured, dark green lawns were gone and the flower beds looked unkempt and unloved, but I could imagine how good life must have been for the resident Dutch officials and traders.

We drove to the port. Along the road leading down to the harbour were clusters of thatch-roofed houses built on stilts and set in groves of coconut, banana and rubber trees. These villages were hives of activity, with children playing in the dirt outside their homes and women in silk sarongs and jackets moving gracefully through the laneways, carrying baskets of food or wet washing.

In the harbour, dozens of sailing ships that looked like Portuguese galleons bobbed on the water. With the light blue sky in the background and the sea a deep green, it was like looking at a painting of paradise. We watched the sun go down, a red ball shimmering in the heat, sinking behind the white sails of the boats that rocked on gentle waves. It was the most magnificent sunset I had ever seen. I was content, sitting with Julius at a small table outside a shabby little Chinese restaurant, sipping tea and gazing out across the harbour to the horizon where the sun was fast disappearing into the ocean. I wished that my parents could see me. I wished I could tell them how happy I was.

When Julius kissed me goodbye two days later and headed off to the airport for his flight to Jakarta, I was not happy at all. I was miserable. I knew no-one in Macassar; I could speak only a few words of Indonesian and even fewer in Dutch; and I was expected, as the wife of a minister in the East Indonesian government, to join other ministerial wives later that day on an official visit to the local leprosy facility on the outskirts of Macassar. I was terrified, less about coming into contact with people who had leprosy – in those days, it was thought to be more infectious than it actually is – than of having to meet the wives of Julius's fellow ministers. I had never had to do anything like this before. These women I was sure would have more poise and sophistication than I could ever hope to achieve.

Late in the morning, the presidential limousine arrived outside our front door. I was waiting on the verandah, having put on my best dress and the little hat with flowers on it that I had worn to my wedding. The president's French wife greeted me outside the car. She looked stunning in a tight-fitting yellow dress with a white orchid tucked behind each ear in striking contrast to her lustrous dark hair. A nightclub dancer in Paris, Gilbert Vincent had met the president when he had gone to France on an official visit. All of a sudden she had gone from being a chorus girl to living in this magnificent palace surrounded by gorgeous Balinese servant girls. It was really like a fairytale.

Gilbert greeted me warmly – her English a little more fluent than my French – and invited me into the car where I was introduced to the other wives – I think there were four of them. Then we headed off on what was to be my first official duty as Julius's wife. I have attended countless functions over the years, many of which I can no longer remember, but this visit to the leprosy complex remains vivid in my memory because it signalled the start of a new way of life for me. I cannot say that I've always looked forward to the functions I've attended, but after a while, I have found that I get on well with people from all sorts of different backgrounds and that I do enjoy meeting them.

The leprosy complex was on the edge of Macassar – a large, scrubby block of land surrounded by a wire fence. There were several dilapidated looking buildings surrounding a slightly larger one which was the complex's main hospital. We were greeted by the director and several of his staff who led us into the building. I was wearing sandals and had collected some sand in them from the path outside the hospital. As we walked down the corridor towards the wards, the sand made it feel as if I was walking on tiny shards of glass. All I could think of as the director spoke to us was: what if sand carries the leprosy bug? Could I catch it?

Once we were in the wards, however, my fears more or less disappeared. Men and women sat on beds, some with fingers missing, others with no toes, staring at us as we passed. Most of the patients were middle-aged and were in the early stages of the disease. We were not taken to the wards that housed the really serious cases.

After visiting the hospital we went outside and met the

patients who tended the small vegetable gardens. They greeted us with smiles, and while I could not understand much of the conversation, I could sense the genuine warmth that existed between them and the director of the hospital. I wanted to tell them that I too had worked in a hospital, that I was a dentist with an interest in medicine, not just a politician's wife, but there was no way for me to convey this. So I just smiled and did my best to catch the gist of the conversation. When we left after about an hour or so, the director thanked us effusively for coming. But I wondered whether I was truly cut out to be a minister's wife.

Alone in the dining room at home, I ate lunch – or at least I picked at some fried fish. I had nothing to do and no-one to talk to. Having worked hard for much of my life – first at school, later at university and then at the dental hospital – I found being idle difficult. Julius had tried to get me voluntary work at the dental clinic attached to the Macassar hospital, but the Dutch dentist who ran the clinic wouldn't have a bar of it, even though I wasn't asking to get paid. I think there was a certain amount of vindictiveness about his refusal to allow me to work. I suspect the old dentist resented the way things were changing, the way Indonesians like Julius were starting to run the East Indies.

When I went to see the dentist myself, his manner was cool and distant. He told me there were enough dentists in the clinic and that he did not need my help. I told him of my extensive experience in Melbourne but it was no use:

professional jobs were for the Dutch and the Dutch alone, however many Indonesian teeth might be suffering from neglect. As he spoke, I thought of the words attributed to Jonkheer de Jonge, who was the Dutch governor-general of the East Indies in the 1930s: 'We have ruled here for 300 years with a whip and a club, and we shall still be doing it in another 300 years.'

I was bitterly disappointed by the Dutch dentist's refusal, for I had planned all along to continue practising dentistry in Indonesia. I had even brought with me my set of dental instruments, which my father had given me as a graduation gift. Now I would not need them, at least for the foreseeable future. I would have to adjust to a life without work, a life I had never lived before.

It wasn't easy. I spent days walking around the neighbourhood in which we lived. Julius had offered me the use of his car, and his driver took me on short trips into the scrubby, flat countryside around Macassar. Most afternoons, I wrote letters home and then spent an hour or so practising my Indonesian. Within weeks, I was able to understand most things people said to me and I could even engage in rudimentary conversations with our staff, who would fall about laughing when I made mistakes.

When Julius was home, there were official receptions to attend virtually every night of the week. These were with local diplomats and government officials and most of the time, my role was to be with the wives and make small talk.

I had to be very careful about what I said because if I was too outspoken, it could affect Julius. I didn't mind: at least we were together. Julius was driven, a man who worked harder than anyone I had ever met. There was so much that needed to be done before the revolution in Indonesia was over. I became intensely interested in local politics and can remember conversations in which I told him he should abandon the East Indonesian government and join Sukarno's Republic. Julius disagreed. He was inspired by Ghandi's example in India and wanted a peaceful, non-violent revolution. Looking back, I think he was right. There had already been too much bloodshed in Indonesia.

We spent nine months in Macassar. Slowly, I learnt to make myself understood in Indonesian and even in Dutch. While I still suffered from boredom when Julius was away, I could at least communicate with most people I met, even if our conversations were full of awkward pauses. The heat and humidity bothered me less as time went by. I grew to love the countryside and would often get Julius's driver to take me out to a *kampong* on the outskirts of town. These villages were always a hive of activity punctuated by the laughter of children at play. Sometimes, in the late afternoon, Julius and I would go down to the port together to watch the sun set over the harbour. I always felt I was in paradise.

Some things remain very vivid in my memory. Not long after I arrived, an excursion was arranged for us which may have been intended to test me – to measure how adaptable I was to new and strange customs. The excursion was a deer hunt, and after travelling a good distance from Macassar along bad tracks in a jeep, we walked for miles across rough, stunted country. Our hunters were a wild crowd of tough men and it was not until after dark that they stopped, slung a hammock for me under the trees and lit a fire. Some of the hunters then went off after deer; others sat around the fire, talking for hours. There was much hawking, farting and spitting into the fire, and much smoking of aromatic clove cigarettes. I lay in my hammock, thinking, 'It's a long way from Ascot Vale!' If it *was* a test, I trust I convinced them all that I was not the squeamish type who would faint at the sight of a mouse.

This was not my last deer hunt. Some years later, we made an expedition to the dry and rugged coast of Sulawesi. The men who made up the hunting party had rifles slung over one shoulder and sarongs over the other and rode bareback on wild horses. Their women, who travelled with them, were kind and gentle and hospitable. On that excursion, we were put up for the night in a thatched communal longhouse, the elevated floor of which was reached via a steep ladder. Julius and I were given the privilege of a double bed and a highly dubious set of blankets. In one corner of the longhouse, a baby was being born and in another, women were doing the cooking. Our dinner was deer meat, cooked in bamboo tubes. It was tough and tasteless.

That night I needed (as usual) to visit the toilet, a need which Julius explained to our hosts. They could not have been more obliging. With bright torches of burning bamboo, a group escorted me from the longhouse to a little trickle of water where such matters were conducted, and stood close by while my need was served. I was hardly assisted by such public attention, but at least it removed any inclination to linger. Back near the house, I indicated that I would like a wash. They pointed to a drum of water near the steps, whose refreshing (but stagnant) contents I splashed liberally into my face, with the result that a few days later my eyes became horribly inflamed with an infection.

During our nine months in Macassar, Julius took me with him on three or four of his official visits to some of the islands that formed East Indonesia. In many ways, these islands are amongst the most beautiful and exotic parts of Indonesia. Each island has its own culture and traditions, and is a miniature world unto itself. These islands have been trading centres for many centuries. Not just Dutch traders but the Spanish and Portuguese once came here. Some of the traders married local women and these marriages have produced the most beautiful people imaginable.

Perhaps the most memorable trip we made was a six-day visit to Ambon – the island Julius represented in parliament. Both of Julius's parents came from Ambon and, despite the fact that he had been born and had grown up in Surabaya, the Ambonese regarded Julius as one of their own.

We travelled to Ambon on an old Dutch bomber. The plane had a hole cut into the floor and through it we could see the islands we flew over. Ambon, even from the air, looked stunning. It had an inner and outer bay and then, seemingly out of the sea, rose these stark, jungle-covered mountains. The sea itself was as clear and still as a sheet of light blue, tinted glass. At the airport, we were greeted by thousands of cheering, singing Ambonese. Beautiful little girls holding bunches of flowers stepped forward and curtsied in front of me, their smiles revealing the whitest teeth I had ever seen. They handed me the flowers and a great roar from the crowd enveloped Julius and me.

The next six days were full of fascinating excursions to different parts of the island. Wherever he went, Julius was greeted as a great local hero, which of course he was, given his Ambonese background and his war record. The Ambonese have a great soldiering tradition and are fierce fighters who have served with distinction in the Dutch East Indies army. Julius's military achievements were known throughout the island, and everywhere we went people wanted to talk to him about his wartime experiences.

Despite their reputation as the Gurkhas of the East Indies, the Ambonese are a Melanesian people who love singing and dancing. The waltz is their favourite dance, and at a celebration like a wedding or an official ceremony they will dance and sing until dawn, the children free to roam around as they please, laughing and playing all night.

Every night during our visit, a celebration was held at which a feast of local cuisine was served. Unlike much of Indonesia, Ambon's staple food is not rice, but a thin porridge called *papeda* which is made from sago. With that, they eat a thick and spicy fish soup. Luckily, by the time we visited I had grown used to Indonesian food and loved the taste of *sambal* (chilli) in most dishes. Because these were special occasions, roast duck or chicken was also served, followed by a dazzling array of tropical fruit. After the meal, the singing and dancing invariably continued all night. The tradition in Ambon is that it is up to the women to ask the men to dance. Julius was always whisked away before I had time to utter a word, which left me with no option but to choose another partner. Those dancing lessons I gave Julius in Macassar shortly after I arrived stood us both in good stead.

Julius and I also attended a church service during our visit – which was perhaps the most memorable of my life. The singing of the hymns was out of this world. The choir stood at the front of the congregation, the men dressed in white cotton jackets and white pants. The women wore long *kebaya* – a three-quarter length silk jacket – and underneath that, a pink or white sarong. Even their shoes were like something out of a fairytale, long and pointed, with turned-up toes. Their long hair was stunningly beautiful, made incredibly shiny by coconut oil, which was rubbed into it after washing. A flute accompanied their voices, which soared into the rafters of the small wooden church.

George Walters, aged twenty in his Light-horse uniform

Olive Ward, aged eighteen

Me at twelve months

In Wilson Hall, sitting my final exams for dentistry at Melbourne University in 1940

Julius in uniform, October 1942

The Walters family in 1941

Clockwise from left: My mother, Russell, my father and Cliff (seated)

Julius and me at the zoo, Melbourne, 1942

Surrounded by crowds waiting to see Julius during our visit to Ambon in 1947

A bouquet for the minister's wife, Ambon, 1947

The Herald article on our marriage. When I protested, they changed the headline to 'Hero Returns For Wife'

Black Hero Returns For White Wife

TODAY'S PICTURE of Mr and Mrs Tahija.

A COAL-BLACK Ambonese sergeant in the Netherlands Indies Army, who first came to Melbourne in 1942 — after killing 200 Japanese in three hours in the Japanese invasion of Tanimbar — arrived by air from New York yesterday to collect his Australian wife and mother-in-law and fly them to Indonesia on Sunday.

The Ambonese is Julius Tahija (pronounced tar-hee-yah). His wife is the former Jean Walters, a Bachelor of Dental Science of Melbourne University and for five years registrar of the Melbourne Dental Hospital. His mother-in-law is Mrs Olive Walters, of Kent Street, Ascot Vale.

Since landing in Melbourne in tattered blood-stained uniform in 1942, Sergeant Tahija has been awarded the Dutch VC, the Willemsorde, the citation mentioning the slaughter of 200 Japanese;

He has made four submarine landings in enemy-held Indonesia as a member of "Z" Force;

He has, as a Christian, married Miss Walters in 1946 at Wesley Church;

He has been elected to the East Indonesian Parliament as MP for South Moluccas and held Cabinet rank as Minister of Social Affairs and Information; and

He has been on two political missions to Holland as an Indonesian spokesman.

Mr Tahija has just flown to Holland as head of an Indonesian delegation discussing the composition of the Interim Government of Indonesia which will precede the setting up by Holland of the United States of Indonesia.

He returned through the United States to attend to the American end of his family's textile import-export business.

Mr Tahija said the Dutch-sponsored Government of East Indonesia (for whom he is liaison officer in Batavia) contained many friends of the Indonesian Republic. When he periodically visited the Republican capital of Jogjakarta he was received by every Republican Minister.

"We recognise," he said, "that we have the Republic to thank for our being as far as we are on the road to Indonesian independence —which we all seek. But our Government feels we can advance furthest by co-operating with Holland, in the way that Nehru attained India's independence in co-operation with Britain."

'VERY HAPPY'

Mrs Tahija, an attractive young blonde, has been twice already to Indonesia with her husband and has lived in Batavia and Macassar. She returned to Melbourne on holiday two months ago.

She said her husband has a comfortable bungalow in Batavia and she would like her mother to see something of life in the land of Australia's next-door neighbor.

"A lot of nonsense has been spoken in Australia about Australian girls married to Indonesians," Mrs Tahija *said. "I would like to go on record as saying I am very happy. My taking my mother up to see how I live is the most adequate testimony to that."*

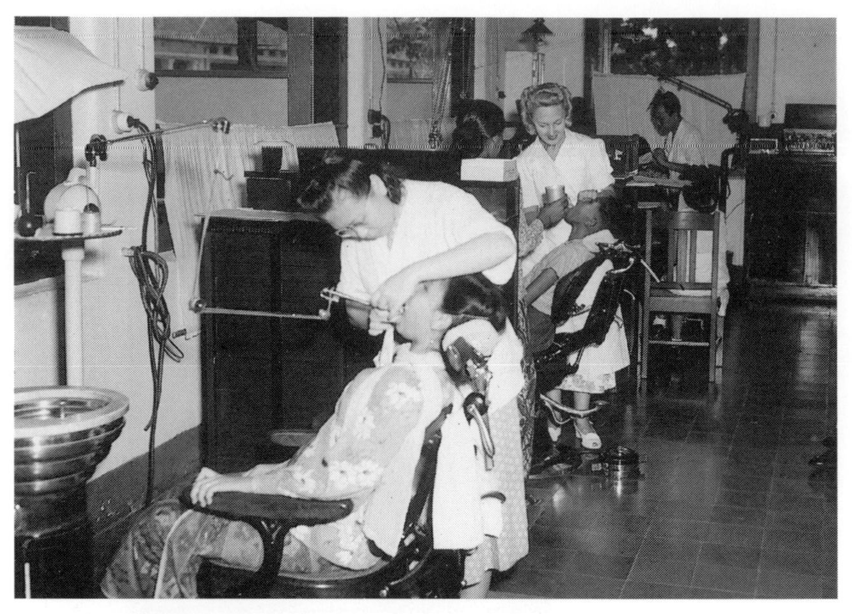

Working at the dental hospital in Jakarta, 1950

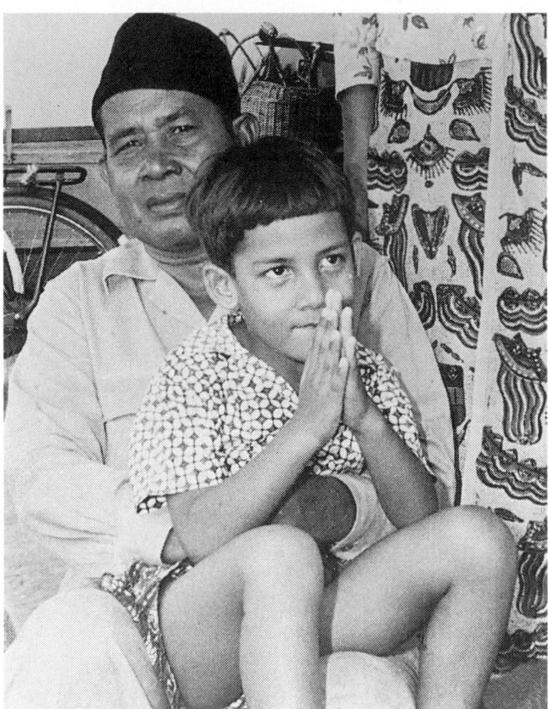

Sjakon with Asro in 1957

Sukarno addresses an angry crowd in front of the presidential palace in September 1950

photograph: UPI

Demonstrators burn an effigy of the American ambassador Howard Jones during an anti-imperialism rally in Jakarta in 1964

photograph: UPI

With George (on my lap) and Sjakon (standing) in 1960

George and Laurel's wedding, 1988
Clockwise from back left: Sjakon, Laurel, George, Shelley (Sjakon's wife), Cindy (our first grandchild), me and Julius

Ambon's population is almost evenly divided between Christians and Muslims. We travelled inland, where the people lived in small villages reached only by four-wheel drive vehicles travelling along dirt tracks. They still lived as they had for hundreds of years – growing vegetables and hunting for deer and wild pigs. Up in the mountains, I felt as if I was living out some sort of childhood fantasy.

More often than not, my whole life in Macassar felt like a fantasy. Indonesian politics was often fiery. There were endless crises and endless meetings that went on late into the night, many of them in our house. I would lie in bed trying to shut out the sound of raised voices in a futile effort to get some sleep. I remember the prime minister one night storming around our lounge room in a towering rage at the way the Indonesians who wanted a federation and those who supported the Republic were in constant disagreement. In the government of East Indonesia, cabinets rose and fell in swift succession. Within a period of weeks I was, in turn, the wife of the Minister for Economic Affairs, for Social Affairs, and for Information.

Julius was away a lot on government business, and at one stage he went to Holland for three weeks. I talked to practically no-one but the domestic staff during this time. I was bored. I missed my work. I wanted to feel like I was a useful member of my adopted country. Even when Julius came back, politics intruded on our reunion. A large crowd of his supporters escorted him home from the airport and then rushed into the house with him. For almost an hour, he couldn't get through the crowd to greet me.

And yet there were many times when I really loved my new life. On one such occasion, I remember one of the domestic staff rushed into the room crying, 'Come! Come quickly! There is someone important to see you!'

I went immediately to the front door where I was greeted by a group of emissaries of the Sultan of Bone. For centuries, Bone had been a powerful kingdom. It centred around the Gulf of Bone, which deeply indents southern Sulawesi. Its sailors had ranged the seas of the Indies. Many had been pirates. They had regularly visited the northern shores of Australia long before white settlement. The Sultan's ancestors had waged war for centuries against the people of Macassar and he was still a ruler of considerable importance.

Now on my front doorstep were about a dozen emissaries dressed in beautiful, multicoloured ceremonial robes that swept the floor. All of them were sheltered from the sun by delicate umbrellas. They bore an invitation to Julius for a special audience with the Sultan. I accepted the invitation and smiled. In unison, they all bowed slightly and departed, their robes flowing behind them.

What a different world I had reached! I felt like Alice in Wonderland where everything was curiouser and curiouser. I knew that I loved this place, loved its people, its food, its smells, its lush plants and flowers. Here was my *lakon* – my destiny.

fifteen

Towards the end of 1947, Julius was appointed the East Indonesian government's representative in Jakarta. He was about to move onto the national political stage at a time of great uncertainty and turmoil. His role was to negotiate on behalf of the government with the Republicans and with the Dutch, as well as to liaise with a special United Nations committee that had been set up to try to break the impasse between the Dutch and Indonesian nationalists on a timetable for independence.

It was not only the Dutch and the Republicans who were in conflict however. There was no agreement among Indonesians about what sort of government they wanted – a federation of regions or a central unitary government based in Jakarta. They were not even agreed on their national boundaries. Indeed, parts of the archipelago wanted to remain under Dutch rule. There was fighting between the

Dutch and the Republic's armed forces in central Java and in parts of Sumatra. In fact, there were outbreaks of violence between opposing political factions all over the former Dutch East Indies.

The Dutch were in no hurry to leave. They would not easily give up their prized colonial possession. Four hundred years of rule – twice as long as the 200-year history of white Australia – had given them the impression that they could stay in the East Indies forever. In July 1947, the Dutch launched a so-called police action against the Republic in east Java, parts of central and west Java, and parts of Sumatra. Two weeks later, the United Nations forced the Dutch into a cease-fire, with the Republic still in control of its capital, Jogjakarta.

We left Macassar in December 1947, travelling to Jakarta by cargo boat. Her Dutch commander, a certain Captain Oegers, was on board – in his coffin. His wife, understandably distressed, sat by his side on the ship's deck. The captain had succumbed to a fatal strain of malaria, which had been treated as an attack of commonplace influenza. This was not an uncommon mistake in those days.

Jakarta was very different from Macassar. It was a hot, steaming city of perhaps a million people, most of them living in small *kampong*. There were porters on the streets, balancing huge loads on their poles, and *betja* – pedi-cabs which were basically bicycles with a double-seat attached behind them for passengers. There were hundreds of hawkers selling a bewildering array of shoddy goods and thousands of beggars. About the only motor vehicles on the roads were tired-looking trucks left over from the war. Jakarta felt like a big, hot country town bursting at the seams. Within a few years, the population was to grow to over three million as people streamed into the city from the countryside after independence. Vast shanty towns sprang up all over the city. Squatters invaded any house left vacant for even a day. At night, Jakarta was in virtual darkness because of the unreliable electricity supply.

The Dutch influence in some parts of the city was obvious. They had built thousands of villas along tree-lined streets in an effort to reproduce a piece of the Netherlands in the tropics. The villas had steep roofs, small windows and brick walls – an architecture that made sense in northern Europe but not necessarily in Asia. They had even built canals, like those in Amsterdam, which, by the time we arrived, were like open sewers in which people bathed and washed their clothes. Chinatown, like its counterparts in Saigon or Bangkok, was an area full of hand cars and bicycles, narrow streets and thousands of shops – their red banners announcing their wares to the milling crowds of people below.

It was almost impossible to find a house when we first arrived in Jakarta. We stayed with an old friend of Julius's father, an elderly Chinese merchant and trader called Mr Tan who lived in a vast colonial mansion in Matraman, a tree-lined street in central Jakarta. The domestic arrangements were curious – at least for this young woman from a small and conventional Australian family. Mr Tan's first marriage had been arranged. His wife was a quiet, homely woman with whom he had seven children. Mrs Tan spent much of her day playing cards or mahjong with her friends – the jolliest crowd of elderly ladies I ever saw. They all wore delightful white jackets – called *kebaya* – trimmed with lace and beautiful floral sarongs. 'Come in, come in', they would cry, their cheeks bulging with chewed betel nut, the bright red streams of which they spat into nearby brass spittoons.

In middle age, Mr Tan had fallen in love with Anna, a beautiful Chinese girl of eighteen, who promptly joined the Tan household. I took an instant liking to Anna, who has remained my closest friend for fifty years. She was happy, charming, and a talented artist and writer. Mr Tan adored her. He had a great appreciation of beauty and the finer things in life. In the evenings, he would sit like a mandarin, wrapped in a long white silk robe, pouring Chinese tea for his guests into delicate little porcelain cups. His morning garb of loose white wraparound pants made him look as if he was wearing a large sail. He was a fascinating man and even now, in his nineties, remains active and interested in everything.

Our room in the Tan mansion was huge, with very high ceilings. Nevertheless, it was stiflingly hot and the mosquito net that enveloped the bed made it even hotter. At nightfall, the servants would close all the shutters and lights would be lit in every room, as was the custom. Night air, it was believed, was dangerous and the lights kept thieves away. One night I begged Julius to open the windows, which he did. Soon we heard shuffling steps outside, and the shutters were promptly closed – gently but firmly – by Mr Tan himself.

Once again, I felt as if I had entered a fantasy world. Once again, I was left alone in this world for much of the time, my days taken up with watching the exotic goings-on in the Tan household, or wandering the streets nearby, absorbing the sights, sounds and smells of this tension-filled city. Once again, I wrote letters home to Australia every day, letters that did not arrive. Everything in Indonesia was in chaos, including the postal service.

Julius went straight to work upon our arrival in Jakarta. He worked out of an office in the centre of the city, and though he often came home for lunch, he travelled regularly, moving between Jakarta and Macassar – where the East Indonesian government was based – as well as going to Jogjakarta to consult with the Republicans. The negotiations between the various Indonesian political factions, the Dutch and the United Nations special committee, were tortuous and tumultuous. They consumed his time and his energy.

The Dutch constantly made agreements on a timetable for independence and then immediately broke them. Julius became increasingly outspoken in his criticisms of the Dutch. At one stage, he told the international press based in Jakarta: 'The Dutch will stand face to face with the whole of Indonesia and not merely the Republic if they do not redeem their several-times given promise to transfer sovereignty to the United States of Indonesia by early 1949.' Given that the Dutch East Indies army was still overwhelmingly Indonesian, Julius's views as those of a war hero and former senior officer had to be taken particularly seriously.

Eventually we moved to our first house in Jakarta, a pretty, white Dutch villa in Jalan Minangkabau. 'Jalan' means street, but in fact we were on a wide boulevard bordered by a canal that was lined with elm trees. The villa had that typical sense of spaciousness and grandness that was at the centre of Dutch colonial design at the turn of the century. It seemed odd to me, however, that all the houses on our street were built so close together. I was told that the Dutch felt comfortable this way, as if the density of housing made them feel they were still in Amsterdam. When we moved to Jalan Minangkabau, we were the only Indonesian family in the street. No doubt the Dutch families that surrounded us saw our arrival as a reflection of the shape of things to come. And it was. As Holland's imperial fortunes declined, the Dutch families moved out one by one and were replaced by Indonesians.

Although all the houses and gardens in Jalan Minangkabau had obviously been beautifully maintained before the war, our place had been totally stripped either by the Japanese or subsequent squatters. Even the taps, basins and toilets had been removed, and the government had to install completely new plumbing and drains before we moved in. The garden had also been ruined, but I welcomed the challenge and soon had it in a fit state – or so I thought – to invite the Belgian ambassador onto the lawn for pre-dinner drinks.

He was a large, heavy man who was soon dripping with sweat, despite the cooler evening air, and after several minutes I suggested that we go in for dinner.

'*Ja graag*' he responded, rose, and disappeared waist-deep into a hole. It would not have helped his already wounded dignity if we'd told him that the hole was the old, dried-up septic tank which the government plumbers had failed to fill in properly.

Around this time I renewed my friendship with Tuska Donskoi, the airline stewardess who had comforted me on my first flight to Indonesia. I had asked Tuska, when we parted in Macassar, to get in touch with me sometime. She did so in Jakarta and within weeks we were firm friends. Tuska had married a Dutch tailor, which had apparently caused something of a rift with her parents. She was a down-to-earth woman with a great sense of humour and there was much about Indonesian life that I learnt from her. Together with Anna, I had, at last, two friends with whom I could talk freely. It had been a long time since I'd had anyone I could really talk to, apart from Julius of course.

Most of the time I had to constantly watch what I said in case it might embarrass Julius. That is the lot of a politician's wife and I accepted my role mostly without rancour as we attended seemingly endless rounds of diplomatic functions.

There were times, of course, when people said things that made me want to scream, but I kept myself mostly under control, though I would certainly let Julius know later what I thought.

My Indonesian was more or less fluent by the time we arrived in Jakarta and I could speak Dutch reasonably well. Almost imperceptibly, I was assimilating into Indonesian life. I was no longer aware of that special pungent smell that characterises so much of Asia. I had grown used to the heat and the humidity, though Jakarta, when we first arrived, felt like the hottest, most humid place on earth. And I had certainly come to love Indonesian food and its great variety – although most of all I enjoyed those hot and spicy dishes that seemed so perfect for the tropics.

In April 1948, my mother came to visit us – the first of several visits she was to make to Indonesia. She fell in love with Jakarta almost immediately. She would sit on the front verandah of our house and watch the show of humanity pass. There were few cars, but there was a constant procession of porters and hawkers with their loads of bananas, mangoes and dried fish, their baskets bobbing gently up and down from either end of the bamboo poles across their shoulders.

Like me, my mother loved the food even though she had never eaten anything like it and she would spend hours in the kitchen with the cook and the other domestic staff laughing and joking. Hilarity was universal when, absorbed one morning in her usual study of the street's passing show, Mum felt the cold, slithery form of a gecko lizard fall straight down the neck of her frock. The harmless little creature had lost his footing on the verandah ceiling but his impact supplied a whole day's entertainment for the Tahija household. Later, on other visits, my mother would help me decorate our little house at Tugu in the mountains. She even sewed the curtains for the windows – curtains which lasted until very recently, when we replaced them with an identical set.

My father never visited us. I don't know why. He kept on saying that he would make the trip eventually, but he never did. When we finally convinced him that he should come to see us, he developed cancer before he could visit and died without ever seeing his daughter's adopted country. This is one of my life's great regrets. Not that I didn't see my father regularly. I would return to Melbourne several times a year and stay with my parents in Ascot Vale. In the early 1950s, they bought a small holiday house in Dromana on the Mornington Peninsula, about an hour's drive from Melbourne, where they stayed for the Christmas holidays. Some years, I would join them there and I would be struck by how different my home was from this peaceful Australian beachside suburb. Was there any way, I often wondered, for Australians to understand what Indonesia was going through – what it meant for people to have been under colonial rule for 400 years and then have to go through a bloody revolution to gain independence?

In the end, I don't think there was any way Australians could comprehend what all this meant for Indonesia. Even today, there is little appreciation of the challenges that confront the country. Right from the start, there were forces threatening to tear the new nation apart. And often, only the armed forces stood between order and chaos. Australians who today express doubts about the continuing army influence in Indonesian life should be grateful that, except in its earliest years, Australia has always been a civil society where civil power sufficed. Indonesia without its army would have collapsed into anarchy, with a thousand islands warring amongst themselves. It is true that Indonesia has never been a democracy along Australian lines, but then such a democracy would have been entirely unsuitable for a country that was desperately poor, ethnically diverse and spread across a huge archipelago. This is not to say that Indonesia will never embrace democracy. It will, I am convinced of that. So too is Julius. Increasing wealth and a growing middle class make that inevitable. I hope I live to see it happen.

There was very little wealth in the Jakarta we lived in during 1948 and 1949. Everything was in short supply, from food and medicines to housing. Julius earned a good salary, but there was virtually nothing on which to spend it. The first time my mother came to visit us, she brought with her a dozen eggs which she cradled in her arms during the three-day trip to Jakarta. We hadn't seen eggs for a year. Nothing was stable and nothing could be taken for granted. Despite intense negotiations, the Dutch were determined to hang on to their colony for as long as possible. There was another, even bigger, Dutch police action against the Republic in December 1948, which began with the bombing of Jogjakarta. Dutch paratroopers seized the city from Republican troops and captured Sukarno and his deputy, Hatta. They established control over most Republican areas in Java. However thousands of Republican soldiers escaped and began an intense guerrilla struggle.

The United Nations established a three-nation 'good offices' committee to help the Dutch and Indonesians resolve their dispute and bring an end to the fighting. Belgium represented Holland, Australia represented Indonesia, and the United States was nominated as the third, neutral party. A month after the police action, the United Nations Security Council passed a resolution demanding that the Dutch transfer sovereignty to the Indonesians, return Jogjakarta to Republican control, and release Sukarno and Hatta. The Dutch dug in. They imprisoned Sukarno and Hatta, declared that the Republic of Indonesia no longer existed, and announced that they would set up an interim government of the United States of Indonesia to replace the colonial administration. The Republicans and Sukarno would be excluded from this federation.

The East Indonesian government headed by Julius's friend Anak Agung Gde Agung launched a campaign to convince the other governments of the proposed federation to reject the Dutch proposal. Julius was away for weeks on end, lobbying politicians, travelling to Jogjakarta for secret meetings with Republican politicians and working desperately hard to build a united front against the Dutch. When he was in Jakarta, we would talk late into the night about what was happening. Often, I would ask Julius how long this uncertainty, fighting and chaos would last. He would smile and say, 'Not too long I hope, darling, not too long.'

In the end, the Dutch caved in and agreed to a round table conference at The Hague in the Netherlands where representatives of Indonesia and Holland, under the United Nations' supervision, would work out a timetable for the transfer of sovereignty to Indonesia. Julius was to attend the conference as an aide to General T.B. Simatupang, the chief of staff of the Indonesian armed forces. This was quite a unique achievement: it meant that Julius had served the commanding generals of both sides in Indonesia's fight for independence.

For me, there was the excitement of knowing that, after such a long struggle, Indonesia was about to become fully independent, something Julius had worked for with such passion and commitment. On top of that, I would travel to Holland with him. We would tour around Europe for a month or so before the conference – visiting England, Italy, Switzerland and France – with nothing to do but enjoy ourselves for the first time in our married lives.

I cannot remember much of that month except that we were happy. We loved Switzerland, Julius in particular, especially its snow-covered mountains. We drove around England, young and carefree. I could not imagine a better life. I could not imagine a better time.

There was only one thing missing. For two years, we had been trying to have a baby without success. I had visited doctors in Australia, but after numerous tests they could not establish why I was finding it so difficult to fall pregnant. I had organised to have further tests in Holland and, while Julius was at the conference, I spent most of my time in clinics being examined by various doctors. I wanted more than anything to have children, but it would take another three years before Sjakon, my first son, was born.

The round table conference lasted two months. Most days, I went for long walks around The Hague. At night, there were diplomatic receptions. I got to know Tom Critchley, the head of the Australian delegation to the talks and a man of great charm who played a key role in helping the Indonesians gain independence. It is forgotten by a lot of Australians – or perhaps they never knew – that their country made a crucial contribution to Indonesian nationhood. That Australia was seen as the nationalist movement's most trusted supporter is shown by the fact that the Republic chose Australia to represent the Indonesian position on the United Nations-sponsored 'good offices' committee. I was, of course, proud of this Australian contribution to my adopted country's independence.

There was great joy in Indonesia when the round table conference reached an agreement that would see sovereignty transferred to the Republican government on 27 December 1949. I remember that day so well. We were back in Jakarta by then and the streets were packed with cheering crowds waving the new Indonesian flag. At government house, which was soon to become the presidential palace, hundreds of diplomats and heads of state gathered for this official end to 400 years of Dutch rule. I can remember seeing India's Prime Minister Nehru standing in front of me on the manicured palace lawn with his young daughter Indira and her two small boys. I could not believe that fate had granted me the privilege of being a witness to this dramatic, historical event.

When the Dutch flag was finally lowered and the red-and-white Indonesian flag raised high, I was so overcome with emotion that I began to cry. Julius was off somewhere, talking to his political colleagues, savouring this magnificent moment in his life and in the life of the nation for which he had worked so hard. I didn't mind. I was grateful just to be there. I thought that perhaps the worst was over, that we could start to lead a relatively normal life.

I was wrong. That is not the way things turned out. In a sense, the turmoil and uncertainty were just beginning. Indonesia had been born at last, but what lay ahead was a childhood and early adolescence filled with great tension and a lot of bloodshed. The Sukarno era had begun.

sixteen

Sukarno dominated Indonesian life and politics for almost twenty years after independence. For twenty years before that, he had been the driving force behind the independence struggle. He was a phenomenon, a unique individual whose charisma, charm and energy captured the imagination of everyone who met him. Sukarno was a dashingly handsome man, invariably dressed in a tropical army officer's uniform, complete with medals and other decorations, though he never actually served in any army. He always wore a black Muslim cap, a *pitji,* on his head and dark glasses. He carried a small black-and-silver swagger stick.

Sukarno's charm was captivating. He had large brown eyes and a brilliant smile, and when he talked to you, he made you feel like you were the most interesting person on earth. He loved women, lots of women, and women loved him. Apart from his four wives, he was known to have numerous mistresses. None of this was hidden. Sukarno would talk openly about women and his relationship with them. In the main, this did him no harm. In fact, the people loved him even more because his success with women proved that he was an extraordinary man, a man of destiny.

He also loved art and he covered the walls of the presidential palace with his favourite paintings. Sukarno had spent a total of twelve years in jail, during which time he read everything he could get his hands on. He was widely read in political theory and philosophy. His speeches, which could last for up to eight hours, were full of quotes from Marx, the French Enlightenment philosophers and great Asian thinkers like the Indian philosopher, Vivekananda. He was a spell-binding speaker who could hold an audience enthralled for hours without a prepared text or even a set of notes.

Sukarno loved music and dancing and parties. He had prodigious energy, which meant he could spend the day in meetings and in making long speeches and then dance the night away, before waking the next morning looking better and fresher than ever. Sukarno, in those early post-independence years, was truly a sort of embodiment of the hopes and aspirations of the Indonesian people. They called him *Bapak* – Indonesian for 'Papa' – and that's what he was back then: the father of the Indonesian nation.

I met Sukarno several times during the early 1950s, mostly at small social functions at the presidential palace, a beautiful, white colonial mansion surrounded by lawns and garden beds full of the most dazzling displays of tropical flowers and shrubs. One time, I sat next to him at a screening at the palace of an American musical which starred Betty Grable.

'Magnificent legs, just magnificent,' he cried, looking straight into my eyes. 'I love a woman with magnificent legs.' Then he laughed, his eyes not leaving mine for even a split second. Sukarno radiated charm. The atmosphere was always electric when he was around.

Julius had great respect for Sukarno as the father of Indonesian nationhood. He doubted that any other leader could have moulded all the disparate ethnic groups across the far-flung Indonesian archipelago into one people. It was Sukarno who promoted *Pancasila,* which means 'five principles', as the basis of Indonesian nationhood. These five principles are: belief in one god; humanitarianism; national unity; democracy through consensus; and social justice. *Pancasila* remains to this day the underlying national ideology of Indonesia. Julius also admired the way Sukarno had been prepared to go to jail and to give up his life, if need be, for the cause of independence. He had suffered much for his beliefs and had remained steadfast in his resolve. There was much, Julius believed, for which Indonesians had to thank Sukarno.

Still, from early on, Julius was concerned and troubled by Sukarno's antipathy towards the West and his opposition to an open-market economy. Julius had always believed that only through the development of a market economy and the promotion of international trade could Indonesia ever fulfil its great economic promise. He was a staunch anti-communist and he thought Indonesia desperately needed an influx of foreign investment to get the economy moving. None of this interested Sukarno. Having spent most of his life fighting imperialism and colonialism, he had no great affection for the West, although he certainly admired much about the United States and often said that the American Revolution had been a source of great inspiration to him. He was not a communist, but he tried to have good relations with the PKI, the Indonesian communist party, which in the early 1950s, was a significant political force.

In the immediate post-independence euphoria, none of this mattered much. Julius was offered a commission in the new Indonesian armed forces by Sukarno. He accepted with some reluctance. What he really wanted to do was develop his business interests. Business had always been his great passion, what he thought he did best. But he was prepared to put his business career on hold for his beloved Indonesia.

Julius's job was to integrate the soldiers of the old Dutch East Indies army with the Republic's armed forces and mould a new modern army for an independent Indonesia. He became a Lieutenant-Colonel, the second highest rank available. The job involved constant travel around the country as Julius had to convince some very conservative elements of the old East Indies army that their future lay with the new Indonesian military. He had to persuade them that they would not be penalised for having served the Dutch so faithfully. In those early years, there were minor rebellions in Ambon and in other East Indonesian islands where the people were wary of ceding central control of their lives to Jakarta. Julius managed to put down many of these minor rebellions without any blood being spilt. He understood the concerns of the island people who felt their interests might be ignored in faraway Jakarta, but he believed in the new Indonesia and was opposed to anything that threatened to split the country apart.

They were happy domestic years, those years immediately after independence. Julius was often away, but not as often as when he had been a politician. He would come home for lunch when he was in Jakarta, often bringing with him a group of officers who needed to be fed.

I had by this stage grown used to having domestic help and relied upon their assistance. Our cook, Amina, was with us for thirty-four years before she died a few years ago. Both Julius and I were heartbroken. So were our sons, who looked on Amina as a favourite and much-loved aunt. Harta, who is my personal assistant, and who has been with us for thirty-eight years, is like a grandmother to my boys. When my mother had a stroke in 1968 and I returned to Australia to nurse her, Harta came with me. She spent most of her time in Australia shivering, rugged up in many layers of clothes, but she loved the place, especially my parents' holiday house in Dromana.

There were still shortages of all sorts of things in Indonesia after independence, including clothing and medicines. Trying to buy antibiotics meant standing in line outside the chemist, often for hours. Jakarta, however, continued to grow at an alarming rate, with people pouring into the capital from the countryside in search of non-existent jobs. The shanty towns quickly spread, covering large areas of the city. There was mass unemployment and very little economic activity. Foreign investment was banned, imports were prohibited and Sukarno was becoming increasingly autocratic, attracted to the idea of state-run businesses rather than free-enterprise ones.

At the end of 1950, I finally managed to return to dentistry, which had been my wish since I arrived in Indonesia. Jakarta's old public hospital had been built in the last century by the Dutch. It was a large, ugly red-brick building in the centre of town. By today's standards – and even by the standards that existed in Australia at that time – its accommodation was primitive and overcrowded, its shabby wards filled to overflowing with patients. The doctors did their best in the face of limited facilities and terrible shortages of medicines. I was shocked when I first went to the hospital to see whether I could organise some voluntary work in the hospital's dental clinic.

Professor Ouw Eng Liang, the head of dentistry, welcomed me with open arms, putting me to work immediately, even supplying me with an oversized, though relatively clean, white coat so that I looked the part. Professor Ouw had degrees in medicine and dentistry. He was a tense and excitable little man, no doubt made more tense and excitable by the fact that he was President Sukarno's personal physician. We became good friends. As part of the presidential retinue, Professor Ouw went on many trips with Sukarno. The president considered this to be such a privilege for the professor that the poor man received no payment for his work.

'I have not practised for three weeks,' he grumbled on his return from one presidential trip. 'I need money. Look at this. A cigarette case as payment for all my work. That will not feed my family!'

When Sukarno was toppled after the attempted communist coup in 1965, Professor Ouw fled to China. He hated it. He went on to Holland, which he hated too. Years later, I saw him in Hong Kong where he lived in a slum, his surgery a curtained-off half of a big room. In the other half of the room, he lived with his wife and two daughters. He was a broken man who died shortly after I visited him. His was a tragic story. He had fled Indonesia, terrified that he would be jailed by the government, but this was highly unlikely, given that he had never been involved in politics. I had urged him not to leave, but he wouldn't listen.

I worked with three other dentists at the clinic, all of them of Chinese descent. We practised in a large room in which the light was so poor that I sometimes had to use a flashlight to look into my patients' mouths. The equipment was primitive to say the least and I was thankful that I had my old instruments from Melbourne with me. But I still had doubts about the strength – and age – of the local anaesthetics and about the safety of the clinic's hypodermic syringes, which were the old-fashioned metal ones with fearfully blunt needles. The syringes required sterilisation after use, but quite often the water in which they were washed seemed not to be boiling. Outside the treatment room, hundreds of people waited each day to have their teeth attended to. There was no time to worry too much about sterilisation standards, bad lighting or poor equipment. I was overwhelmingly glad to be back working.

I saw things at the clinic that I had previously only read about in textbooks. There were many patients who came in with tumours the size of footballs in their jaws. They were terribly poor people who had often travelled for days by foot or carts to come to the hospital. They were petrified. Some of them had never been out of their villages.

Professor Ouw would operate on them using only a local anaesthetic. At times, in the middle of an operation, the electricity would suddenly cut out and the overhead fans would stop. With virtually no lighting and in stifling heat, Professor Ouw would continue the surgery.

One young woman came in with a tumour that was about the size of half a watermelon. The tumour had forced one of her eyes shut, had blocked an ear, and had extended down into her throat, threatening to choke her. The surgery couldn't be done at the dental clinic, so Professor Ouw and I piled into his car with the patient, while the other three dentists travelled on their motorbikes to a larger hospital.

The heat at the hospital we took our patient to was unbearable. The perspiration poured off all of us, even the poor young woman who lay stoically on the table as Professor Ouw prepared to cut out her tumour. People wandered into the room to see what was going on – nurses, cleaning staff, even other patients – and many stayed for the duration of the surgery.

The operation took at least two hours. I had never seen anything remotely like it. I kept backing off, feeling faint because of the heat, but Professor Ouw kept urging me to come closer so that I could see exactly what he was doing. The whole procedure was done under local anaesthetic. The young woman lay there silently, in total acceptance of what was being done to her. I marvelled at her quiet, dignified endurance. When the surgery was finished, she was placed in a cubicle for a couple of hours after which she was collected by her husband and taken back to her *kampong*.

'Now,' said Professor Ouw, 'we will go to the Hotel des Indes and have a beer', which we did.

Two weeks later I asked him how the patient had got on. 'Oh, splendidly,' he replied. 'No problems.'

Over the two years that I worked in the dental clinic in Jakarta, I was often struck at how little fuss people made about what were often quite painful treatments for problems which far exceeded anything I had seen in the dental hospital in Melbourne. We regularly had to remove pieces of rotting jaw or treat infections that had been allowed to fester for weeks before medical help was sought. People had to travel such great distances to see a dentist that they almost always put off seeking treatment until the pain became unbearable. I was shocked by all this, but I quickly realised that these were normal conditions in third-world countries and that I would have to get used to them.

I did. I would actually look forward to going to the clinic each morning. Work started at 7.30 a.m. and finished at 1.00 p.m. By that time, I was exhausted and completely wrung out by the heat. But I was happy. Years later, my son Sjakon studied medicine and did his internship at the same hospital where I had worked. By the time he arrived there, the old place had been renovated and modernised.

I visited the hospital once, ostensibly to see Sjakon, but what I really wanted to see was the dental clinic where I had practised all those years ago. It was still there and it still looked much the same as it had looked in 1951. I could picture myself at one of the old chairs working in the semi-darkness, the perspiration running into my eyes and making it almost impossible to see. I felt a twinge of regret. I didn't know it back then, but this was to be the last time I would practise the profession for which I had trained and which I enjoyed so much. After a while, I even gave my precious instruments away to someone who had a greater need of them than I.

seventeen

In 1951, I discovered I was pregnant. The pregnancy had come after four years of trying, and after countless visits to doctors and clinics in Australia and Europe. We were thrilled. We couldn't wait for the baby to be born. Then when I was seven months pregnant Julius suddenly had to go to Europe for three weeks on a military mission. I cried and complained and asked him to stay. He couldn't. This mission to Holland was crucial for Indonesia's future. He had to go.

I could not have the baby alone in Indonesia, so I flew to Melbourne to be with my parents. It was a rough trip that took three days, and I was ill most of the way. I went to see the obstetrician who, after examining me, told me that my baby was no longer alive. I went through a twelve-hour labour to deliver the dead baby. My doctor advised me against seeing the child and to this day I don't know whether this was the right thing to do.

The next day, I had to call Julius in Belgium to tell him what had happened. A faint and scratchy telephone connection made it very hard. So did the fact that I was consumed with grief.

'The baby was stillborn,' I cried.

'Is it still to be born?' he kept asking.

It was perhaps one of the darkest moments of my life.

Despite the blow of the stillbirth, my life had settled into a pattern that I enjoyed. We now knew that I could fall pregnant and that in time we would have the children we both wanted so much. Our four years of married life had been happy ones despite the uncertainties we'd confronted. The more I lived with Julius, the more I knew that there could never be any other man for me. There were sides to him I hadn't really seen before we lived together and these drew me to him even more.

Julius is at heart a fiery man with a quick temper who doesn't suffer fools gladly. He can be endlessly calm and patient in political or business negotiations, but at other times he can erupt in fury at some small problem or perceived slight. When I tell people who do not know him intimately that he has a terrible temper, they do not believe me. In public, he seems to be the calmest, most controlled man on earth.

At the same time, Julius is the most generous, soft-hearted man I know. While he can be very tough in business and has a long memory when people let him down, he has always been there when people needed help. And not just friends. I have seen Julius go out of his way to help people who were more or less strangers to him, but who he felt deserved a chance in life. He has always been aware that his life, in some ways, has been privileged, and that he has a duty to help those less fortunate.

Julius and I know we have been lucky right from the start. While in the early years of our life together we did not have the luxuries that most people took for granted in Australia or the United States, we always had a decent house in which to live, a car, domestic staff and enough money to cover all our needs. Julius had promised my parents that he would care for me and look after me; he kept this promise to an extent that even they could not have expected. He denied me nothing, not even my dream of a house in the country where I could plan and construct my own garden.

While Julius was still in the army, we used take off for the weekends to Patjet, about two-and-a-half hours' drive from Jakarta, through a pass in the central mountains in west Java. We would stay in a small *kampong* house, sleeping on a bare-board bed covered with an old army blanket. Rats would poke their heads through gaps in the walls and, if they were unlucky, would fall victim to Julius's air rifle which he kept by the bed. We loved it there. The house was surrounded by thick, overgrown tea bushes that sloped up the sides of the mountains, many of which were extinct volcanoes. But travelling to Patjet through the mountain pass was dangerous in those days. The tea plantations and thick undergrowth provided cover for gangs of bandits who fired on passing cars, sometimes killing their occupants.

In 1950, we discovered a small hotel at the foot of Pangarango mountain, an extinct volcano which was about 1000 feet above sea level and only one-and-a-half hours' drive from Jakarta. It was run by a German man and his Eurasian wife, and from that base we would walk along narrow tracks into the hills. The countryside was dotted with the ruins of Dutch villas, looted and destroyed by local anti-Dutch nationalist groups during the revolution. The Dutch owners had long since fled to Holland, though they remained the legal proprietors of the villas and the land that surrounded them.

On one of our walks we saw a villa that had been built on the slope of a hill and that had views of Pangarango. The villa had no internal walls and no windows and its exterior walls were covered in bullet holes. I fell instantly in love with the place. The view to Pangarango was magnificent, the air was fresh and cool, the tea plantations, though overgrown and neglected, formed a dark green blanket over the hills leading to the foot of the mountain. The several acres of land that surrounded the house had once been rice paddies, but were now overgrown with weeds and wild grass. The irrigation ditches were clogged with rubbish and every tree on the property had been cut down and used for firewood.

Nevertheless, I saw that this place could, with work and imagination, become something wonderful. I felt something about this spot that I had felt about no other place I had ever been to. This was my special place, where I could put my heart and soul into making it a true, physical reflection of my deepest feelings.

The nearby *kampong* was called Tugu, which means statue. There had once been an old Hindu statue carved of stone near the entrance to the village, but during the revolution the statue had been reduced to rubble. The revolution was of course over by the time we first saw the villa in Tugu, but in the surrounding hills, bands of Muslim fundamentalists held up passing travellers, invaded houses and regularly shot those who resisted. After the Dutch had been driven out, these gangs turned their attention to government officials, business people and expatriates whom they considered their enemies. They were opposed to the Sukarno government, which they considered far too secular.

I didn't care. I was so enchanted by this little villa and the land surrounding it that, after we returned to Jakarta, Tuska Donskoi and I spent weeks at the chaotic titles office searching for its owner so that we could offer to buy it from him. We finally tracked him down in Amsterdam. He turned out to be a former director of the Dutch-owned Java Bank. He had been interned by the Japanese during the war and had returned to Holland when the war ended without ever seeing his house in Tugu again. He agreed to sell it to us. We paid

25 000 rupiah – the equivalent of about A$2000 – which was quite a sum of money in 1951. For me, it was the most rewarding purchase Julius and I ever made.

The Dutch owner had called his villa 'Carrie' after his daughter. Julius had a new wooden sign made, which we placed at the peak of the gable at the front of the house. It said 'Nusa Ina' which means Mother Land. That wooden sign, a bit battered and worn after almost fifty years, still sits in the same spot, facing out across the garden I have created over three decades. Today, tropical flowers bloom in garden beds that flow down the rolling green lawns of the terraced hillside to the irrigation ditch and the vegetable gardens where the local people grow carrots and cabbages.

As soon as we bought the villa, we employed local tradesmen to repair its interior walls and build new windows. The outside walls, which were covered in white render, we patched and painted. The steep roof was more or less intact: all that it needed was for some tiles to be replaced. During this time I travelled to Tugu at least once, and sometimes twice, a week – often staying alone overnight but for the old caretaker, Pak Suhardi and his wife Mahiti who were living in the garage behind the villa when we bought the place. Pak Suhardi and Mahiti were Sundanese, the main ethnic group of west Java, and spoke only the local dialect which was very different from Bahasa Indonesia, the national language. We made ourselves understood through hand gestures and facial expressions. Bent, wrinkled and toothless, Pak Suhardi was a lovable rogue.

We hadn't owned Tugu long when his wife Mahiti came and sat silently beside me as I was resting in the garden one day. She said nothing for a long time. Then she spoke. 'Pak Suhardi is going to take a second wife,' she confided.

I said nothing. In the Muslim tradition, men can have up to four wives. Multiple wives were a not uncommon phenomenon in Indonesia in the 1950s, though it was increasingly discouraged by Indonesian women who had been active in the revolution. Though Indonesia is the world's largest Muslim nation, its form of Islam has always been tolerant and moderate, unlike some Muslim countries, where women have not always been treated equally with men. In my experience, Indonesian women have in many ways played a more active role in the country's affairs than in Australia. Some of the great heroes of Javanese culture have been women – warriors who led their armies to great victories over their adversaries. Today, Indonesian women are playing an increasingly active role in politics and in business. There may still be some remote areas of Indonesia in which polygamy is practised, but it is frowned upon, especially amongst the growing middle class.

I certainly frowned upon it when I heard the news from Mahiti. This was something that Julius would have to deal with, a real challenge to his diplomatic skills. Julius immediately called Pak Suhardi aside and told him how much we appreciated him and how lucky the Tahijas were to have such a lovely couple working for them. 'Especially,' he added, 'when so many older men take younger wives.'

'Yes,' agreed a rather crestfallen Pak Suhardi. 'It is unfortunate. Many of them do. Of course I would do no such thing.'

One day, a young boy who was perhaps twelve years old came by looking for work. He appeared as if from nowhere, a lad not yet in his teens who had been born during the Japanese occupation and had lived through the misery of the revolution. His name was Amat and I took an instant liking to him. Amat worked for us in Tugu for four decades. He married and raised a family there and his life revolved around the property, where he was the chief gardener and general supervisor. The Tugu garden is as much his work as mine. He really was like one of the family. When Amat developed a life-threatening liver disease, we brought him to Jakarta and had him admitted to the Metropolitan Medical Centre close to where we live and where he could be watched over and given the best care. Julius and I visited him every day as his life slowly ebbed away. His death was one of the saddest occasions of my life.

Two of Amat's daughters still work for us and his son is employed in one of our businesses. His widow, who continued to live at Tugu for several years after Amat died, has now retired to her *kampong,* living on the pension Julius pays her and which she so richly deserves.

I have a photograph of our Tugu house taken at the end of 1951. It seems to be set in the middle of nothing. Here and there you can see ruined villas in the distance, surrounded by scrub and weeds, with a few vegetable patches scratched out by the local *kampong* people. There is not a tree in sight. When I set about planning the garden, I read as many books on tropical plants as I could get my hands on. I visited the botanical gardens at Bogor, an hour's drive from Jakarta, and bought plants for Tugu. I was also determined to plant gum trees, not just because they would always remind me of my old home but because they were beautiful and fast growing and would screen our little house from nearby properties.

There were, of course, no gums to be had in Indonesia. So when I returned to Australia at Christmas in 1951, I bought twelve little eucalypts about a foot high. The night before I left to return to Indonesia, I shook the dirt off their roots and wrapped the plants in wet newspaper and then plastic. I tucked them in amongst my clothes in the suitcase. The day after I arrived home, I rushed to Tugu to plant my little trees. They have never looked back. Today the gums are giant trees scattered across the gardens. I sometimes sit beside a clump of them and if I close my eyes and breath deeply, it's as if I am back in the Victorian bush somewhere – perhaps with my father, on a warm spring day.

My first initiative in the garden was get to work with Amat and Pak Suhardi, together with some young men from the *kampong*, to clear the scrub and weeds so that we could plant grass across the former rice fields that made up our terraced garden. The work was done by hand, with the most primitive of tools. It took months. Finally, the land was ready for planting. The local grass was not too bad, a variety of couch grass, but an American friend smuggled in a coffeepot full of Kentucky bluegrass. This didn't go far on six acres. Over the years, however, it has spread across the lawns, giving them a startling bluish tinge and ensuring that even in the dry season, the grass gets soggy.

A lot of the planting was just a matter of trial and error. I planted European fruit trees, but they were a failure. So I pulled them out and planted two lychee trees which bore no fruit but which, after forty years, have a lovely shape and superb green foliage. The altitude at Tugu is 1000 metres and trying to plant coastal trees quickly proved useless. My gums were fine, tree ferns of all varieties thrived, as did avocado trees, cinnamon trees and, of course, lots of bamboo.

The cinnamons, which I brought back from Sumatra wrapped in wet newspapers, have become a feature of Tugu. As they thrived, their seeds spread, and their distinctive, delicate pink foliage was soon to be seen in many other spots in the district where no gardener's hand had ever placed them. They were welcome arrivals. When my original plants grew decrepit I begged fresh seedlings from others, who had no notion of how these beautiful trees had come to the Javanese hillside.

Cinnamon too is responsible for the Tahijas' one modest appearance in the literature of botanical science. After a new species was discovered in Borneo, it was described and named by the eminent botanist A.J.G.H. Kostermans at Bogor's famous botanical gardens, not far from Tugu. He called this beautiful tree *Cinnamomum tahijanum* in honour of Julius, who had been generous to the garden's herbarium 'and whose wife is immensely interested in plants and in maintaining a beautiful garden up country from Bogor'.

In the garden beds at Tugu, I planted impatiens, marigolds, salvia, begonias and zinnias. I tried numerous other exotic plants, but it was the old standards that never let me down. I tried to grow rhododendrons but with no success. A type of clerome did well. The flowerbeds change over the years as I continue to experiment with different plants and shrubs. Gardens are living creations. Some things thrive and grow, others struggle to survive and often die. In part, good gardeners are ruthless, prepared to quickly get rid of plants that are clearly failing and experiment with new ones. Though the garden at Tugu was designed and built almost fifty years ago, it is still evolving, still changing. I wouldn't have it any other way.

The garden at Tugu became my obsession before the birth of my first son. Even after Sjakon was born, I would go to Tugu at least once midweek to do my planting, taking my son with me. Julius was often too busy to come during the week, but we almost always spent Saturday and Sunday at Tugu. Looking back, I am amazed at my foolhardiness, heading off to the mountains with a small baby, unconcerned about the gangs of Muslim fundamentalists and bandits that roamed the nearby hills. There were regular shootings and armed hold-ups, but I was so determined to work on my garden that I ignored the dangers. There were times when, late at night, we could hear machine-gun fire coming from the tea plantation. I would grab Sjakon and take him into the bathroom which had thick brick walls and we would wait there – a little chilly and nervous – until things quietened down and it seemed safe to go to bed. Sometimes, if Sjakon wasn't with me, I would swallow a sleeping pill in the middle of the shooting and drop off happily to sleep, thinking 'to hell with them all'.

While Tugu absorbed much of my time before Sjakon was born, his birth changed my life utterly and forever. I was thirty-six years old. We had been trying for at least four years to have a baby and Sjakon was like a gift from God. He was born shortly after Julius had resigned his commission in the army and had joined Caltex Indonesia as an assistant to the managing director.

At the end of 1951, after two years in the army, with his job of integrating the old East Indies soldiers into the new Indonesian armed forces complete, Julius had decided that it was time for him to start a new phase of his life. Business had always been his most passionate interest. While he had enjoyed army life and had found politics fascinating and challenging, he felt that the business world was where his future would lie. I was not so sure. Indonesia was still in turmoil. The country was poor and the government was hostile to both the free market and to the West. Julius, were he to go into business, would inevitably have to battle against government officials who were almost entirely ignorant of what needed to be done to get the economy growing so that ordinary people could prosper. Julius, however, was adamant that he could best serve Indonesia by going into business.

When he decided to leave the army, Julius went to see the president to tell him personally of his decision. Sukarno was very understanding. He told Julius that the country needed businessmen.

'Why don't you get involved in the oil industry?' Sukarno suggested. 'One day, it will be our most important industry. We need Indonesians with the proper expertise to run it. You, Tahija, should be one of them.'

'But I don't know anything about oil,' Julius replied.

'Doesn't matter,' Sukarno said. 'Learn. Our country is rich in oil. We Indonesians need to know about it. We should not be dependent on foreigners. It is most important.'

Up to this point, Julius had had no plans to enter the oil industry, nor did he expect to get a job offer from an oil company. He was a soldier and a trader, already involved in the import of textiles. Julius's trading business had grown, even while he was still in the army, and when he quit the armed forces he expected to work full-time building up his import-export company. Sukarno's suggestion that he get involved in oil preceded, by about three days, a job offer from Caltex Pacific. This conjunction was entirely coincidental – unless, of course, one believed in Sukarno's psychic powers.

Our lives were about to change again. Caltex Pacific was to be a dominant interest in Julius's life for the next forty years. In a way, it still is. When Julius started with Caltex, it was Indonesia's smallest oil company. Today, it is the largest oil company in Asia, Indonesia's biggest foreign exchange earner and amongst the four or five biggest oil companies in the world.

That Caltex even survived during the turbulent Sukarno years was in large measure due to Julius. Even when the threat of jail hung over him, when his own private businesses were taken from him, when he was humiliated by communist trade union officials allied with the government, he stuck by the American shareholders of Caltex Pacific. He refused to allow the takeover of the company by the state. These were years of great stress and worry and there were times when we wondered whether we would survive.

eighteen

Sjakon was born in December 1952, at the Protestant Tjikini Hospital in Jakarta which was run by a group of efficient Dutch sisters. He was named after the son of a seventeenth-century Ambonese freedom fighter whose family was banished to Ceylon after the freedom fighter was sentenced to death by a Dutch colonial court. I thought it a beautiful name. My mother came to Jakarta to be with me. Virtually all the medical people in Indonesia at that time, apart from the most junior, were Dutch trained. As far as giving birth was concerned, this meant natural childbirth with no painkillers or any other sorts of drugs for that matter. But my only concern was that the baby be healthy.

Sjakon was a brown baby with a thin face and a long nose – the image of my brother Russell. Clearly this baby would grow up dark like his father, rather than blonde like me. Like his father, he would be an Indonesian. I would make sure that he knew of his Australian grandparents, but I knew, from the moment Sjakon was born, that his home would be in Indonesia and that Australia would most probably be a place that he visited every now and then, but not much more.

I felt no regret at this. Five years in Indonesia had changed me. It had deepened not only my love for Julius, but also for my adopted country. I loved its ethnic and cultural variety, and I loved its many peoples. Scarred by the Japanese occupation and later by the trauma of the revolution, Indonesians were still suffering, many of them deprived of the basic necessities of life. Yet the ordinary people had a dignified stoicism about them that was wholly admirable. They were also friendly and welcoming, steeped in their local cultures and in the lives of their villages.

I used to laugh and then get angry when I read Australian newspaper reports about Indonesian imperial ambitions and the danger of an Indonesian invasion of Australia. It was so much prejudiced nonsense. In the main, Indonesians have always loved their country, their island, their *kampong*, and few have entertained thoughts of leaving. Even now, how many Indonesians apply to emigrate to Australia?

Julius began work with Caltex six months before Sjakon was born. He had taken the job on the understanding that it was for a six-month trial period and that he would draw no salary during that time. At the same time, he would be free to develop his own personal business interests. At the end of six months the arrangement would be reviewed and Julius could decide whether the oil industry suited his skills. Right from the start, he made it clear that his private companies would have no dealings with Caltex in order to avoid any perceived conflict of interest. This rule has been adhered to for the last forty-five years. None of the family businesses – not our insurance company, our bank, our plantation interests or our mining interests – have ever had any business association with Caltex.

Caltex Pacific was – and remains – jointly owned by the American oil giants Texaco and Chevron, but it was one of the country's smaller oil producers, well behind Royal Dutch Shell. The shareholders of Caltex realised that in the volatile political climate of post-independence Indonesia they would need someone, an Indonesian, who understood the country and had good political contacts, if the company was to prosper. They chose Julius.

For his part, Julius was unwilling to become a salaried employee, even a senior one. He wanted to develop his own businesses. From childhood on, that had been his dream. The war and later the revolution had intervened before his dream could be realised. Now he was in a hurry to make up for lost time. The Caltex shareholders agreed to his terms and what began as a six-month trial has lasted to this day. Julius, even when he became managing director of Caltex Pacific, was not a salaried employee and remained free to run his own, expanding business interests.

Julius quickly grew to love the company and the oil business.

When Julius joined Caltex, its oilfields were in the wilds of central Sumatra. The company's main camp was a place called Rumbai, which was a half-hour journey by boat down the Siak River from Pekanbaru, a small town with a small airport that consisted of a tin shed and a narrow, pot-holed runway. Rumbai had a few makeshift buildings and was surrounded by thick jungle and mangrove swamps. There were large clearings amongst the trees where the drillers worked twelve-hour shifts, around the clock, seven days a week, searching for oil.

Before the war, a famous American geologist called Richard Hopper had been employed by Caltex to explore the Rumbai region, despite the fact that his first five years of work in the area had yielded virtually nothing. Hopper and his team had drilled thousands of holes but had come up with disappointing results. Hopper, however, remained convinced that there was oil at Rumbai, and lots of it. He persuaded the shareholders of Caltex to invest over a million American dollars – a fortune in those days – to ship new drilling equipment to the site, a daunting task given the thick jungle terrain.

By 1941, Hopper had his equipment in place and he was about to begin drilling when the Japanese invaded the East Indies. The oilfield and the equipment were abandoned. The Japanese, however, continued the exploration and struck oil. Though unsure of how big a find it was, they forced thousands of Sumatrans to work on building a pipeline that would connect the oilfield to the coast. The pipeline was never completed and the drilling was abandoned. Thousands of forced labourers – *romushas* – died because of maltreatment and brutal beatings, and were buried in mass graves around Rumbai. In the 1960s, Julius had Caltex build a special memorial to the *romushas* at Pekanbaru.

Caltex returned to Sumatra after the war to develop the Rumbai fields. When Julius joined the company, it was just starting a new drilling programme. It was still unclear how large the oilfield was, though Richard Hopper – who had served in the US forces during the war mostly in New Guinea and Kalimantan – returned to Rumbai to supervise the drilling. We became close friends. Richard had led a fascinating life, exploring for oil in the most forbidding places. At Rumbai, before the war, he and his geological team had lived in the jungle in tents, with snakes, crocodiles, leeches and malaria-carrying mosquitoes. They kept kerosene lamps lit all night to keep away the elephants and tigers. Despite their gigantic height, jungle trees have shallow roots. During one storm, one of these trees toppled over, killing several of Hopper's men.

I first went to Rumbai when I was four months pregnant with Sjakon. We flew to Pekanbaru from Jakarta. It was a short trip of two-and-a-half hours, but once there we entered a different world. Pekanbaru was a raw, ugly town of prefabricated huts. It was dusty in the dry season and a muddy mess in the wet. But it was always unbearably hot.

From Pekanbaru we travelled by steamer down the Siak River – a broad, brown waterway enclosed by thick, primeval jungle, interspersed from time to time with rubber plantations. We had to keep alert for floating logs, but even more for the local people in their shallow, dugout canoes. The men wore loincloths and carried sharpened spears. The children were naked, laughing and frolicking as they canoed downstream in search of fish. The water was full of crocodiles: you could see them swimming around the canoes. At dusk, hundreds of hornbills would fly in flocks from one side of the river to the other, their huge beaks set against the blue sky, their wings creaking in that curious way that makes you think they need lubrication. The jungle covered every inch of ground. Huge trees of all kinds rose up into the sky, laced together by creepers. Their heads poked up like umbrellas and the orange flowers of the vines grew around them like coronets.

Mining camps and oil camps have much in common. They are all throbbing centres of excitement, of bustle and activity, of improvisation and a clear determination to get things done. They are also rough and ready – the workers living in tents, and the kitchens made up of open fires surrounded by packing cases on which the men eat their food. I loved the atmosphere of the oil camp and I loved the jungle that surrounded it. I had seen some wild areas of Indonesia when I had travelled with Julius from Macassar, but I had seen nothing like this.

The local people and the company's American contractors worked on the oilfields together. The contrast between the locals – who dressed in their loincloths and who often carried baskets hanging from their headbands – and the burly Americans – who ate steak and ice-cream three times a day and didn't mind a drink after work – was startling. But they all seemed to get on wonderfully well. The locals – or *Sakai* as they were called – were excellent hunters, their preferred weapon a spear of sharpened bamboo. They hunted mainly for deer and wild pigs which they roasted over huge open pits. The mouth-watering smell would waft around their wooden houses, built high on stilts to protect them from wild animals.

Sometimes, Julius and I would wander off into the jungle and follow the tracks of monkeys, tigers, bear, deer and elephants. Julius would carry his hunting rifle just in case we got into trouble. He never needed to use it, though there were times when we spotted elephants and monkeys in the thick undergrowth. This, I thought, was truly paradise. After Sjakon was born, we often took him with us to Rumbai. He would ride around in the Caltex jeep with local Sumatrans, and sometimes they would take him out hunting. What a life for a young boy!

The closest oilfield to Rumbai was called Minas and it was to become the biggest oilfield outside the Persian Gulf. By 1960, Caltex was by far the largest oil company in Indonesia. From its inception, Julius was there with his vision for the future: Caltex would be an American-owned oil company, but one that was run by Indonesians and which invested heavily in the social and economic life of the country. That vision has been fulfilled. Caltex Pacific has been run by Indonesian executives from the time Julius was appointed chief executive in the mid-1960s. The company has contributed mightily to social and cultural programmes not only in Sumatra, but all over Indonesia. It has helped train thousands of Indonesian oil industry workers and sent hundreds of promising young Indonesian executives overseas, to America and Australia, to study and develop new skills.

Meanwhile, our family's private enterprises continued to grow, even in the difficult environment created by the Sukarno government. Julius bought a small insurance company that he took into a joint venture arrangement with British Royal Insurance. That company has grown into one of the largest private insurance firms in Indonesia. Julius went into manufacturing, making soap products and palm oil. He bought tobacco plantations in east Java, employing thousands of local seasonal workers. Julius worked like a man who was driven. I suppose he was: driven to achieve something for his family and for his country.

Just before Sjakon was born, we moved to Jalan Imam Bonjol in Jakarta's diplomatic district. I was only slightly sorry to leave our old villa. It was at our Jalan Minangkabau house, however, that Julius, both symbolically and literally, buried a link with his wartime Z Special service. He had kept as souvenirs some of the 'instant suicide' pellets he always carried in the field. Now, with baby Sjakon on his way, there was no place for anything so dangerous. We dug a hole in the back garden and buried them.

Our new, two-storey house had high, white ceilings and polished tile floors, its balconies overlooking a street lined with Tanjung trees. Next door was the Bulgarian embassy and, further down the road, the British and American embassies.

We took our domestic staff with us to our new house – I could not imagine living without our cook Amina and our rogue of a driver, Asro. Asro adored Sjakon. He would go swimming in the sea in the Bay of Jakarta with Sjakon hanging on to his neck. He taught Sjakon to fly kites and how to 'fight' with other kite flyers. Ground-up glass was stirred up with *kak,* a Chinese glue, and the kite string would then be dipped in this mixture. When it hardened, the string became as sharp as a knife. By skilful manoeuvring, it could be drawn across an opponent's kite string to sever it. Any kite which had a tail attached to it was regarded as a non-combatant and would never be attacked.

Today, in the tea plantations beside our property at Tugu, the children from the *kampong* still have kite fights which I can watch for hours. I sit on the lawn, with the nearby mountains shrouded in mist and floating cloud. A cool and gentle breeze rustles the leaves of the gum trees. Sometimes these trees seem to me to be a reflection of my own life. Transplanted into an alien environment, they have nevertheless survived and thrived, growing strong in their new home.

nineteen

Julius never had a major falling-out with Sukarno. Through the early 1950s, he had regular contact with the president and we were invited not only to small social functions at the presidential palace but to most of the formal functions that Sukarno hosted. He was the most captivating of hosts. The air was always electric when he was around. Women, including the wives of ambassadors, fell over themselves to be near him. He adored the attention and radiated such warmth that some women were rendered speechless by his attention.

Of Sukarno's four wives, I liked his first wife, Fatmawati, the most. She was a sweet and genuine person who clearly loved Sukarno deeply. While he took three more wives and had many mistresses, he always treated Fatmawati with respect, often staying with her at weekends in a gracious colonial mansion he had purchased for her.

I did not know Sukarno's middle two wives very well and had little to do with them. His last wife, Dewi, was perhaps the most beautiful woman I have ever seen, and she always wore the latest in haute couture. But she was Japanese and, with the war still bitterly remembered, not very popular. After Sukarno was deposed by Suharto, Dewi disappeared from view. She lived in Europe for a time before returning without fanfare to Indonesia in the 1970s. I still see Dewi sometimes in Jakarta, looking lonely and forlorn, though still attractive.

Most of the time, the contact I had with heads of state and members of various European royal families was fairly superficial. However I can recall meeting India's Prime Minister Nehru at a function at the presidential palace. He noticed me standing apart from the eager, thrusting reception line and came across especially to greet me. I was touched. We chatted about Indonesia and about India. He had hypnotic eyes and a calmness that quickly put me at ease.

I also still remember a private audience Julius and I had with Queen Beatrix and Prince Bernhard of the Netherlands. How ironic, I thought, for Julius to be sitting there, chatting amiably to them in Dutch, when for years he had been so actively involved in the independence movement which worked to remove their sovereignty over Indonesia.

While Julius may not have had a direct falling-out with Sukarno, it was clear by the mid-1950s that my husband was not a supporter of the form of government that Sukarno was presiding over. Sukarno had developed what he called 'guided democracy', which in essence meant that the president became the supreme political authority in the country. It was the president who installed the prime minister and his cabinet; censorship of newspapers became widespread; and the government controlled virtually every facet of economic life. Private businesses were increasingly taken over by the state and a thousand different regulations made life almost impossible for expatriates and for foreign-owned companies. Indonesians could not hold foreign currency of any sort and people coming into the country had to declare the money they were bringing in and exchange it for Indonesian rupiah.

As the economy deteriorated, there were food riots in Jakarta almost every week. Inflation was out of control. Corruption was widespread. The rupiah was being devalued so fast that in order to contain the anger of civil servants, the government often paid them in rice and other foodstuffs so that at least their families would have enough to eat.

Julius, working for one of the biggest foreign-owned companies in the country, was increasingly vulnerable. He had always been a firm believer in the private enterprise system. In his view, Indonesia would only grow and prosper through the development of a capitalist economy that emphasised individual achievement. These beliefs were an anathema to Sukarno and to the PKI, the Indonesian Communist Party, which was growing in strength and was increasingly allied to, and supported by, the Chinese government in Beijing. Large numbers of Chinese 'advisers' were coming to Indonesia and the PKI was moving ever closer to playing a significant role in Sukarno's government.

Julius was under constant pressure during this time. Although he rarely spoke directly to me about the strain he was under, I could see it in his face, in his eyes and in the way he slept fitfully at night – his sleep increasingly full of nightmares from his war experiences. Julius was convinced his phone was being tapped, so whenever he needed to talk to the shareholders of Caltex in America he would fly to Singapore. With people he did not know well, he forced himself to remain calm and acted as if he was confident that things would work out. He was determined to keep his nerve in the face of subtle and not so subtle pressure from government officials and ministers.

Once again, our home became a hive of activity, with meetings of Caltex executives and government officials stretching into the night. There was a constant flow of people in and out of the house. I would sit upstairs with Sjakon, playing games with him, and listen to the raised voices, the slamming doors, the arguments. There was nothing I could do to help Julius except to listen to him and comfort him and try to make our home as tranquil a place as possible. There was no-one I could talk to about what was happening because I could never be sure that something I said would not cause Julius harm. The American executives of Caltex were very jittery and they were confused by

Sukarno. They were unsure of what he wanted and unsure about how to deal with him. Julius was their interpreter and key adviser. It was Julius who had to deal with government officials who were contemptuous of Americans and looking for ways to humiliate them. He spent countless hours in the offices of ministers, waiting to talk to them, only to be turned away after a three- or four-hour wait because the minister was too busy to see him.

On one occasion, Julius sat all day outside the minister of finance's office for an appointment that the minister himself had organised. Julius believed that what the minister really wanted was for Julius to leave, so that he could then tell the newspapers that Caltex had refused to meet with him. In the end, seeing that Julius was prepared to wait all day and into the night, the minister ushered him in to the room. Julius knew the man well from pre-independence days, when Julius had been negotiating with the Republicans on behalf of the East Indonesian government. The minister was all graciousness and smiles. He asked about Sjakon and me. Then he said, 'Caltex will find things are easier to conduct if it donates to our political party'.

This was a moment of truth for Julius, one that would determine the way he conducted business for the rest of his life. He knew that corruption was widespread and that paying what amounted to a bribe would undoubtedly smooth over some of the problems Caltex was experiencing. But he also knew that once he crossed that line there would be no turning back, that he would be caught in a web of corruption from which he could never extricate himself.

'No way,' he replied. 'If Caltex did that, I would resign.'

The minister looked momentarily surprised, then continued with the conversation as if nothing had happened.

By the late 1950s, the Indonesian economy had ground to a halt. Sukarno had expelled all Dutch companies and had made it so hard for other foreign enterprises that companies were quitting Indonesia in droves. Indonesia had virtually no exports and lacked sufficient foreign currency to buy essentials like building materials and medicines. Sukarno's behaviour became increasingly erratic. Every day, he broadcast interminably long speeches on the radio that were full of venom against the West. Invariably, these speeches provoked mobs of radical, communist-led trade unionists and students to rampage through the streets of Jakarta screaming anti-American and anti-British slogans and daubing the offices of any foreign company they came across.

The mobs would regularly march down the street past our house on their way to the American and British embassies where they would hold loud and aggressive demonstrations. These became more and more violent. British embassy vehicles were burnt and the US embassy was invaded twice. On the second occasion, the mob left only when the ambassador, a dignified, elderly man called Howard Jones, who Julius and I knew well, confronted them and agreed to meet with a small delegation to hear their grievances. Ironically,

Jones liked Sukarno and Sukarno liked him, but that didn't stop the president from railing against the 'US imperialists', which was always a signal for the demonstrators to head for the American embassy.

From my balcony I could see the mobs attacking the embassy compounds. Sometimes humour would be used to lighten what might have otherwise become very grim events. On one occasion when the mob threatened to set the British embassy on fire, the ambassador – a Scot – put on his kilt and marched up and down the first-floor verandah playing the bagpipes. My enjoyment of this splendid spectacle was interrupted by Julius's urgent cries of 'Get inside! For God's sake get inside!'

The meetings at our home became ever more frantic and urgent. There were secessionist rebellions all over Indonesia and it was common knowledge that some of these were financed by the American Central Intelligence Agency. Anti-American feelings grew to a fever pitch. The Indonesian communist party, the PKI, by the late 1950s, had several million members and millions of sympathisers. It is hard to believe now, but those were the days when the outright incorporation of Indonesia into the communist bloc seemed a distinct possibility. Increasingly, the PKI became a major player in Indonesian politics, with leading communist officials taking up key posts in Sukarno's cabinet. Sukarno himself was never a communist, but he was an autocrat who moved ever closer to the communist party because he feared the power of the armed forces and needed allies to counterbalance their influence.

Things were particularly dire in 1958, just before our second son, George, was born, when there was a secessionist rebellion in Sumatra and the insurgents seized control of a large area of eastern Sumatra that included the Caltex oilfields.

Many Sumatrans had long resented the fact that so much of their wealth was flowing to the central government in Jakarta. The rebels, led by a group of army officers, wanted to make Sumatra a separate country. They told Julius that they were happy to allow Caltex to keep operating, but they wanted the revenues to remain in Sumatra rather than be sent to Java. While they controlled the area where the Caltex oilfields were, the rebels did not stop oil production. Julius continued to fly to Sumatra and go to the oilfields unimpeded.

He had made it clear to the rebels that Caltex would continue to pay taxes to the central government and would not pay them. Still, rumours circulated in Jakarta that Julius was financing the insurgency. Simply because he was associated with a large American-owned company, Julius was vulnerable to this sort of dangerous speculation. The fact that the CIA was helping the rebels was openly confirmed when, in May 1958, a CIA-financed plane carrying military supplies to the insurgents crashed and its American pilot was captured by Indonesian soldiers.

Nothing Julius said or did could dispel the gossip about his involvement. He knew that he was under serious threat when senior army officers, friends from his old service days, called him to say that they had heard he was about to be arrested. From then on, Julius went to work with a small bag of clothes and his toothbrush. If he had to go to jail, I insisted that he do his best to look after his teeth. We would joke about this, but my heart sank every time he left the house.

The rebellion ended several months later, though Julius's safety remained far from secure. Shortly thereafter, in August 1958, our son George was born. Soon after his birth I returned to Melbourne with both children so that they could get to know their grandparents. I returned regularly to Australia, at least twice a year, so that my children could have a relationship with their Australian family. I had no doubt that my children would grow up as Indonesians, but I wanted them to know of their Australian heritage. My father loved the boys and adored having them around. He renamed the family's holiday house on the Mornington Peninsula 'Dromana Tugu' and he would tell the boys stories about his bush childhood spent on the dairy farm near Wangaratta.

More and more, however, I felt like a visitor to Australia whose home was elsewhere. Despite the troubles we were experiencing, I missed Indonesia – the smells, the bustle, the heat and the food. Australia seemed so quiet, so sanitised, compared with my new home where life, for so many people, was lived on the edge.

During that visit with my sons, the Mornington Peninsula seemed a world away from the turmoil that gripped

Indonesia. I would sit on the beach at Dromana Tugu and watch Sjakon play in the shallows with my father, while George lay beside me in his basket under an umbrella. Holiday-makers camped on the foreshore amongst the ti-trees, their clothing strung across wires hung between caravans. How peaceful it all was. I would sit looking out across the bay, the waves gentle, even timid, as they lapped onto the beach, and I would wonder whether Australians realised how lucky they were to live in a country with no major traumas to confront. To most Australians, Indonesia was just another poverty-stricken Asian country that didn't know how to govern itself. They were not interested in what 400 years of colonial rule could do to a proud people.

While I was happy to spend time with my parents, I was anxious to get back to Indonesia because I knew the pressure Julius was under. In these foreboding days, one never knew when a friend might disappear into prison for years on end because they had criticised Sukarno. Old friends who had been part of the East Indonesian government with Julius in the 1940s were arrested and thrown in jail without trial. These were old independence fighters, many of them members of the royal families of Bali or Java. The police would come for them late at night and take them off to prison. Just what they had done to deserve such treatment was never revealed to them.

When Anak Agung Gde Agung was arrested and jailed, Julius was grief-stricken. Agung had been prime minister of

East Indonesia and Julius a minister in his government. He came from Bali where his family were local royalty and lived in a magnificent Balinese mansion. Agung, while not a Republican, had been a key player in the independence movement. He, together with his whole cabinet, had resigned in protest when Sukarno was arrested in 1948. In 1949, when the Dutch wanted to set up an Indonesian federation that excluded the Republicans and Sukarno, Agung had refused to co-operate. Yet now he was unceremoniously thrown into jail where he stayed for six years until, in the aftermath of the attempted communist coup, he was freed by President Suharto and appointed Indonesian ambassador to Belgium.

Today, Agung lives in Bali on the family estate, an old, dignified man who calls Julius every few months so that they can reminisce about old times and new.

twenty

Although our lives were fraught during these years there were still times we spent together as a family that were times of joy. We would often sail our small yacht to Pulau Nirvana – Paradise Island – in the Bay of Jakarta. It was a tiny island, uninhabited and covered with small trees. We would leave home at dawn and spend the morning swimming and fishing off the island's lovely beach. By noon, as the breeze freshened, Julius would proclaim, 'The white caps are up!' and we would pile into the boat to return home. You cannot find Nirvana today. The trees have gone, cut up for firewood. Indeed, the very island itself has been carted away for sand to make concrete for Jakarta building projects. Only a lifeless reef sulks beneath the surface of the sea. So much for paradise.

Tugu remained our main retreat – though there were times when the unrest that gripped Jakarta reached us even there. I can remember one terrifying night when we were woken up by the sound of trucks pulling up outside our house and a tumult of voices. Julius went to see who it was while the children and I locked ourselves in the bathroom. At the front door, Julius was confronted by two dozen armed Ambonese who had come over the mountains to seek his advice about whether they should join a rebellion against the central government in Jakarta. They crowded into our little house, cold and wet through from their all-night journey in open trucks. All we had to warm them up were a couple of bottles of Dutch gin which were quickly emptied.

Julius advised them not to join any rebellion and to return quickly to their villages. Warmed by the alcohol and by the open fire I had lit, each one of them embraced Julius before they clambered aboard their trucks and drove off into the darkness, the tropical rain pelting down on them.

Most weekends, I would force Julius to abandon his business concerns and his worries about the state of Indonesia's economy and government, and come to Tugu with me and the boys. Even when there was gunfire and shouting at night, I felt safe there most of the time. I loved to sit on the verandah with Julius, while Sjakon and George played at our feet, taking in the breathtaking scenery.

Tugu is more or less surrounded by ancient volcanoes, and their great conical peaks seem calm in their grandeur. But who can tell when they might erupt? Heavy clouds and mist hang around them. Downpours of rain accompanied by violent thunder and lightning characterise the wet season.

The ground is soon sodden by the inches of water that the sky dumps suddenly upon it, but the volcanic country and the steep slopes combine to drain it quickly. When the sun breaks through, the air has an extraordinary clarity, showing off the blue shades of the mountains. The evenings are cool and I almost always light an open fire in the corner of the living room as the fog swirls down from the mountains and envelops the house.

If I am to leave anything behind that is a true expression of my personality, and even of my soul, it will be the garden at Tugu. I look at the sweeps of lawn that fall away from the house in great, descending steps and remember how they were once rice terraces, cultivated for hundreds of years by the Sundanese before the Dutch arrived in the sixteenth century. The rushing, man-made watercourse – *slokan* in Indonesian – which once carried irrigation water down the mountains and which could be turned on and off as the rice culture demanded, dates back perhaps a thousand years. Its unending, tranquil song is one of the joys of Tugu, especially in the quiet of the evening. All this I love passionately.

I also love the stone statues which I have brought from Bali and other places to sit in the garden. They have blended quickly into their surroundings, encrusting mosses making them seem as if they have not been disturbed for hundreds of years. Sly Balinese humour finds expression in sculpture. The stone sentry at the verandah's edge, a musket slung over his shoulder, is yawning, about to drop off to sleep. There are statues of round old men with ferns growing out of their nostrils. Others have tendrils of vine tucked cosily under their arms.

I love the sound of the *muezzin* at nightfall, calling the faithful to prayer at the nearby mosque. I love the sounds of children laughing and frolicking in the tea plantation. I like to walk beneath the shade of the gums, grown big and sturdy in the cool mountain air. I love to sit with Julius at night by the open fire, the fog swirling around our little house, and watch the flames dance for us. This has been my joy for half a century. Though our sons and their families now also have small houses in Tugu, I wonder what will happen to my garden when I die.

It was only in Tugu that Julius could relax a little during those terrible times. He would spend the weekends playing with the boys, teaching them the bushcraft that had saved his life during the war. He taught them to hunt and to shoot. He was determined to pack in as much time with his sons as possible in case he was whisked off to jail. I remained as calm as I could. Yet every now and then I would lie awake at night with Julius awake beside me, and I would ask him, in a whisper, 'How long with all this last, darling?'

'Oh,' Julius would answer, his voice so quiet that I could hardly hear him, 'another ten or fifteen years. No longer than that.' Then he would laugh although there was no joy in it, but rather a sort of resigned weariness.

Perhaps our worst fears were realised one day when we arrived at Tugu, and found nailed to the door an army proclamation stating that the property had simply been seized and taken over for military use. Fortunately, it turned out to be a case of a local commander getting too big for his boots and, upon further enquiries in Jakarta, we heard no more of it.

We tried hard not to show the boys how concerned we were about what was happening. George, who was still a toddler, was unaffected by the pressure on Julius, but Sjakon knew that these were difficult times.

As the situation in Indonesia had become increasingly unstable, Asro, our driver, had begun taking Sjakon to school on his bicycle – the small boy sitting on the seat while Asro pedalled furiously. Because families like ours were targets for abuse from angry mobs stirred up by local communists, Sjakon could not be driven to school without the risk of the car being stoned. So Asro took him on his bike. Every morning when they left, I would pray for their safe return and I would wonder whether Julius would be in jail by the time his son got home from school.

Eventually, however, it even became too dangerous for Asro to take Sjakon to school and my son had to be kept at home. I did what I could to keep up his education. I continued to teach him to read and write, and we hired tutors for those subjects in which I was not proficient. Our domestic staff, most of whom had been with us for more than a decade by then, were regularly abused by the mobs of demonstrators who were always on the streets. They were called traitors for working for us, because we were 'agents of US imperialism'. Not one of our staff left or ever complained about the abuse they were subjected to. I was very moved by their loyalty and had tears in my eyes when I told them how I felt.

Things got steadily worse. We had a factory in Surabaya where we produced Palmolive soap products under licence and palm oil products. The factory employed several hundred people and was reasonably profitable. The workers in general were well paid and happy. Then, without warning, the factory was taken over by militant trade unionists with the open support of local government officials. The managers Julius had trained and encouraged were sacked. So was half the workforce, basically because they were not fervent enough in their support for the militants. We were told that the factory still belonged to us, but that we could longer run it, visit it or take any share of the profits.

There was nothing we could do. It would have been futile to complain, perhaps even counterproductive. At least Julius was not in jail – not yet anyhow. Julius felt responsible for the people who were suddenly left without jobs and with no means of supporting their families. He quickly decided that he would have to keep paying his employees, despite the fact that the factory was no longer in his hands.

Only recently has Julius told me that at times during those years he thought about sending the boys and me to live in Australia where we would be safe. There were even occassions, he said, when he had considered leaving himself because the future seemed so bleak and he could see no end in sight to the growing anti-capitalist hysteria.

Julius never said anything to me about this at the time and had he done so I would have refused to leave Indonesia without him. What if he had been jailed? Who would have visited him? How would he have known what was happening to his children? It is unthinkable that I would have abandoned him at such a time. Indeed, I would have done everything in my power to talk him out of leaving. We had gone through too much, struggled too hard for this country to abandon it so easily. I also know that, if we had left, a big part of Julius would have withered and died. I simply cannot imagine him living anywhere else.

Caltex, however, had become a major target for the militant mobs. Slogans were painted on the company office buildings in Jakarta. Demonstrators regularly surrounded the building, hurling abuse at employees. Windows were smashed by rock-throwing thugs and every evening Julius would have to run the gauntlet of screaming protesters as he left his office to go home. Caltex's American shareholders were increasingly inclined to abandon Indonesia in the face of mounting pressure from Sukarno and his communist allies. Julius urged them to remain patient. Caltex, he told them, was Indonesia's only meaningful source of foreign currency and one of the country's largest employers. Even Sukarno, with his seemingly blind hatred of foreign companies, wouldn't dare seize the Caltex oilfields.

In his heart, however, Julius was not sure this was true. Sukarno's anti-American and anti-western rhetoric was becoming more and more extreme. His speeches became even longer than they had been – and that was quite long enough. The communists grew more and more active in all walks of Indonesian life. It was well known that they were drawing up lists of 'enemies' who would be eliminated when the time was right. No doubt Julius Tahija, arch-capitalist, was up near the top of one of those lists.

Meanwhile, Sukarno and his ministers continued to incite the mobs against America and, by implication, Caltex, which was increasingly seen as the main symbol of American involvement in Indonesia. Eventually a decree was issued which placed Caltex under the temporary control of the government. Communist party officials were given the power to run compulsory lectures in socialist theory and practice which the whole workforce had to attend.

Julius was told that the company would eventually be taken over and that he could remain and run it for the state. He answered that if the oilfields were expropriated, he would resign immediately. His punishment for such defiance was humiliation. He was forced to sit beside his drivers and other low-level staff and listen to crude lectures on the evils of capitalism and American multinationals. The staff canteen was closed to executives and Julius had to buy his food from street hawkers. In Javanese culture, such insults cut particularly deep.

The state-controlled newspapers regularly ran stories critical of Caltex and, by implication, of Julius. Friends in the army and in the government kept telling us that Julius was in danger and that he should be prepared to leave the country at a moment's notice. He made no such plans. He was a fatalist. If it was his fate to end up in jail, then so be it. Several of his Caltex colleagues were arrested and jailed, dragged away from their family homes by police, without explanation and without arrest warrants. When this happened, Julius would make sure that the salary of the jailed executive continued to be paid so that at least his family wouldn't suffer financially.

There were times when I was mistaken for an American and abused on the streets. I can remember an angry group of demonstrators bailing me up outside a shopping centre where I had gone with a group of American women, the wives of some visiting oil company executives. The protesters hurled insults at us in Indonesian. I stood there listening in silence and then told them in fluent Indonesian, 'You should be ashamed. These people are visitors to our country. They deserve to be treated politely.' The crowd fell silent, looked sheepish, and moved on to their next target.

I grew sick of Sukarno's speeches and his sloganeering. I grew tired of the demonstrations, the angry mobs, the violence that seemed more and more to characterise their protests. The British embassy was set on fire. The American ambassador's residence was ransacked, and his clothing was thrown onto the street. The ambassador had to stand there with his wife and say nothing while all this happened. He did it with great dignity, smiling as he and his wife's clothing was piled into the gutters outside his home.

We still attended embassy receptions, though both Julius and I would have much preferred to stay at home. By the time his day ended, Julius was suffering from nervous exhaustion. Nevertheless, only those close to him would have known it, so determined was he not to show any signs of weakness. Julius and I were at one such reception when we met Aidit Dipa Nusantara, the leader of the PKI. He knew Julius well and approached him with a big smile on his face. He was a small man with intense eyes who greeted Julius as if he was a long-lost friend. He told Julius that Indonesia was about to go through major changes and that Julius ought to get with the strength and admit that the private enterprise system was wrong for the country. He had his hand on Julius's shoulder as he said this. He smiled and Julius smiled back before moving away a little so that Aidit's hand fell off his shoulder.

'Believers in private enterprise like me,' Julius told him, 'bear a special responsibility. We can neither ignore social inequities nor address them through giveaway programmes. We must offer opportunities for people to help themselves.'

'Let's see who will survive,' Aidit replied. 'Either you or I will disappear by the time this is over.'

Aidit was one of the organisers of the attempted coup in 1965. When the coup failed he went underground, but within a month his hideout was discovered by soldiers loyal to General Suharto and he was shot. Photographs of his body were published in several Indonesian newspapers. I do not condone nor cheer the killing of any human being, but I can't say that I shed too many tears over Aidit's death.

Eventually the constant tension took its toll. In 1963, Julius began to suffer chest pains and shortness of breath. A heart specialist told him that unless he removed himself for a while from the stresses of his business and public life he would die. I insisted that we had to leave Indonesia for an extended holiday. We went to Europe where we stayed for two months, travelling and relaxing, just spending time with each other. This was one of those rare times in our lives when we were together as a family and I loved it. We could never forget about what was happening in Indonesia, but at least we had the chance for a respite together. Julius recovered and quickly became anxious about what was happening at home. He could not abandon Caltex nor the people who worked for the company, for whom he felt responsible.

So we went back to Indonesia. By the early 1960s, almost all the foreign-owned companies had fled Indonesia and I believe Caltex too would have sold up its operations to the Indonesian government and got out of the country had it not been for Julius's determination to see things through. He continued to encourage the American shareholders to keep faith in the company and they took his advice. Caltex continued to fund exploration and various social and economic programmes designed to help small local businesses develop.

The economy was by then in ruins. Inflation was running at over 600 per cent. The government's response was to simply print more money. On every street corner in Jakarta, black-market currency dealers plied their trade, exchanging foreign currency for bucket loads of rupiah. Ordinary people found that they couldn't even buy their most basic food requirements. Their money was more or less useless.

Our home seemed to be constantly invaded by hordes of government officials and company executives whose meetings would sometimes last until dawn. Every few days, Julius would fly to Singapore so that he could talk to Caltex's American shareholders. He hardly slept and neither did I. The children knew we were under pressure, but in the main, I managed to be there for them, to calm them down, to listen to their problems even when all around us was chaos.

In Australia, Indonesia was increasingly seen as a threat to the whole region. When Malaysia was created in 1963, there were Australian troops and airforce squadrons based in Malaya helping the British combat communist guerrillas active in the region. Sukarno saw Malaysia's emerging nationhood as a western imperialist plot. His speeches were full of belligerent threats against the new country. This was the period of 'confrontation' when there were fears that Indonesia was an expansionist power that would one day threaten Australia. I do not believe that this was ever a possibility, but my family were certainly worried about me and there was little I could say to reassure them. My concerns were not about Australia but about my adopted country, about where it was headed, and about my husband, who – if things turned out badly – would pay a terrible price for his beliefs and his loyalty to Caltex.

When President Sukarno declared 1965 'the year of living dangerously', I was fearful about what that would mean for Julius. It turned out to be a prophetic statement, though hardly in the way Sukarno had intended it.

twenty-one

In September 1965, Julius had to attend an international business conference in San Francisco. The whole family were to go with him, after which we planned to go on to London for a short holiday. We wanted to go by ship to Southampton from New York, a trip we had made before and had enjoyed a lot. To this day, the family never travels together on one aircraft. In those days, I would fly ahead with the children, set ourselves up in the hotel and then Julius would join us. The boys and I flew to San Francisco three days before Julius left Indonesia.

On the day we flew out, Julius was contacted by General Parman, the head of army intelligence. General Parman was an old family friend whom Julius had known for thirty years, from the time he joined the Dutch East Indies army before the war.

'I hear that you plan to take your family abroad,' the general said.

‘Yes,’ Julius replied. ‘In fact, Jean and the boys have just left. I shall join them in the US in a couple of days.’

‘That’s good,’ his friend answered. ‘I just wanted to make sure.’

General Parman took Julius to the airport. It was as if he wanted to make sure that Julius was really leaving. Julius did not ask the general why he was so concerned to see Julius go, nor did Parman ever hint at why he was so adamant that Julius leave. These were times when one asked as few questions as possible.

At the time, Julius imagined that Parman had information that Julius was about to be arrested. Perhaps that was indeed what Parman thought, though we can never be sure. Perhaps he had an inkling of what was about to happen, for there were factions of the armed forces and of the airforce in particular, that had communist sympathies and that had made those sympathies clear. What I do know is that we never saw Parman again. A week later he was dead, together with five other generals, killed by communist thugs and communist-leaning army personnel. The generals were tortured and mutilated before they died, and their bodies were tossed down a well in a village aptly named Crocodile Hole on the outskirts of Jakarta. This was the beginning of the attempted communist coup that was to have far-reaching repercussions on all our lives and that was to change Indonesia forever.

In the space of several weeks following the coup attempt,

tens of thousands of people would die. The PKI, the largest communist party outside the communist bloc, was destroyed and outlawed. Sukarno's dominance over Indonesian politics was ended and the Suharto era was begun. With it, Indonesia took the path of economic reform based on encouraging free enterprise and foreign investment. It was a path which Julius had long advocated and which, within two decades, transformed Indonesia from the sick man of Asia into one of the fastest-growing economies of the region. There would be a burgeoning middle class and the country would have the chance to achieve what Julius had always believed was possible: an Indonesia that was the Asian equivalent of the United States.

None of this seemed likely when we heard, on board ship en route from New York to Southampton, of what had happened in the early hours of 30 September 1965. The coup attempt, which involved sections of the armed forces and bands of armed communists, began at 4.00 a.m. with raids on the homes of the six generals who were killed, as well as on the home of General Nasution, the defence minister. Nasution managed to escape when the assassination squad assigned to kill him arrived at his home and was greeted at the front door by his wife. But as he scaled the walls of the nearby Iraqi embassy, his five-year-old daughter Irma was killed in a spray of bullets meant for him.

At the same time as this was happening, the conspirators took control of the presidential palace, the Indonesian radio station and an air base just outside of Jakarta. For reasons that remain a mystery, the assassination squads did not target General Suharto who, at the time, was the chief of the elite strategic command. Shortly after the coup attempt was put down, Suharto speculated that perhaps he had been spared because the conspirators felt that his command was 'not important enough'. This was the coup leaders' fatal mistake. Within hours, Suharto's troops had regained control of Jakarta, and a day later the coup leaders surrendered. President Sukarno, whose role in the coup attempt is a matter of debate, remained president, but with no authority and no power. His era was over. Within a year, General Suharto would replace him as president.

When the bodies of the murdered generals were discovered in the well at Crocodile Hole, people were outraged. We had arrived in England by then and were disturbed and concerned about what had happened. The murder of the generals was a shocking crime, made worse by the mutilation of their bodes which, in Javanese culture, is considered to be a form of desecration. That one of those murdered was a close friend made it even worse.

We returned home as quickly as we could. A week after the coup attempt, Jakarta seemed more or less back to normal. There were no soldiers on the streets and no tanks guarding strategic buildings. Nor were there any mobs demonstrating outside the American or British embassies. For the first time in more than a decade, Jakarta seemed to be at peace.

It wasn't of course. Aidit, the PKI leader, was dead within a month, shot by soldiers loyal to General Suharto. The other coup leaders were arrested, put on trial and sentenced to death – though these sentences were later commuted to life imprisonment. During the year that it took for General Suharto to take over as president from Sukarno, there were mass killings in Indonesia on an unprecedented scale, certainly in the country's history this century.

On every island of the Indonesian archipelago, in every region, in virtually every *kampong*, there were killings. In some parts of the country where the communists had been strong, there were battles between armed communist bands and anti-communist, pro-Suharto groups. But in other areas there were simply mass slaughters as local communities wreaked their revenge not only on communists and suspected communists but sometimes on entirely innocent people. Many ethnic Chinese were killed during this period because they were suspected – falsely, I believe – of having contact with the communist government in Beijing.

I vividly remember one of our drivers telling me how, when he was working in Bali after the coup, he was pressed into the service of armed groups on the island. These groups forced him to use his truck to carry the bodies of those killed in the anti-communist frenzy to mass graves where they were dumped and covered over with soil and rocks. I was horrified by this. To this day, no-one knows exactly how many people were killed. Estimates range from half a million down to 200 000, but we will never know the exact figure or just why or how this fury was unleashed. Certainly the murder of the generals and the mutilation of their bodies enraged many people. But there was more to it than that.

There is a Caltex executive with whom we are friendly who, in 1965, was still a teenager. For years, local communists had threatened to kill his entire family because they were Christian and active in the local church. A communist mob had once forced his father to dig a series of graves beside the family home which, they said, would be where his family would be buried at the appropriate time.

When the coup failed, this young man saw crowds slaughter the communists who had terrorised his family. While he did not take part in the killing, a part of him was glad when it happened.

I come from a country where such passions and such killings are alien and, in a sense, I could not understand why this happened. Yet when I recall that Julius was probably on the top of a list of people who would, like those generals, have been murdered had the coup succeeded, I thank God that it didn't, even if the cost of failure proved to be so high.

At Crocodile Hole, statues of the murdered generals have been erected. They face the well where their bodies were found. Beneath the statue of the most senior general who was slain is an inscription which reads: 'Be alert. Make sure this does not happen again.' The statues are a national shrine. They are monuments not only to those who died, but to a turning point in Indonesian history. From the time the Dutch flag came down at that special ceremony in the grounds of the presidential palace in December 1949 until the attempted communist coup, Indonesia had gone through almost two decades of political drama, intrigue, bloodshed and uncertainty. Its people had suffered all sorts of deprivations. At different times, the very integrity of the nation itself had been in doubt.

Sukarno had been a great Indonesian freedom fighter and the most charismatic leader the country is ever likely to have. It was his flamboyance and drive that helped forge the Indonesian nation. There is no doubt that in the early days of his presidency the people saw him as the personification of their hopes and aspirations. They loved him and, in his own way, he loved them too. But his strengths were also his weaknesses. Sukarno wanted to be a major world leader, but he ignored Indonesia's economic problems. He was more interested in fine rhetoric than in the hard work of actually getting the country on its feet. He believed that, no matter what he did, the people would always love him. This is a fatal mistake for a politician to make. Such love is always conditional and always likely to be withdrawn. By the time Sukarno realised that he had lost the support of a majority of the people, it was too late for him to resurrect his presidency.

It took a year for things to settle down after the coup attempt. During this time, Sukarno remained president even though his days were clearly numbered. There were still large street demonstrations and elements of the armed forces remained committed to Sukarno. Curfews were imposed regularly, so that after 7.00 p.m. the streets of Jakarta were empty of people. Gradually, peace was restored. Foreign companies started to return to take up their former businesses. We went back to our Palmolive factory in Surabaya that had been taken from us by the government. It was a sorry sight, run-down, dirty and badly in need of work.

Those times have become like a dream, distant, otherworldly, and yet at the same time vividly real. So much is different now about my adopted country. So much has changed. When I look at my grandchildren, I wonder whether they will ever be able to understand that only a generation ago Indonesia was a country that seemed to have no future. I wonder whether they will be able to understand what their grandfather went through, not just in the latter part of the Sukarno era but during the war and during the revolution when the nation was being born. By the time of the communist coup attempt, I had known Julius for twenty-three years and had been married to him for eighteen. We had never known a time when things were stable, settled or clear. The shape of his life, and mine, had been determined by the war, by the Indonesian revolution and by the volatile Sukarno years. We could hardly ever plan for the future with any certainty that such a future would arrive.

Now that we were in our middle age it seemed that at last the dream Julius had for Indonesia – and for us – might have a chance of becoming a reality. General Suharto, whom Julius had known since the days of the revolution when they were both senior officers in the newly formed post-independence armed forces, was in many ways the antithesis of Sukarno. He was a quiet, modest man from a humble background whose diffidence was very much a part of his Javanese heritage. This does not mean that he was weak or vacillating. On the contrary, General Suharto was clear right from the start about the path he thought Indonesia had to take if it were to become a prosperous nation capable of providing a basic level of material comforts for its 200 million people.

That path was one that Julius had urged for the country from the time that it became independent. Suharto too was convinced that Indonesia's future could only be secured through the development of a free enterprise economy, one that encouraged foreign investment and rewarded initiative and risk-taking. Suharto asked Julius to formally spread the message overseas that foreign investment would now be welcomed in Indonesia.

The first conference Julius addressed on the subject was in Sydney in 1966. He then travelled to the United States and to Europe to tell business groups and governments that Indonesia had fundamentally changed. Foreign investment started to roll in. For the first time in more than a decade, tourists started to come to Indonesia, particularly to Bali. The skyline of Jakarta began to change. Soon the horizon was dotted with building cranes. Import restrictions were lifted so that, for the first time, basic medicines were available for the treatment of common illnesses. Both Julius and I felt that finally there would be peace and stability in the country. Julius could be what he had always wanted to be: a builder, a creator of wealth, not so much for himself – for even back then we had enough to keep us comfortable for the rest of our lives – but for his beloved Indonesia.

In 1966, Julius was appointed managing director and chief executive officer of Caltex Pacific. It happened shortly after his fiftieth birthday. He was the first non-westerner anywhere to head a major transnational oil company. After what he had been through, I thought that this was a just reward for his loyalty to Caltex during the traumatic Sukarno era. But more than anything, it was recognition of his great talent, his good judgement and his vision.

From the start, Julius had always believed that Caltex could be a tremendous force for good in Indonesia. And it has been. The company has donated millions to development projects. It has helped local people establish small businesses that, in turn, have become suppliers of all sorts of goods to Caltex. As part of a deliberate policy, Caltex has trained hundreds of Indonesians in a range of skills needed to successfully run the Sumatran oilfields. The company's American shareholders, Chevron and Texaco, have upheld Julius's plans to make the company a truly Indonesian one. There has always been a need for American expertise and technology – there still is – but in all other respects, Caltex

Pacific has been run by Indonesians for more than thirty years. If you were to ask him, Julius would say that this has been his greatest achievement.

In some respects, my life did not change very much. There was less tension and uncertainty. I no longer had to lie awake at night wondering what was going to happen to us, wondering whether Julius would end up in jail or worse. I no longer had to put up with insults from angry pro-communist mobs or watch those thugs attack western embassies and burn cars, the smoke from their vandalism covering our neighbourhood. But Julius was busier than ever, both with Caltex and with the family's private business interests which, by the late 1960s, included tobacco plantations, manufacturing, insurance and banking. I was often left alone with the boys and, I must say, I never completely got used to it. I often felt lonely. Despite the receptions and dinner parties and ceremonies we had to attend, I was never a great social butterfly. I always loved meeting people, but parties left me cold. My passions were reading and gardening and, of course, Julius and the children. I have never been able to spend as much time with Julius as I would like.

Nor did I ever spend as much time with my parents as I would have liked before they died. In life, we make choices – or choices are made for us – and we must live with them. My mother visited us often in Indonesia and I regularly went back to Australia. Julius came whenever he could. He loved my mother and father as if they were his own parents; they were a replacement for the family he felt he never had. Yet because our lives were in Indonesia, because that is where my destiny compelled me to go, I felt a deep sense of guilt when they died. Perhaps children always feel such guilt when their parents die.

At that point I too felt that my ties to the country in which I had been born and grown up were severed. It was as if I had been finally cut loose, and I was now, in some fundamental way, alone. I had been going back to Australia for visits for almost twenty years and with each visit I'd noticed how much the country was changing, and not in every way for the better. I noticed the destruction of so much of Melbourne's fine Victorian architecture, especially in beautiful Collins Street where I had, a half-century earlier, strolled with my father in his police uniform. He had loved the grey Victorian façades that dominated this gracious street. Those façades, those buildings, had disappeared by the 1960s – replaced by modern office blocks that were often hideous.

Happily the faces of the people had changed too. Suddenly, more and more Australians were not Anglo-Saxon. They were from southern and central Europe, and from Asia. So many different languages were being spoken on the streets, on buses, trains and on my beloved trams. Melbourne was no longer a predominantly British provincial town but a cosmopolitan city with the most bewildering range of foods and restaurants, catering to every imaginable taste and beyond.

I loved visiting this new Melbourne. Still, after a couple of weeks away, I would long for a fiery Indonesian curry. I also missed the soups. Julius and I have always loved soup, and no meal is complete without it. There are literally hundreds of different types, from every province in Indonesia. Our favourite is probably *soto babat,* a thick soup of tripe in coconut milk. There is nothing like fresh coconut milk, which is not the water inside the coconut but the flesh, grated and squeezed into a rich cream. The soup that is meant to have magical medicinal powers is *sayur asem* or sour soup, which, when I first ate it, tasted and looked to me like washing-up water. Now, no week goes by without us having at least one serve of *sayur asem.* It is made from maize, young jackfruit and nuts from the Melinjo tree. One of Julius's favourite dishes is *pindang serani,* which means Christian soup. I have never been able to discover why it has that name. It is a sort of bouillabaisse, a hot fish soup with lemon grass, chillies, garlic, onion, tamarind (for sourness) and *terassi* – a fermented fish sauce.

What made my trips to Australia special was that my boys could spend time with their grandparents. When my parents died – first my mother and, shortly afterwards, my father – some of the joy went out of my visits. A month after my father died, I returned to Melbourne to tidy up our old house in Ascot Vale. It was so quiet that I burst into tears. My father's old woollen cardigan hung in the hallway. I touched it and held a sleeve to my face. The smell brought back a flood of memories of the times we had spent together in this house, this house where I had met Julius and where my life, as a result of that meeting, had been changed forever.

We sold the house in Ascot Vale in the 1970s because we simply couldn't get anyone to look after it. Julius did not want to sell it, but I insisted. I could not bear the thought of it becoming a run-down shell of what it had once been. It was still heartbreaking. Julius had tears in his eyes when the sale went through. So did I. After all, this house had played a crucial role in our lives.

We bought a small apartment in North Melbourne, the suburb in which my mother had been born and in which my grandfather had had his 'Ward Bros.' shop, selling sewing machines and pianos. I took my father's beloved books with me and the writing desk he had made for me when I first started university. There are ghosts and memories all around me when I visit Melbourne. I like to wander down the city streets where I used to walk with my parents. It brings back wonderful memories. It keeps me connected with the past. Most of my relatives have died. The only ones left are a sister-in-law and an old aunt, my father's sister, who is 104. Her memory is remarkable. Every time I am in Melbourne, I visit her and we talk about my father and their lives back on the dairy farm.

Some of my university dental school colleagues are still alive and I try to stay in touch with as many of them as possible. A few years ago, we had a reunion at a golf club outside of Melbourne. How different my life is from theirs, I thought. I have kept up my Australian dentistry registration which means I can still work as a dentist in Australia, although of course I never will. I have done this for my father, in his memory.

But Australia is not my home. My home is in Indonesia. When I die, that is where I will be laid to rest.

twenty-two

Though he had already turned fifty when he was appointed chief executive of Caltex Pacific, Julius worked harder than ever. His day was even longer – if that is possible – than it had been before. He would often wake up at three in the morning to begin making his phone calls to the American shareholders of Caltex in America. He would then spend the morning on Caltex business before heading off to our family's company offices where he would be based for most of the afternoon.

In between his Caltex commitments and his work for our family holding company, Julius managed to fulfil his obligation to President Suharto to promote Indonesia as a place where foreign investment was welcomed and embraced. He travelled the world, at his own expense, addressing business conferences, meeting with government officials and with politicians, always selling his vision of the new Indonesia. He was in his element and determined to make up for the time lost during Sukarno's final years.

My life revolved around our home, our children and, of course, Tugu, where the garden was starting to take shape – the reality starting to match my original fantasy of what I wanted to create there. We bought some more land around our property when it became available and the garden grew to about ten acres of lawns, flowerbeds and trees. Some of the land we set aside for our children. Today both Sjakon and George have houses at Tugu where they come with their families, though not as often as Julius and I. They are not passionate gardeners like me.

The rounds of receptions and embassy parties and business lunches became even more hectic at this time and I accepted that it was my role to be by Julius's side – to entertain for him and to spend evenings with the wives of politicians, executives and ambassadors while the men were in another room talking politics or business. I did not mind. I had long ago decided that this would be my role in our family and I played it willingly. There were still times when I missed my professional life. There were times when I wished I could develop my interests in painting and architecture. But I would not have chosen another life – nor would I now.

While men still predominate in Indonesian politics and business, this is no more so than in Australia or the United States. There are several women in President Suharto's cabinet, and in Surabaya there is a bank run and staffed entirely by women, where even the security guards are female karate experts. In the professions, more than half the graduates in medicine are women and over 60 per cent of those in dentistry are female. Every oil company, including Caltex, has a significant and growing number of female engineers, and more and more women are holding senior positions in commerce and industry.

Among the poorer mass of people, a woman's life is still all too likely to be a struggle. In the countryside, girls are usually married by the time they are fifteen, their marriages arranged by their families. Though there has been a variety of birth control programmes since President Suharto came to power, these girls still tend to have too many children and, as a result, are old before their time. In the cities, the poor salaries paid to so many male workers mean that wives have to battle to keep their families fed and clothed. They take in boarders, sell snacks in the markets, and most of them will do any sort of job to earn a few extra rupiah. But this arises from poverty and not from discrimination. Is it really any different in Australia where feminism has been a middle-class movement of middle-class women whose victories have, in the main, done little for working-class and poor women?

While Indonesia is probably the most religiously tolerant Muslim country in the world, there are still some aspects of Muslim culture that are prevalent in the countryside that cannot be condoned. I remember my horror when, one day at Tugu, I noticed an old woman coming out of the staff quarters at the back of our house. Her mouth was stained scarlet with betel nut and she gave me a broad grin as she scurried past.

'Who was that?' I asked Amat.

'Oh, she's from the *kampong*,' he said. 'She has just done a *sunat*.'

Sunat means circumcision. One of Amat's daughters had given birth to a baby girl two months previously. The little girl, I discovered, had had her clitoris cut out to ensure that she would have no sensual feelings and would therefore not be distracted from her family duties and domestic chores.

A campaign is being waged by Indonesian women's groups to stamp out this ghastly practice, but old customs die hard. Some of the Muslim religious leaders still encourage it and in some villages it is still considered to be the right and normal thing to do to baby girls. I recently asked one of the young women who work for us at Tugu whether, if she had a daughter, she would have her circumcised.

'Oh, yes,' she said, 'of course. Otherwise my daughter would be a prostitute.'

It is difficult to influence such beliefs.

Unlike Australia, Indonesia remains a country where religion is very important and where the concept of a secular society seems alien and strange. But there is no state religion in Indonesia despite the fact that 95 per cent of the population is Muslim. Muslims, Hindus and Christians all have the same religious rights and freedoms.

Not long ago, I had a spell in an intensive care ward of a

hospital in Jakarta. Several people came to my bedside and asked if they might pray for me. They included an old man from the local Chinese Methodist church who was accompanied by his daughter-in-law.

'Could Mary pray for you?' he asked. I was touched to tears by this young woman's warmth and sincerity as she prayed by my bedside.

On the other side of the ward lay a very old lady, perhaps in her nineties. She was Sumatran and she was constantly surrounded by a group of Sumatran women. Some wore traditional dress – a loose sarong and *kebaya* – and the younger ones wore miniskirts – they were office workers on the way to work. The old lady was deaf, but one young miniskirted girl bent low to one ear and another girl to the other as they read from the Koran to their great-grandmother.

Anyone who wants to understand Indonesians, I thought, should never underestimate the role of family and religion in the lives of most of the people.

They should also consider the influence of more than three centuries of Dutch rule. To my mind, modern Indonesia's roots lie in the revolution against the Dutch straight after the war: that revolution bound Indonesians of every ethnic and cultural group together in one cause – to rid the country of their colonial rulers and their influence.

However, 400 years of history cannot be cast off easily. In quiet times up in Tugu, or when Julius is away, I like to let my mind run back over those four extraordinary centuries.

I do not in any way, I hope, glamorise the period of Dutch rule. Its essential purpose was to make Holland rich, no matter what the cost to the indigenous people. Yet what a remarkable people they were, from a tiny country almost sunk beneath the cold seas and fogs of northern Europe. Sometimes colonised themselves by the conquering Spanish and French, they navigated their small, wooden ships to the other side of the world and established their empire over a large expanse of the Indian Ocean.

When I first went to Indonesia, I met many Dutch business people who made it easy for me to understand why the Indonesians wanted their country back. They were absurdly arrogant and full of self-importance. A few Dutch officials were more sensitive to the demands of the indigenous people for a greater say in their country's affairs, but even they could not understand that throughout the world the colonial era was ending.

Nevertheless, Dutch colonialism can not be compared to the brutality that characterised, for instance, Portuguese colonial rule. The Dutch, for one thing, did not allow the alienation of indigenous lands, which could be leased but never bought. They were tolerant of regions and of ethnic variety and allowed local laws to govern many customary matters. Their fine public buildings still stand and the best of them – unlike their former homes – remain an example of what tropical architecture can achieve. Though they themselves are gone, their footprints on Indonesia can still be felt and seen in the country. There is a sort of symbolism in the fact that President Suharto's official residence – a splendid white palace – is the former seat of the Dutch governor-general of the Indies. Even the Indonesian legal system derives from the Napoleonic code, introduced by the Dutch.

But the Dutch echoes grow ever fainter. Few young Indonesians can speak Dutch or have any interest in the history of Dutch colonial rule in Indonesia. To them, Holland is just another country in faraway Europe. This is true of my family. Although Julius and I can both speak Dutch, we never use the language at home and our children cannot understand more than a few Dutch words. (In fact I hardly ever use the language. Julius still speaks Dutch to a couple of his old friends, but otherwise speaks Indonesian or English.) Apart from my old Dutch books on the Indies and their enduring fascination, Holland has been reduced for me to the consumption of rollmops (herring in spiced vinegar) and *oude Genever*, a potent Dutch gin, of which I take two small but powerful glasses, well chilled, every night before dinner.

What the Dutch never gave the indigenous people was a democratic political system. Neither did the revolution nor the Sukarno years, which began with ideas of democracy but quickly degenerated into an autocracy that was on the verge of embracing communist totalitarianism when the army intervened and turned the country in an entirely different direction. Only those of us who have lived here, through the revolution, through the Sukarno years, and through Suharto's presidency, can truly understand how great Suharto's leadership and vision have been.

But President Suharto is nearing the end of his career and it is not clear who will replace him, or whether the succession will be smooth and peaceful. Corruption is widespread, though not as bad as some in the West believe. The growing middle class – perhaps bigger already than the entire population of Australia – will inevitably want more freedoms. There are still enormous numbers of poor people, but the poverty in Indonesia is not the same as the poverty in India or parts of Africa. There is no famine in Indonesia, no widespread starvation. Wages, while still low, are rising. Increasingly, children of working-class parents are taking the opportunity to gain an education and move into the middle class. They too will demand political change.

I came to Indonesia from a country with a history of Westminster-style parliamentary democracy. There is no such democracy in Indonesia. I don't believe a democracy like Australia's would suit us, not yet anyway. I want Indonesia to move down the road towards democracy. I certainly think that the media should be free from political interference. But the country's history suggests that a Westminster-style democracy is unlikely in the foreseeable future.

Since independence, the armed forces have played a vital role in keeping Indonesia together. They have built bridges and roads, and have kept the peace. The army will remain at the centre of Indonesian social and political life, of that I am certain. There is simply no other organisation to take its place as a unifying force in a nation that consists of 16 000 islands, hundreds of different ethnic groups and scores of different regional cultures. In a sense, Indonesia was a post-war, post-colonial invention which is still in the process of becoming a reality. It could still, conceivably, be torn apart.

twenty-three

My first visit to the Ijen Plateau of East Java was in the 1970s. It is the place where Julius and I go whenever we feel the need to completely get away from civilisation – a place that is still wild and in some parts inaccessible, even today. I have probably travelled through the islands of Indonesia as much as anyone during the past fifty years. I love the great variety of cultures and environments that go to make up my adopted homeland. The Indonesian archipelago is endlessly fascinating and I have, in my travels, managed only to scratch the surface of what it has to offer.

We first went to the Ijen Plateau because we had heard that there were ancient Hindu temples in the area which had not been explored for centuries. To get there, we flew to Surabaya and then travelled by four-wheel drive until even the dirt road disappeared, leaving only narrow tracks through the hilly, scrub-covered country. We hired horses from a *kampong* and an ex-army tracker was employed to take us further inland. I learnt from him to distinguish between the tracks and traces of pigs, deer and jaguars, all of which were plentiful in the area. After a day's ride, we reached a remote *kampong* and asked the people about the ruins.

They took us to a steep canyon and pointed down the sheer walls. We could see a ledge of sorts some ten metres down from the lip, but the only way down was by rope. The rope was secured to a tree. I held my breath, shut my eyes, and slid down it. There was no temple, but there was a cave beside the ledge with Hindu inscriptions on either side of the entrance. Inside the cave, there was nothing except rubble and tree branches.

Having photographed the inscriptions, I was then faced with the problem of getting back up to the top. There was no way I could climb back up the rope. My heart sank. The villagers, however, were unconcerned. Within a matter of minutes, they had constructed an emergency ladder using two thick bamboo poles which were long enough to reach the ledge. Laying them parallel, they knocked holes at equal intervals and through these holes and inserted thinner bamboos in the manner of rungs. It was a shaky old ladder and no doubt I would not have survived a fall down the canyon wall, but with my eyes firmly focused upwards I scrambled to the top.

When we returned to Jakarta, the Museum of Indonesia managed to decipher the words on the cave's entrance. It seems that, centuries earlier, the cave had been occupied by a group of Hindu hermits. There was little else they could tell me, but my photographs became part of the museum's collection.

The Ijen Plateau has changed a lot during the last two decades. The population has grown considerably and what was once horse country is now covered in motorbike tracks. But much of the Ijen Plateau remains studded with antiquities and remnants of ancient occupation. In one place, the local people offer you yellow glass beads which they have taken from centuries-old stone coffins. The stone slabs which once sealed them as lids have been removed and are used as bridges over small streams, while the boxes themselves make mangers for holding cattle feed. I sent some of the beads to Holland for study and learnt that the glass originated in Persia or northern India.

We have a little shack at Jampit on the plateau where we go at least twice a year. The hour's flight from Jakarta to Surabaya is only the beginning of the journey we must make to get to there. The next eight hours are testing, packed inside a jeep with all our supplies. Usually we make the journey in a day, but sometimes we stay overnight at a spot on the wild coast called Pasir Putih, which means 'white sand'.

Our usual routine is to buy bread, rice, biscuits, tinned butter, vegetables and fruit in Surabaya. Then, as meat cannot be kept without refrigeration, I buy a dozen live chickens and they are piled into the back of the jeep for the journey to Jampit. For the chickens, sadly, it is a one-way trip.

Julius loves to go hunting with the locals, and when they bring back a wild pig he helps them skin it, gut it and prepare it for roasting on a spit over an open fire. As the smoke rises, I follow its journey upwards and I am always awed by the sky, filled with more stars than I have seen anywhere in the world.

There have been times when I have gone to Jampit on my own, with just a driver and the short-lived chickens for company. When I am alone, I stay in the upstairs room of our ramshackle little house. But our trusty caretaker Sandun always sleeps below, his sharp *golok* – sword – handy. For a long time there was no toilet in the house, and climbing down the steep, slippery steps to go outside on a dark, rainy night was quite dangerous. One night I almost fell, much to Sandun's alarm. Shortly afterwards, with much respect and politeness, he gave me a present, carefully gift-wrapped in newspaper. Nothing could have been more kind or more thoughtful, but it was hard to preserve the solemnity of the occasion when I unwrapped a brilliant pink chamberpot bearing the cheery inscription, 'Hi, Kitty!'

The soil and climate around Jampit are perfect for the cultivation of Arabica coffee, and not all that far from our shack there is a factory that processes the local beans for the export market. Our own coffee needs, as well as those of the *kampong*, are produced by more primitive means. The fresh coffee beans, placed in a long, steel cylinder, are cranked slowly round and round by hand over a low fire of charcoal. Nobody who has observed this patient process can forget the exquisite aroma of the roast. When done, the beans are transferred to a stone or wooden mortar and pounded incessantly with a long pole until they are reduced to fine powder, like Turkish coffee. It does not need to be brewed for drinking: one simply puts a heaped dessert spoon in a glass with plenty of sugar and pours on boiling water. The finest coffeeshops and restaurants in the world cannot produce a cup of coffee to compete with it.

In Jampit, the pounding process was usually performed by Ma Jima – a toothless old lady who managed nevertheless to chew constantly on a cud of tobacco. On one occasion I took a jar of her produce with me back to Jakarta and, on making myself a coffee, was surprised to see in the glass a walnut-sized lump of fibre. The coffee tasted putrid, and then it dawned on me what had happened. Ma Jima had clearly lost her tobacco and hadn't troubled to retrieve it. Imagine if I had been making coffee for a guest! Back at Jampit they all screamed with laughter at my story.

With Tugu and Jampit, I am truly blessed. Tugu satisfies my passion for gardening, for transforming a fantasy into my own personal reality. Jampit is wild, untamed and, I hope, untameable. My fascination with the Ijen Plateau and its natural and man-made treasures is endless. When I am away from Jampit for any significant period of time, I long to return.

Some of the places I have visited I probably never would have gone to had it not been for Julius's business interests.

In the mid-1960s, just after the demise of Sukarno, the American Freeport Sulphur Company was in search of new mining ventures. At the time, they decided that copper should be their major focus.

In the 1930s, a Dutch geologist named Jacques Dozy set out to climb an unconquered peak in Western New Guinea's Jayawijaya Mountains. Dozy was a fanatical mountaineer and his interest in climbing the mountain had nothing to do with any geological interest in the place. But during his climb he discovered a massive black outcropping close to a glacier – the only glacier to exist in the tropics – and recognised it as a huge copper deposit. He named the outcrop 'Ertzberg' – Dutch for 'Ore Mountain'. It lies near the peak of Mount Zaagkam which, at 14 500 feet, is the highest mountain between the Himalayas and the Andes.

Dozy wrote a report of what he had seen during his climb, but for the next twenty years it lay gathering dust at the University of Leiden in Holland. Even Dozy did not imagine that this massive ore deposit could ever be mined. Ertzberg is more than two miles above sea level and about seventy-five miles of mountains and mangrove swamps separate it from the coast.

In 1959, researchers for Freeport stumbled across Dozy's report and the company received permission from Dutch officials – Western New Guinea was still a Dutch colony – to explore the area. Their geologists confirmed that Ertzberg was a huge deposit of copper.

But for the next six years, nothing could be done to exploit the Ertzberg find. During that time, Indonesia came close to going to war with Holland over West Irian, which Sukarno claimed was a natural part of Indonesia, but which the Dutch insisted was a separate colony. The dispute was finally settled shortly before the attempted communist coup and Irian Jaya – as it is now called –was incorporated into Indonesia.

Julius was in America on Caltex business when he was contacted by Freeport executives to discuss Irian Jaya and the Ertzberg copper deposit. For the next four years, Julius worked with Freeport raising the money and getting Indonesian government approval for a mine at Ertzberg. It was a mammoth project. The cost of building the mine, which took three years, from 1969 to the end of 1972, was US$150 million.

Bechtel Corporation, which did the construction work, had to build seventy-four miles of road through forty miles of jungle and twenty-five miles of mountains. Mining facilities would include a new town named Tembagapura at the base of Mount Zaagkam. Three computer-controlled tramways would connect the town with the mine. One tramway would carry workers up to the mine, the others would carry ore down to the processing plant. Six miles from the town, the rock would be crushed and processed and then sent along a four-inch thick pipe the seventy miles to the coast. On the coast, landfill dredging would transform a mangrove swamp into a port for ocean-going vessels.

Our family company became a significant shareholder in the Freeport mine which today is the largest gold and copper mine in the world. I had counselled Julius not to get involved with Freeport. Indonesia had just emerged from fifteen years of chaos and the new era of President Suharto promised a period of steadiness. It seemed to me to be a time of consolidation rather than one of rash adventuring and striking out in new and unpredictable directions. I was wrong.

For one thing, nobody knew better than Julius the hazards of operating in Irian Jaya, for he had fought the Japanese there during the war. He knew first-hand the terrible swamps, full of crocodiles and disease, where he had spent weeks chest-deep in water and where a change into dry clothes was only an exercise of imagination.

Then there were the mountains: limestone ridges that are among the highest and most rugged in the world. How, I wondered, would a mine ever be built there? But when I listened to the Freeport geologists and the engineers of the Bechtel Corporation as they discussed their plans, when I saw their enthusiasm and dedication, I realised that this dream was destined to become reality.

In March 1973, I went to the Freeport mine with Julius for the official opening by President Suharto. We went a few days early so we could explore the mine site and its surrounds together before the official guests arrived. On the journey to the mine, I was fine until the final half-hour helicopter ride to the mining camp. Having crossed the swamps, our chopper suddenly entered a deep, sheer gorge, almost as if we had passed into the mountains through a gateway. There was hardly width enough for the rotor blades to spin without clipping the rock walls. I stared at my feet in an effort to avoid seeing what lay outside. I was terrified.

The camp was at a breathtakingly dramatic spot. From the main dining mess, I looked up at the mountain towering over our heads. It was awesome and frighteningly close. With most camps, there is some way out, but here, if there was a landslide, the camp would be obliterated.

As I travelled up to the mine site on one of the trams, the views of the nearby mountains were as stunning as anything I have ever seen. We even managed to fly by chopper to the glacier, perhaps the most incongruous sight I have ever beheld: a large, tropical snow field.

For the indigenous Irianese, the mine has been both a curse and a blessing. The shock of sudden acquaintance with bulldozers and helicopters before they had even met a bicycle or a wheelbarrow has shattered their world view. In the villages which we visited, where the Stone Age was still alive and well, and the integrity of their way of life remains intact, they were a proud people. With their bodies greased and shiny with pig fat, and plumes in their hair, the only attire the men wore was a penis gourd. The women wore only a girdle of reeds around their waist. They had few possessions but their social organisation and natural confidence remained intact.

Around the mine and in the town of Timika near the

coast, however, some of the people seemed dispirited, clad in dirty rags, demoralised, lost. Yet others, in clean shorts and T-shirts seemed to have adapted well to the presence of the mine and the miners. They were buying goods at the small supermarket, including sliced white bread and cornflakes like veteran suburbanites everywhere.

Many Irianese still live in their traditional villages shut off from the rest of the world and it is always fascinating to visit them. They are the most friendly, open people I have met. Others have moved to the mining town for work and have adapted, for better or for worse, to life away from their villages. While the mine has brought the benefits of education and modern medicine, and I know that Indonesia cannot afford to lock Irian Jaya's riches away from the 200 million Indonesians who will – have already – benefited, it nevertheless troubles me that things have changed so fast and that the local people have had to so quickly adapt to what, for them, had been unimaginable.

Much of Indonesia, especially the more remote, smaller islands, remains virtually untouched by what we call progress. Flores is one such island. It lies east of Java, strung like a green bead on the nation's necklace. It is long and rocky and has been Catholic for 300 years. When Sjakon graduated from medical school in Jakarta in the late 1970s he was sent, like other graduates, to an isolated area to do a sort of internship as a way of paying back the government for its investment in his education.

Sjakon was on Flores for three years. He lived with his wife Shelley and their baby daughter, Cindy, in a shabby little house next door to his medical clinic.

We visited Sjakon and his family several times while they were on Flores. Their house had no running water, and their toilet was a hole in the ground at the back of their house, screened off by a small, rickety, wooden fence. There were rats everywhere. Sjakon and Shelley had to coat the legs of Cindy's cot with a thick glue to catch the rodents as they tried to climb into where the child lay sleeping. The cot was a gruesome sight most mornings.

But there was much more to Flores than that. For a start, I loved the market. Horses were tied up everywhere, for that was the only mode of transport for most people. There were dogs and pigs, too, tied to stakes. Both animals were considered a delicacy on the island, as well as rats and often monkeys, which were skinned and hanging from hooks. While Sjakon had become used to eating dog, he could not bring himself to eat monkey. I could eat neither and mostly settled for chicken, if it was available, and vegetables if it wasn't.

There was a monastery on Flores run by Franciscan nuns who were practical, humane human beings who did not try to change the local culture. Sister Anne, who had come to Flores from Austria, often helped Sjakon with his medical work. I saw her one day galloping across the prairie like a cowboy, her habit flying in the wind behind her, revealing blue jeans and riding boots.

Several years ago, my son George decided that the family should have an ocean-going vessel. While the rest of the family were pretty keen on the idea, I did not warm to it at all. I could not see how it would be fully used and thought it would cause us more trouble than good. But I was out-voted and George went ahead and commissioned a boat, designed by a prominent American designer, to be built in a Taiwanese shipyard.

It took three years, and in 1994, we took delivery of our boat, a 62-foot, 55-ton motor cruiser, which can go 3000 nautical miles without re-fuelling. It sleeps six, plus two crew, very comfortably, but one Christmas, friends from Perth took the boat on a cruise around Bali with fourteen guests and they managed quite well. Upon my first sight of the boat, all my doubts vanished. I could not wait to take her to sea. It required all of George's qualities of persevering firmness to achieve this family success, through a welter of problems over which today he modestly draws a veil.

We called our boat 'Saumlaki', after the place in the Tanimbar islands where Julius had fought off the Japanese against overwhelming odds. In all the years since the war, he had never revisited the pier where the action had taken place and which troubled him still in his dreams. A voyage to Saumlaki was one of our first in the new boat, a poignant and moving return to a place which, even after all these years, remains so vivid in Julius's memory.

Our boat has opened up a new world for Julius and me. We sail around the Indonesian islands, stopping where we please, exploring our country's extraordinary beauty and variety. The most unexpected things happen on our travels. We have made hundreds of trips and have even journeyed to Darwin and Brisbane. But that first trip to Saumlaki sticks in my memory. We fished on the way from Ambon and then used the ingenious barbecue, which swings outward from the boat, to grill our catch fresh. No food can match the flavour of freshly caught fish quickly grilled on a barbecue at sea.

Although I was seasick on the first leg of our journey, the sea from there on was calm and we sighted many whales and hundreds of dolphins. The Moluccas or the Spice Islands are amongst the most beautiful islands on earth. Banda still has many seventeenth-century houses and old forts and the rows of nutmeg trees are a gorgeous sight. Manuk, shaped like half a coconut, has thousands of seabirds hovering over it, so that it looks like it is floating, quivering, on air.

Going ashore at Saumlaki, on Jamdena Island, was an emotional experience – not just for Julius, but also for George and me. Many things had changed in the fifty years since the war. The long timber jetty where Julius and his men had inflicted such heavy casualties on the Japanese had been replaced by a concrete one; there were substantial buildings on the beach, right over the places where Julius's men had dug their trenches in the sand and from where they had fired on the Japanese. But George and I could easily visualise what it must have been like for Julius during those frightening, uncertain hours, waiting for the Japanese to arrive.

Julius searched for and found islanders he had met during the time he had spent on the island and these reunions were deeply affecting for everyone. They stood silent for a minute in memory of the two Indonesian soldiers who had died during the action. For me, it brought back a rush of memories: memories of my loneliness, my desperate fear, my uncertainty during those years when Julius was away on missions and I had no idea whether he was dead or alive. It brought back memories of those early days when I first fell in love with him, days that are still fresh in my memory, and that set the course of my life forever.

twenty-four

Is life simply a voyage, like a train trip, with fresh scenes rushing constantly past the window? Does it add up to something more coherent than a mere progression of small journeys through a series of railway stations? Or is it just 'one damn thing after another'?

In a way, my destiny in life has been to be an eyewitness to history, to the birth of the new nation of Indonesia. I was there from the earliest days, before the country's birth struggle against its Dutch rulers was finished. Julius was an active player in that struggle. His life – and therefore mine – has been shaped first by the fight for Indonesian nationhood and then by Indonesia's movement towards prosperity and material wellbeing for its 200 million people. It has been a tumultuous half-century and, thanks to Julius, my family has been somewhere near the centre of that tumult for most of that time.

Yet I have retained, over the fifty years that I have lived in Indonesia, the detachment of an onlooker. In no sense have I been a public person and I have had no real part as an actor in the history I watched unfolding. I was a foreigner – at least in the early days – and, to a certain extent, I remain one still. Part of me is still an Australian who will always ask herself whenever something momentous happens, 'How would they have handled that back in Australia?'

To many Australians, Indonesia has long been a place of menace, of yellow hordes eyeing a vast and empty continent, ready at any moment to move southwards and fill those unpeopled spaces. Perhaps some Australians still see Indonesia that way. Certainly, there is little understanding in Australia of how complex and diverse a country lies just to the north of the Australian continent.

The Indonesian archipelago stretches like a constellation across Australia's northern coastline and beyond, its 16 000 islands home to hundreds of millions of people with different ethnic and cultural origins. Just keeping them all together as part of an Indonesian nation has been a major achievement over the past fifty years. Australians often talk about their multicultural society and yet, from the vantage point of Indonesia, Australia is essentially a homogeneous society, bound together by a common language and a common culture. Australia, unlike Indonesia, has never had to contend with the constant threat of ethnic tensions tearing the country apart.

As I have watched Indonesia take its perilous journey to independence and, later, survive the upheaval of the Sukarno years, I have had a strange sense of being prepared for these events. Long ago and far away, my father – a humble police sergeant in Melbourne – had been able to take far-sighted historical views. He had foreseen the deaths of the European empires and would often say to me, 'It'll only take a war in Asia for those colonial governments to topple. And a good thing. No people should be ruled by foreigners.'

The upheavals of independence, however, took their toll on my family, not least on my sons' education, which suffered many a hiccup as a result of the general unrest. This was particularly true in Sjakon's case. George, being six years younger, enjoyed somewhat more settled times, although there was an alarming incident when an unknown man tried to grab him, as a little boy, from the car which was taking him to school.

We were fortunate that we could, when necessary, afford private schools and could also engage tutors from time to time. Sjakon's passion for hunting, and for other outdoor pursuits, also affected his study. Nevertheless, he graduated from Jakarta's excellent medical school and went on to undertake eye research at the University of Wisconsin and in Perth.

George took his Bachelor of Science in mechanical engineering in 1983 from Indonesia's Trisakti University, then an institution of mixed standards which has since improved considerably. When he went to the University of Virginia for his MBA, he described the experience as 'like heaven'.

Both careers, one in medicine and the other in banking, have been successful, but I still shudder slightly when I look back on the educational shoals and rapids we had to negotiate in the years of trouble.

I have no doubt that Indonesia's last fifty years have been a half-century of progress. It has been far from steady progress and it has been punctuated by terrible mistakes. From my vantage point, much of what was valuable and lovable about this great country has been lost forever as it increasingly embraces the ways of the West. Perhaps that is inevitable. Perhaps the price for material wellbeing and development is the destruction of old ways and ancient wisdoms.

The *kampong* is vanishing and, with it, traditional village life. I miss the *pijit*, those old ladies skilled in the traditional art of massage. Their understanding of the aches and pains in human muscles was miraculous and the feeling of bliss that would follow a session with one of them remains a cherished memory.

The old Indonesian herbalists too are dying out, and their secret potions that could cure virtually any ailment are fast being lost, probably forever. The little eating places, tiny wooden stalls that sold deliciously spicy snacks of dried salted fish or pickled vegetables, are in retreat – constantly under threat from the international fast food chains like

McDonald's. There are so many McDonald's in Jakarta now that no New Yorker wandering the streets of this city need ever feel far from home. And the traffic in Jakarta is even worse than in New York. The old days, when I could stroll down the wide, tree-lined streets of Jakarta, along its network of Dutch-built canals, are long gone. Jakarta is a city almost choked by smog. Five minutes in the traffic brings on red, tear-filled eyes and asthma.

Little things are sometimes the clue to larger truths. Traditional dress – the *kebaya* and sarong – that once gave Indonesian women their distinctive grace and beauty, have made way for the miniskirt and T-shirt. The tyranny of television rules in Indonesia as much as it does in the West, and with similar consequences. But Indonesia's story is also one of triumph, often against the odds.

So is that the path I chose for myself, to be an observer of history? Did I set out to bridge the cultural and political and even racial gaps between Australia and Indonesia, as if my life were a metaphor for the destiny of these two countries that are geographically so close and yet so distant in many ways?

Lives, except in retrospect, are not metaphors. They are lived moment by moment. The path down which a life travels is unclear and indiscernible until one looks back and imposes order on what is essentially the chaos of existence. So, I suppose, it has been with my life.

Was the path of my life just an accident, set by chance, by some throw of cosmic dice? I cannot answer these questions definitively. I grew up in an Australia that has now more or less vanished. My family's roots in Australia go back almost to the beginning of European settlement. My father came from the rural poor, those who struggled to scratch out an existence on small land-holdings, their lives ruled by fire and drought and back-breaking work. My mother's ancestors were city people, British migrants who settled in Victoria in the 1800s, shopkeepers and traders who became relatively prosperous in the years when Melbourne was a boom town built on golden dreams.

Yet my father had dreams beyond the small dairy farm on which he was raised. Where those dreams came from is a mystery, but those dreams, which remained unfulfilled, had a deep and lasting impact on my life. And, in some profound way, my mother must have loved him for those dreams, because a humble policeman would not have been her family's preferred choice of partner. These two seemingly simple people were, in reality, not simple at all.

My father, from childhood on, loved books and ideas. His soul was filled with poetry, with an overwhelming love of words. He dreamt of worlds far beyond the little farm near Wangaratta. He dreamt of visiting the great cities of the world. He read and absorbed and wondered at a world which he could never fully enter, but which he could never entirely abandon.

From as early as I can remember, his dreams became mine. I knew, even as a small child, that my father had been denied that which he was determined would never be denied me. No matter what his material circumstances, no matter what the cost, I would achieve those things that he knew were beyond him. All the doors that were closed to him would be open for me. And I rushed through those doors, eager to explore this world that was so important to my father.

I wonder whether it was those dreams that set me on the path that involved me abandoning my home, my profession and my family for a life that, for some time at least, would leave me a stranger in a strange land? When my father talked to me of foreign lands and faraway places, was that the beginning of my search for a life beyond the comfortable suburbs of Melbourne and the easy rewards of a professional career?

All I know is that the path of my life cannot be understood without an acknowledgement of the power of love. I met Julius fifty-five years ago and we have lived together for half a century, and I loved this man from the moment I saw him. We met at a time when both our worlds were under threat and when, every day, it was uncertain whether Julius would live to see another. Perhaps our love was so intense because we really did not know whether there would be a tomorrow.

But that cannot be the whole story. Love, like so many other things in life, is a mystery. I can still clearly remember how I felt when Julius walked through the gate towards our front door in Ascot Vale. This was no moment of infatuation, for it has lasted a lifetime. I knew nothing about Julius when I first saw him – nothing of his country, his culture, his family, his dreams – and yet I knew everything, not with my mind, but in my heart. By the time he left that first evening, I knew that the course of my life would be set by my love for this man.

And so it has been. My life, which began along one path, has ended up going along another, entirely different one. With some reluctance, I gave up my profession for the role of mother and wife. My career had been hard earnt – achieved, I believe, against the odds. I loved my work and the sense of being useful and productive it gave me. I even loved it when people invariably thought I was a dental nurse rather than a dentist when they came to the hospital for treatment.

There are people who would argue that I have given up much for Julius – my family, my country, my professional career. That, they would say, has been the lot of women for far too long a time. In a sense, it is true, I have given up a lot for Julius; but then, in every life, there are choices to be made that involve sacrificing some things in order to gain others. I followed my heart as far as Julius was concerned, but I followed it with my eyes open. Sometimes we look at each other, Julius and I, and we both know that we are thinking the same thing: how lucky we have been to have each other.

My family has prospered in this new Indonesia. Sometimes, when I sit on the terrace of our home in Jakarta or on the verandah of our country house in Tugu, I marvel at what can happen in a lifetime. While I have never played an active role in the family businesses, I have always known what was going on and Julius has often come to me for advice, especially about people. Our sons Sjakon and George are now active partners in Aust-Indo Corporation, our family holding company. Sjakon divides his time between business and his busy medical practice as an eye specialist, while George concentrates fully on the management demands of what has become an amazingly diverse group of companies with interests worldwide.

While I have left the running of the company to Julius and then later, to Julius and my sons, that does not mean I have no interest in business. But I made a decision early on in my life with Julius that I would not meddle in his public life. I would be his partner and supporter; I would raise our children; I would play the role of executive wife to the best of my ability. There was a cost for this, a not insubstantial one. It may sound strange, but I have never written a cheque nor driven a car.

No life, however, not even one as fortunate as mine, is without its moments. While I was prepared to sacrifice much for the love of a man, I paid a price for that love that many women have paid. Loneliness has been part of that price. There have been times when I felt so alone that all I could do was cry. There have been times when I desperately wanted Julius to be there, but he wasn't. His public life constantly and necessarily took him away from me.

Some young women ask me whether I feel I have lived a life too much in Julius's shadow. I answer that I don't for a moment believe that Julius thinks he has been living for fifty years with a submissive woman who lacked a mind of her own. My advice to him on a whole range of matters is always offered in private and I am always taken seriously. We have been, and remain, partners in life. Has Julius been the head of the Tahija family? Yes he has. I believe every family needs a head, but that does not mean that I have somehow been the junior partner. We have just had different roles.

It was not my role to attend the fiftieth anniversary celebrations of the end of the Pacific War in Hawaii in 1995 in the presence of the United States president, Bill Clinton. When the US secretary of defence stepped forward to lay an official wreath, one man was chosen to accompany him – the most senior and highly decorated soldier present. To the assembled dignitaries, he was Colonel Julius Tahija. To me, he was the man I have loved for a lifetime. I was content to sit on the sidelines, my heart filled with pride. When Julius told me that he could not have achieved what he has without me, I believed him absolutely.

A life can rush past before one knows it and there can be regrets for things left undone and choices made that proved to be unwise. I do not have many such regrets and if I had my time again, there are few things I would do differently. I do not know why my life took the path it did, but I am content with the road down which I have travelled.

Many people ask me whether, after all these years, I have become an Indonesian. I rarely think about it. On one level, I am Julius Tahija's wife and the mother of his two Indonesian children and the grandmother of their children. I am at home here. But on another level, I am George and Olive Walters' daughter, a fourth-generation Australian. Up in Tugu, high in the mountains of Java, I plant and nurture gum trees. I know where gum trees come from. On cold nights, I toss a handful of gum leaves on the fire. There is no more comforting and familiar smell that I know of on this earth.

index

Aceh 44
Acland Street (St Kilda) 33–4
Aerssen, Baron van 85
Agung, Anak Agung Gde 151–2, 181, 227–8
Amat 202
Ambon island 73
  post-war visit 166–9
American Freeport Sulphur Company 271, 272; *see also* Freeport mine
Amies, Professor 47–8, 65, 94, 141
Amina 189, 217
Anderson, Harry 54–5
Anna 174, 177
Anne, Sister 276
Anzac Day parades 100
Ascot Vale 1, 5
Asro 217, 233
atomic bombs, Japan 105
Aust-Indo Corporation 288
Australia
  perception of Indonesia 113, 281
  role in Indonesian nationhood 183

Ballini, Mario 47, 48, 94
Banda Island 278
Bayer, Sybil 124
Beatrix, Queen, of the Netherlands 219
Bechtel Corporation 272, 273
Bernhard, Prince, of the Netherlands 219
Biak 12, 13
boat trips 277–8
Bondan 116, 117, 118, 119
Bram, Oom 125

Caltex Pacific Indonesia 19, 206, 207, 208, 210–13, 216, 225, 235–7, 239, 251–2, 257
Camp Pell (Melbourne) 53, 54, 80, 83, 85
Chevron 19, 211, 251
Chifley, Ben 8
Chinatown (Melbourne) 27–8
Cinnamomum tahijanum 205
circumcision (*sunat*) 260
coffee making 269–70
Collins, Stella 28
Cowra prison camp 11, 117, 121
Critchley, Tom 124, 183
Crocodile Hole (Jakarta) 243, 247
Curtin, John 46

Dakota *see* DC3 cargo plane
Darwin bombing 46, 80
DC3 cargo plane (Dakota) 8
dental hospital (Spring Street) 34–5, 47
domestic staff 19–20, 149, 150–1, 152–3, 156–7, 200–2, 217, 233–4
Donskoi, Tuska 13, 14, 146, 177, 199
Dozy, Jacques 271
Dutch colonial rule 5–6, 16, 39, 171–2, 181
Dutch East Indies army 6, 43, 53

East Brunswick primary school 31
East Indonesia 6–7, 181
Eastern Café (Chinatown) 64
Edgar, Jean 121–4, 126, 127
epic theatre (*wayang*) 42–3
Ertzberg 271, 272

Flores Island 275, 276
Freeport mine 12, 273
  impact on local people 274–5

glacier 13, 271, 274
Great Depression 32
Gull Force 73

Harta 189
Hindu inscriptions 267–8
Holland, liberation of (WWII) 101
homes
  Anne Street (East Brunswick) 22, 23, 24–5
  Ascot Vale 1, 5, 254–5
  Jakarta
    current 15–16, 17
    embassy district 216–17
    first house 176–7
  Macassar 149–50, 152, 154, 157
Hopper, Richard 212, 213
household staff *see* domestic staff

Ijen Plateau (east Java) 266–8, 270
Indonesia
  CIA activities 224, 225
  food 43, 157–8, 168, 254, 269–70
  independence celebrations 183–4
  independence struggle 5–6, 106–10, 113–14, 138–9, 171–2, 175–6, 180–1
  influence of Dutch rule 261–3
  Japanese surrender 110–11
  religion 260–1
  role of family 261
  1950s and 1960s 219–212, 223–5, 227–8, 232–48, 240–1
  social change 283–4
  women 258–60
Indonesian communist party (PKI) 188, 220–1, 224, 244
  attempted coup 238, 243–5
interracial love affairs 64–5
Irian Jaya 272, 273

jackets (*kebaya*) 174
Jakarta 15
description 172–3, 180, 190
Jalan Imam Bonjol 216
Jalan Minangkabau 176–7, 216–17
Jamdena Island 73–4, 278
Jampit 268–9, 270
Javanese people 39
Jima, Ma 270
Jogjakarta 6, 124–6
Jones, Howard 223–4
Jonge, Jonkheer de 163

kampong (village) 283
kebaya (jackets) 174
Kostermans, A.J.G.H. 204

MacArthur, General Douglas 12, 46, 51, 101
Macassar (Ujung Pandang) 6, 16, 143–5, 147–54, 158–60
Manuk Island 278
Melbourne 26, 33–4, 253–4
  during World War II 33, 49–52, 71–2, 94, 105–6
Melbourne University 2, 32–3
Merauke 11, 12
Methodist Ladies College (MLC) 31
Minas oilfield 215

Moluccas (Spice Islands) 38, 278
Mount Zaagkam 271, 272

Nasution, General 244
Nehru, Prime Minister, of India 184, 219
Nicholas, Betty 31
Nicholas, Nola 31
Nusantara, Aidit Dipa 238–9, 246

oilfields (Sumatra) 212–16, 225
Ouw Eng Liang, Professor 190–1, 192–3

Pacific War celebrations (Hawaii) 289
Pancasila (five principles) 187
Pangarango mountain 198
Parman, General 242, 243
Pasir Putih 268
Patjet 197–8
Pekanbaru 212, 213
PKI *see* Indonesian communist party
Pulau Nirvana 229

Rumbai 212, 213, 214

Sandun 269
Saumlaki 73–8
  post-war visit 277, 278–9
Saumlaki (boat) 277
Siak River 212, 213–14
Simatupang, General T. B. 182
Sjahrir, Sutan 112
Soekawati 151
Spoor, General Simon 111, 112
Suhardi, Mahiti 200, 201
Suhardi, Pak 200, 201–2
Suharto
  character 250
  opening Freeport mine 273
  suppression of the 1965 coup 244, 245
Sukarno
  antipathy towards the West 187, 236
  centralised government model 113, 220
  character 6, 185–7, 248–9
  communist association 151–2, 220–1, 224–5, 235
  declaration of independence 6, 106–7
  imprisonment by Dutch 181
  oil industry advice 207
  upheavals during presidency 219–212, 223–5, 227–8, 232–48, 240–1
  wives 160–1, 218–19
Sulawesi 6
Sultan of Bone 170
sunat (circumcision) 260
Surabaya 37, 38, 39
soap factory 234, 249

Tahija, Cindy 276
Tahija, George 258, 277, 279, 288
  birth 225, 226
  childhood 158, 227, 233
  education 282–3
Tahija, Jean
  birth 22
  courtship 62–4, 66–70, 80–5, 88–93, 94–9, 102–3
  death of her parents 252–3, 254
  dental career 34–5, 47, 52–3, 70, 94, 190–4, 287
  early life 24, 25–6, 27–8
  education 2, 20–1, 29–33
  experiences of racism 64, 65–6
  father *see* Walters, George
  first meeting with Julius 1–2, 3, 56–62, 286–7
  gardening at Tugu 202–6, 231–2, 258, 290
  grandfather 24–5, 36, 255
  leaving Australia 1, 4, 5, 7–14, 139–43
  life in her eighties 15, 18, 20
  marriage 129, 132–7
  mother *see* Walters, Olive
  official duties 160–4, 166, 219–20
  response to Julius returning to war 70–1, 72, 81, 83, 90–2
  sons *see* Tahija, George; Tahija, Sjakon

stillbirth 195–6
support of Indonesian
independence 83–4, 114
travels 182–3, 242
to Australia 179, 189, 226–7
within Indonesia 166–9, 197–9,
213–15, 229, 266–70, 277–9
view of her life 17–18, 20, 155,
170, 255–6, 280–1, 283, 284–90
view of Indonesia 16–17, 180,
263–5, 283–4
Tahija, Julius
awards 7, 85
birth 37, 38–9
business acumen 40–2
Caltex Pacific Indonesia career 19,
206–8, 210–16, 221–3, 235,
251–2, 257
character 18–19, 196–7
childhood 40–3
copper mining, Irian Jaya 272–4
education 39–40
father 37, 38, 45, 97, 109
life in his eighties 18–19
military service 7, 43–6, 73, 80,
85–9, 99–100, 103–5
duties after World War II
109–10, 111–12, 148–9,
188–9
Saumlaki mission 73–9, 83
mother 37–8
political career 6, 7, 112–13,
129–30, 131, 155, 169–71,
181–2
private businesses 216, 234, 252,
257
vision for Indonesia 112, 129–30,
138–9, 164, 188, 250
Tahija, Shelley 276
Tahija, Sjakon 233, 258
birth 183, 209–10
career 194, 275–6, 288
childhood 206, 215, 217, 227
education 233, 282
Tan, Mr 173–4, 175
Tan, Mrs 174
Tanah Merah (Red Earth) 11
Tembagapura 272
Texaco 19, 211, 251
Tilden, Bill 10
Timika 274
Tugu 179, 199–206, 202, 203, 204,
229–31, 229–33, 258, 290

Ujung Pandang *see* Macassar

Victoria Market 55–6
village (*kampong*) 283
Vincent, Gilbert 160

Walters, Cliff 4–5, 23, 29–30, 35–6,
48, 49, 57, 72, 105, 133
Walters, George 179, 226, 290
background 23–4, 25, 285–6
beliefs and values 2–3, 22–3,
29–31, 32
life during World War II 48–9, 51
love of vaudeville 26–7, 29
marriage 24
police service 24, 27–9
response to Jean leaving home 1, 3
response to Julius 58, 68, 84
Walters, Olive (née Ward) 24, 25
background 24, 25, 285, 290
marriage 25
response to Julius 3, 62, 67, 84
visits to Indonesia 178–9
Walters, Russell 4–5, 23, 29–30,
35–6, 48, 49, 57, 72, 105, 133, 209
Ward, Olive 24, 25; *see also* Walters,
Olive
Warner, Molly 116–21
wayang (epic theatre) 42–3
Wesley Church (Lonsdale Street) 135
Western New Guinea 271
Wunderly, Dr 136–7

Z Experimental Station 87, 88
Z special unit 7, 86, 99, 100, 216
Zakaria, Jack 121–2, 123–4, 125,
126–7, 128
Zakaria, Naraya 127–8

acknowledgements

This book had the humblest of origins, for it was intended for the eyes of no-one but my family. How often, in the course of my long life, have I heard people lament, 'I wish I knew more about my family background!' But they have left it too late, and although genealogical research in the public records, and scrutiny of old family Bibles will help them construct the base branches of a family tree, the life and the breath and the sparkle have been lost forever.

So when my sons, Sjakon and George, began to grow up, I resolved to act in good time. I would set down on paper the story of my life, both before and after it merged with the life of that fiery particle, Julius.

It had been anything but an ordinary life, I realised, as I recorded its details. From time to time, as I mentioned one event or another to friends, they seemed so interested that I began to wonder whether there might not be a wider audience.

And so developed, with the encouragement of both family and friends, this book which you now hold in your hand.

I could not have managed this unaided, and first and foremost, I thank Michael Gawenda, whose editorial skills and understanding helped me to refine my original drafts and to give the book its shape. Towards the end of this labour, he was appointed to one of the most distinguished editorial chairs in Australia – that of the Melbourne *Age* – and I wish him well in his heavy new responsibilities.

George and Sjakon both searched their own memories of early family life, and prepared for me valuable notes of things which had been important when they were little.

For a lifestory which began in Melbourne, I also needed help with things at that end, including with research and with liaising with my publishers. This has been unfailingly supplied, with speed and efficiency, by Margaret Gurry.

So this story of my life has been prepared, as the life itself was fortunately lived, with the kindness and help of others. I thank every one of them.